BLUFF

Publishers Weekly Top 10 Mysteries for Spring 2019

"Jane Hitchcock pulls off another stunning tour de force in her newest crime novel, *Bluff*. Nobody writes high society and its down-low denizens better than Hitchcock—and this book is her best yet. It's all in the cards—and it's masterful."

—Linda Fairstein, *New York Times* bestselling author

"With the heart-pounding suspense of a high-stakes poker game, *Bluff* is a vivid, compelling novel about deceit, seduction, and delicious revenge that will have you spellbound and cheering as you turn the last page."

—Susan Cheever, author of *Home Before Dark* and *Treetops*

"Jane Stanton Hitchcock's *Bluff* is the royal flush of suspense novels! The queen of both writing and poker aces it again!"

—Linda Kenney Baden, celebrated attorney, legal commentator, and author

"This delicious novel of sweet revenge reveals, with wit and stylish vigor, a world—New York high society—that the author clearly knows intimately."

—*Publishers Weekly* (starred review)

"Hitchcock pokes fun at the gossipy upper class, at the verbal tics of crass hangers-on, at the street-smart capability of former strippers and former advertising executives alike. The biggest takeaway: He who underestimates women of a certain age certainly does so at his own peril. Frothy fun with a backbone of feminist steel; as quick-moving and intricate as any heist movie."

—*Kirkus Reviews*

"The axiom 'write what you know' deliciously foretells this poker-themed thriller...A smartly plotted upper-crust caper."

—Karen Keefe, *Booklist*

Bluff

Books by Jane Stanton Hitchcock

Trick of the Eye
The Witches' Hammer
Social Crimes
One Dangerous Lady
Mortal Friends
Bluff

Plays

Grace
Bhutan
The Custom of the Country
(an adaptation of Edith Wharton's novel)
Vanilla (directed by Harold Pinter)

Screenplays

Our Time
First Love

Bluff

Jane Stanton Hitchcock

Published by Poisoned Pen Press, an imprint of Sourcebooks, Inc.
P.O. Box 4410, Naperville, Illinois 60563-4410
(630) 961-3900
sourcebooks.com

Library of Congress Cataloging 2018949096

Printed and bound in the United States of America.
SB 10 9 8 7 6 5 4 3 2 1

For Jim Hoagland, the love of my life,
and for
Jim Fennell
and
Jane Ellis

The Flop

"Poker is the game closest to the western conception of life, where life and thought are recognized as intimately combined, where free will prevails over philosophies of fate or of chance, where men are considered moral agents and where—at least in the short run—the important thing is not what happens but what people think happens."

—*John Lukacs*

Chapter One

Death is colorful in the fall. The trees in Central Park bristle with red and gold leaves, like a beautiful dawn before the dark of winter. On this crisp, sunny October day in New York, I'm all dressed up for a lunch to which I'm definitely not invited. I want to look my very best. I'm wearing a tailored Saint Laurent black wool suit, one I bought in Paris years ago when Yves was still designing. Affixed to my right lapel is a fake gold and sapphire pin in the shape of a flower, a decent copy of the real one from Verdura I had to hock years ago because I was broke. I have on a pair of secondhand black patent leather Louboutin shoes with scuffed red soles I recently bought at a thrift shop just for this occasion. I think labels matter much too much in New York. But, alas, they *do* matter, and I'm on my way to a place where they matter most.

I whisk a comb through my bobbed graying hair and apply a little lip gloss to my lightly made-up face. It's not an unattractive face, just an older one, silted with apprehension. I'm satisfied I look like what I'm supposed to be: a middle-aged lady of means with a conservative sense of style. I re-check the contents in my faux Birkin bag to make sure I have everything I need. It's all there: wallet, glasses, compact, lipstick, comb, cell phone, gun.

My name is Maud Warner. I grew up in New York. Many of the girls I went to private school with lived in the grand houses and apartment buildings of the Upper East Side. My parents' duplex apartment at 1040 Fifth was stocked with fine antiques and paintings. I never thought about how rich we were. No one in my young world thought about such things. Money and possessions were simply the view we'd all grown up with, like farmland to a bunch of country girls. We wore uniforms in my all-girls school so there wasn't the egregious sartorial competition there is today. The only thing I knew for sure was that the girl sitting next to me in class was probably just as miserable as I was.

I pass several haunts of my youth: The Knickerbocker Club, where I attended my very first dance when I was twelve years old and sat like a wallflower until the bitter end, despite having learned how to do a mean foxtrot in dancing school….A La Vielle Russie, the elegant jewelry shop on the corner of 59th, where my stepfather bought me a Faberge pin for my twenty-first birthday which had belonged to one of the last Tsar's kids—so much for a good luck charm… F.A.O. Schwartz, where my beloved Nana took me to sit on Santa's knee every Christmas…The now-defunct Plaza Hotel, where Mummy and I had tea in the Palm Court once a month, and where I lost my virginity to a Harvard boy in a white and gold suite on the tenth floor after he plied me with mai tais from Trader Vic's…And lovely Bergdorf's, where I bought my coming out dress and the wedding dress I burned when I got divorced, plus so many of the clothes that enhanced the great and small occasions of my seemingly privileged life… Tiffany's, where I ordered my pale blue monogrammed stationery… And Trump Tower, which used to be Bonwit Teller, the old department store, where I had my first summer job in the gift department, and learned that the road to hell was actually paved with beaded flowers and gilded frames.

I pass Saint Patrick's Cathedral, where I always went to light candles for the dead. I walk in and light a candle for my beloved brother, Alan, recently deceased. He was the last of my family and one of the main reasons for this outing.

I cross over to Madison Avenue, then Park, where I pause to look up at the elegant Seagram's Building, my final destination. My stepfather knew the architect, Mies van der Rohe. My parents had many famous friends. Their glamorous parties were so packed with celebrities, I used to refer to myself as "the only person there I didn't know."

I turn down 52nd Street toward Lexington and stop at the entrance to The Four Seasons restaurant, that bastion of social climbing in Manhattan. I take a bracing breath and walk purposefully inside. As I climb the marble staircase, I hear the hum of conversation, which is the music of power in this power restaurant in this power city. I gird my loins, as the Bible says, and take the last few stairs up into the airy restaurant where the best tables are reserved for the best bank accounts.

I'm greeted by the famous maître d', who knows who is who and who is *not*. This guy can size up a customer before he or she has reached the top step. That's why I've taken care to dress well. He doesn't recognize me, thank God.

"Good afternoon. Do you have a reservation?" he says, his polite smile conveying a soupçon of suspicion.

"I'm meeting Mr. Burt Sklar," I say. "I believe he's dining with Mr. Sunderland."

"Ah. Mr. Sunderland, of course!"

It is Sun Sunderland's name, not Sklar's, which sparks deference in the maître d'. He inclines his head in the direction of "the Sunderland table," as it's known. It's the best table in the house—a banquette against the wall. Anyone sitting at it can see and be seen from a decorous distance. Four times a week, at lunch, it's occupied by Mr. Sunderland and at least one of an array of prominent guests who comprise the media, financial, political, and artistic elite of New York, the country, and the world. But on Fridays, Sunderland always dines with his best friend and business partner, Burt Sklar. It is their ritual. I know this because it is well known and often commented on.

The maître d' leads me through the restaurant. I recognize a few famous faces which stand out in the crowd like the fresh pepper grinds on the chef's famous white truffle risotto. Out of the corner of my eye, I spot a table of three lunching ladies I used to know quite well. Once upon a time, I would have detoured to air kiss them all. Not today. Today it's eyes straight ahead, one foot in front of the other in a grim gangplank demeanor. Nothing can distract me from this plunge into the depths.

As we approach the table, I see that Sunderland and Sklar are deep in conversation. Sunderland is a stocky man who looks ponderously prosperous in his dark suit, gray Charvet tie, and starched white shirt with knotted gold cuff links. He has a full head of silvering hair and tired brown eyes. He's a solid man who exudes Mount Rushmore gravitas.

Burt Sklar, by contrast, is gym-fit and spray-tanned. Strands of his black hair are carefully combed over a shiny pate. He's dressed all in black—black suit, black shirt, black tie. Contrary to Sunderland's rocklike presence, Sklar is all motion, using his hands to hammer in a verbal point. He reminds me of a bat. I overhear him repeating his mantra, the words he prefaces every sentence with in order to reassure people of his veracity: "*Candidly…? Honestly…? Truthfully…?*"

I'm careful to stay behind the maître d' so the two men won't see me coming. My heart's beating fast. I glance down at my bag to make sure all is in order. It's open in a fashionably casual way, like a pricey tote. The gun is nestled in the side pocket where it will be easy to grab.

I've rehearsed this moment in my mind and in front of my warped closet mirror too many times to count. I know exactly what I want to do. Whether or not I'll be able to do it right there on the spot is the question. Let's face it, no one ever really knows how they will perform until the curtain goes up for the live show.

I hear the maître d' say, "Mr. Sklar, your guest is here."

Sklar looks up, clearly irritated at having been interrupted mid-spiel.

"What?" he asks, puzzled.

"Your guest is here," the maître d' repeats.

Sunderland turns to Sklar. "You invited someone?"

"Hell, no," Sklar says.

Sklar furrows his brow and leans to one side, trying to get a look at me, the uninvited guest. He can't see my face because I'm using the maître d' as a shield until I'm ready. I draw the gun from my purse. Sunderland sees me before Sklar does. His eyes widen as he gasps: "*Lois! No! We killed you!*"

I'm so startled by Sunderland's outburst, I lose my concentration as I pull the trigger. The noise is deafening. Chaos erupts in the room. People are screaming, scrambling, diving for cover. I drop the gun, turn around, and start walking. If I'm caught, so be it. If not, I've come prepared. Amazingly enough, no one stops me. Out on the street, I hail a cab and head for Penn Station, where I board an Acela train back to Washington, D.C.

So it begins…

Chapter Two

This crime is so shocking that even the most jaded reporters are impressed by its brazenness, and even more impressed by the unlikely shooter—a fifty-six-year-old socialite named Maud Warner, who somehow escaped and is now on the run. Sun Sunderland, billionaire financier and philanthropist, was shot while lunching at The Four Seasons restaurant.

Fifty-second Street between Park and Lexington avenues is cordoned off. A gaggle of media is camped outside the restaurant hoping to snag beleaguered patrons as they exit the building, one by weary one, after being questioned by the police. People are phoning, texting, Facebooking, tweeting, instagramming, belching, screaming, practically vomiting the news.

Inside the restaurant, the maître d' has been sedated, sick with the knowledge that this terrible thing has happened on his watch. The Four Seasons will no longer be known as New York's premiere power eatery. It will now be known to the rubbernecking masses as "the place where that billionaire got shot." Tourists will book a reservation there, not for the restaurant's gourmet food, elegant Bauhaus setting, or to mingle with its elite clientele, but to view the scene of high-class carnage.

The maître d' feels responsible because he now realizes exactly who Maud Warner is. How could he have been so stupid not to recognize her right away—he, who never forgets a face or a name? Had he recognized her, he never would have brought her anywhere near Burt Sklar. He never would have let her into the hallowed Grill Room. He would have ushered her straight out the door, or perhaps to the Pool Room, where the lesser-known rub elbows with the unknown.

Maud Warner has famously been proclaiming her hatred for Burt Sklar for years, accusing the "accountant to the stars," as he's known, of looting her family fortune. She has been nicknamed "Mad Maud" for going around predicting doom for anyone associated with Sklar. People think she's nuts to question the integrity of a man who has so many celebrated clients and—most of all—whose best friend and business partner is the honorable, estimable, and immensely powerful Sun Sunderland. Like everyone else who knows the history, the maître d' is convinced that Sklar, not Sunderland, was the intended target, and that Maud Warner is just a lousy shot.

There's an APB out for Warner, who is in the wind after a miraculous escape. Sunderland has been whisked away to New York Hospital in critical condition. Burt Sklar is being questioned by the cops before being taken to the hospital to be checked out.

Sklar talks even faster than his usual carnival patter because he is so damn relieved to be alive. He's suffered a sprained wrist from diving under the table. No social tennis for awhile. He tells officers he knows exactly who the shooter is: She's Maud Warner, this crazy woman who claims he's responsible for her mother's misfortunes, her brother's recent death, and all her family's woes.

"*Truthfully?* Maud Warner's been the bane of my existence for years," he says.

He tells cops he's sure she was aiming only for him, not his "best friend" Sun Sunderland. But by some "mysterious quirk of fate," Sunderland somehow got into her line of fire. The "mysterious quirk of fate" of which Sklar speaks was, in fact, his own arm pulling Sunderland across him to shield himself the instant he saw the gun. In Sklar's mind, his action was nothing more than a reflexive survival instinct, a natural response he could no more help than, say, fleeing a rabid dog. Unfortunately, pulling your best friend in front of you to take a bullet clearly meant for you, might possibly be construed as a cowardly act by those who were never actually in that dicey situation. Better not to mention it, he concludes.

Sklar is humble and super cooperative with the cops. He's a chameleon, able to gauge the colors of those he's dealing with and blend into their sensibilities. He tells detectives, "That bullet was meant for me. I know it was. *Truthfully*…? I'd give anything to change places with Sun. I love the man."

The cops don't comment. They listen. Sklar continues talking to them earnestly, making eye contact with each man, impressing upon them that he knows they have a job to do and can see they are both excellent officers of the law. Sklar is usually very adept at creating camaraderie with people by seeming to put himself in their shoes, however costly or cheap those shoes may be. But right now, his folksy approach doesn't seem to be working. The cops are looking at him like they suspect there's something he's not telling them. Time to crack a joke to get them in his corner.

"*Candidly*, guys? You know the world's gone completely nuts when you're safer in Syria than at The Four Seasons."

That gets a chuckle out of them. And don't they know it too. The world is nuts, all right, full of people who think they can get away with all kinds of shit.

And do.

Chapter Three

As the train rumbles toward D.C., I can't believe I actually escaped from that restaurant. Forget *The Invisible Man*. Older women are invisible and we don't even have to disappear. No one gave me credit for being the shooter. That's why I was able to calmly walk out of there. It used to bug me that I was beyond the gaze of men, overlooked and underestimated. But right now, I'm quite happy no one on this train is paying the slightest bit of attention to me. If they're focused on anyone other than themselves, it's the millennial blonde in the front of the compartment.

As the train rolls on, I replay the scene in my mind. I was pretty cool and calm walking up to that table because I'd rehearsed it so much. But I did get rattled when Sunderland blurted out, "*Lois, no! We killed you!*" like he'd seen my mother's ghost. I must look a lot more like my mother than I thought. I wonder if she'd be pleased to know that. Doubtful. Mummy so loved being one of a kind.

I close my eyes and think, am I really that same prep school girl whose life was laid out before her like a magic carpet of privilege? Was I ever that innocent young debutante who curtsied to New York Society at the New York Infirmary Ball, then went on to marry the very suitable young man of my parents' dreams? It's hard to recognize myself now. God knows that naïve young girl could never have imagined that in her middle age she'd be sitting on a train wondering if she'd killed a man—and worse—not really caring.

Chapter Four

Greta Lauber is with her chef, going over the menu of tonight's dinner party in honor of her dear friend Sun Sunderland when the phone rings. She lets her assistant get it. She has no time to chat. She's much too busy with last-minute details. Greta plans dinner parties the way generals plan battles. Like a social Napoleon, she understands that guests march on their stomachs.

Greta is a famous hostess in New York, known as a grand acquisitor of paintings, porcelain, and people. She has an eye for quality, in life and in art. No "Paperless Post" for her. Invitations to her "small dinners," as she calls them, are handwritten on ecru cards, and much sought-after because, along with the elegant apartment, gourmet food, vintage wines, and glittering table settings, there is always interesting company. Greta coined the phrase, "You are who you eat *with*." She has a knack for finding new people, young people, people of the moment, who add spice to the stew of old regulars. But the thing that has cemented her reputation as a hostess with the mostest are the dinners she gives for really powerful people—politicians, movie stars, media moguls, billionaires—like the one she is giving tonight in honor of Sun Sunderland, who has just donated one hundred million dollars to New York Hospital for a new cardiac research wing.

Greta has recently noticed that many of her wealthiest friends have become as obsessed with science as they once were with art.

The big collectors who used to bring gallerists and fashionable artists to her soirees now bring doctors and research scientists. She attributes this to the fear many of her aging friends have of being themselves collected by the Great Connoisseur in the sky.

Through her long career in the financial capital of the world, she has observed one thing: Money exaggerates who people are. If they are good, they will be better. If they are bad, they will jump right down on the devil's trampoline. If they are fearful of death, they will fund research into the disease they believe they are most likely to die of. Hence, The Sun Sunderland Cardiac Research Center at New York Hospital. She has no idea her august guest of honor is fighting for his life in the very hospital he has just endowed with a fortune. He is not dying of heart disease, as expected, but of a gunshot wound. What are the odds?

Ms. Ellis, Greta's crackerjack assistant, comes into the dining room wearing a long face.

"Mrs. Lauber, Mrs. Hartz is on the telephone. I told her you were busy, but she says it's extremely urgent. She sounds distraught."

"She always sounds distraught," Greta mutters heading for the library to take the call.

"Magma, sweetie, I really can't talk now. What's up?"

"You haven't heard." Magma the Magpie, as she is affectionately known, falls uncharacteristically silent. It is the calculated silence of someone who enjoys the glide before impact.

"*What*?" Greta says impatiently.

Wait for it…

"Sun's been *shot*."

"What do you mean *shot*?"

"I mean *shot*. With a *gun*. That Mad Maud Warner walked into The Four Seasons at lunch and shot Sun point-blank. And she got away! I was *there*! I saw the whole thing! The police questioned me!"

"*Dear God*…!" Greta says, plopping down on the couch.

As Magma Hartz is recounting the drama in detail, Greta grabs the remote and switches on the TV. The five o'clock news is just coming on. The screen blooms with the chaotic scene outside The Four Seasons earlier that day. The shooting is the lead story. A perky blond reporter is on camera giving a breathy account of the incident. Greta turns off the sound. She has no need of media commentary when she's hearing all about it from an eyewitness.

The crime is so bizarre on so many levels that Greta cannot quite comprehend it. First of all, what are the odds that one of your guests would have witnessed the shooting of your guest of honor—even if it is a small world, like people always say? Second of all, she can't believe that Maud Warner, a woman she's known for years, could possibly be capable of such a depraved and brazen act.

Greta feels terrible for Sun, now in intensive care, as well as for his wife, Jean, who is one of Greta's very best friends.

"I should probably cancel the dinner," Greta muses.

"Absolutely *not*," Magma cries. "People want to be together in time of tragedy. Trust me, discussing it will be helpful for everyone."

Greta understands better than anyone that what separates a good hostess from a great one is her record of providing memorable parties. This dinner will be memorable, all right, especially with Magma, an eyewitness, right there to be questioned. On that account alone, she feels she must go through with it.

Greta hangs up and rushes to the dining room. She surveys her round table which is set for sixteen, the most it can accommodate. She instructs Martyn, her butler, to remove two places, which is not as easy as it sounds. Greta's famous round table is known for its elaborate place settings. She likes to create a feast for the eye as well as the palate. Martyn removes two places, then rearranges the wineglasses, the water goblets, the champagne flutes, the crystal vodka shot glasses, the sterling silver placemats and cutlery, the individual Georgian salt cellars, the candlesticks, and Greta's collection of little precious jewel flowerpots which sparkle against the dark mahogany. It's time-consuming, like striking a stage set.

Greta thinks about the new generation of baby billionaires who wouldn't be caught dead setting up a dinner like this, even if they had all the accoutrements. While most dinners today are happily casual, with food and dress to match, Greta clings to her formal entertainments like a passenger aboard a sinking yacht.

Greta doesn't really expect to hear from Jean Sunderland to say she's not coming. But she thinks someone from Sunderland's office should have had the grace to let her know. She reflects sadly that basic etiquette has gone the way of bustles and buggy whips, despite the fact that good manners are the only thing people have entirely within their own control.

As she soaks in the tub, Greta wonders if she should wear the stunning new Michael Kors black crepe dress she bought just for this occasion. Black crepe is always fashionable—except when death is hovering so close.

"I don't want to look like a prediction," she thinks.

No, she'll wear the cheery green taffeta Oscar from last year. She hopes no one will remember she's worn it several times before—not that people care about such things anymore. The world has changed, she thinks. Definitely not for the better.

Chapter Five

I check my iPhone. The news is all over the web. Sunderland's in the hospital in intensive care. He's had heart attack as a result of the shooting. They now know I'm the shooter. But so far they've only managed to dig up an old photo of me from my deb days. No chance of me being recognized now. I call Billy Jakes.

"*Maudie*! What the *hell*?! Are you *nuts*? You know the whole world's looking for you, right?"

"At last. They've ignored me for the past ten years."

"Where *are* you?"

"Never mind. Can you meet me at the Shoe?"

"*Jesus*…" He hesitates. "Okay. But I can't get there 'til late. The game."

"See you there."

I put on my sunglasses and get off in Baltimore. I ditch the phone after removing the sim card. I take a taxi to the Horseshoe Casino, which just opened in August. No one there knows me yet. I figure a casino is the perfect place to hide. There are no clocks. No windows. No one's checking the news. People don't care who you are. They just want your money. I can play poker until Billy shows up.

The minute I enter, I hear the cards singing to me like the Sirens over the jingle-jangle of the slot machines, beckoning me upstairs to the poker room.

"Love the cards and the cards will love you," my grandmother used to say as she taught me poker games like five card stud, seven card high low, and draw.

And I *do* love the cards. The cards are my dangerous friends.

I take the escalator upstairs to the poker room and buy into a two-dollar/five-dollar No Limit Hold'em game. I'm at a table full of men, as usual. When I was young guys used to look at me and think, How do I get her into bed? Now they look at me and think, How do I get into her chips? I'm an older lady who's supposed to play Old Lady Poker. Little do they know.

This particular table is filled with mopes with beer breath and sour attitudes who seem to know each other. As I'm arranging my chip stack on the felt, I see one of them wink at his buddy and whisper, "*Cha-ching*!" like I'm a payday. So I'm thinking, you guys can't even imagine I could outplay you any more than you can imagine you're sitting here with the most wanted woman in the whole freakin' country.

I win the first pot I play.

Cha-ching!

Chapter Six

Jean Sunderland paces the waiting room of New York Hospital. She has been in that sterile hell waiting for updates on her husband's condition ever since a distraught staffer burst into her board meeting at the Museum of Modern Art and blurted out the news he'd been shot. It's hard to believe. Things like this simply don't happen to people like them—not to the wealthy, socially prominent, well respected Sunderlands. If a man like Sun Sunderland ever did get shot, it should be the result of a terrible accident at a pheasant shoot on some grand estate, not at lunch at The Four Seasons.

Jean is a fashionably thin, crisply turned out woman in her mid-fifties. Her attractiveness comes from a combination of meticulous grooming and a lively intelligence. She exudes an aura of competence. She's a person who can be trusted to get things done, and done well. Having been successful in business, she's weathered many a crisis in her life, but nothing near the likes of this current situation.

Burt Sklar was already there when Jean arrived at the hospital. He stayed awhile to keep her company and bond with her in their mutual hour of grief. She finally Garboed him—"I want to be alone"—politely telling him to get lost. Jean has always been wary of Burt Sklar. She has never been able to figure out why her husband liked him so much. She doesn't trust him. In the early days of their marriage, she asked her husband to drop Sklar. Sun defended his old friend, saying, "Jeanie, you just don't get Burt. He's stuck by me through thick and thin. I never forget loyalty."

Sunderland and Sklar have been close friends for years—way back when they were each married to their first wives. Sunderland was married to Pam. Sklar was married to Sylvia. They had many happy times, dining and vacationing together, just the four of them. A tight-knit group. Halcyon days. That is, until Pam ditched Sunderland for her exercise teacher—a woman.

Sunderland was devastated by his wife's betrayal. He didn't know which was worse: the abandonment, or her choice of a female partner. Wherever Sunderland went, he imagined hearing the snickers of his enemies and friends alike. That a powerful man like Sunderland had been left by his wife for a *woman* was simply too delicious a morsel for the gossips not to chew on. You couldn't cut the *schadenfreude* with a chainsaw.

It was Sklar who stepped in to help Sunderland navigate that terrible period in Sunderland's life when his battered manhood was nailed up like a ragged pelt for all the world to sneer at. Grateful for his friend's loyalty, Sunderland confided in Sklar over many a drunken dinner. He told Sklar about certain sexual appetites he had. He described kinky, stamina-requiring episodes which proved he was a strong and virile man, not some wimp whose wife left him for "Daisy Dyke," as he referred to his wife's paramour. Sklar, who knew things about Sunderland that no one else knew or could have imagined, didn't judge; he listened. Sklar was a discreet, supportive, and sympathetic ear. You don't forget a friend like that. You can't. He knows too much.

Eventually, Sunderland met and married Jean Streeter, the creative director of Streeter/Greene, the enormously successful advertising agency she helped build. Jean was a force in New York's ultra competitive world. She was considered a great catch. Their marriage helped erase Sunderland's past humiliation. Over Jean's objections, Sunderland picked Sklar to be his best man in their cozy wedding at Greta Lauber's house.

Later on, Jean was one of the few people who actually paid attention to Maud when she accused Sklar of embezzlement, and worse. Jean warned her husband, "Where there's smoke, there's fraud." Sunderland defended his old friend, assuring his wife that Maud's accusations against Sklar were nothing more than the deranged rants of a bitter divorcee with money problems.

"You know why she hates Burt? Because Lois Warner trusted Burt more than she trusted her own daughter. Simple as that. All our friends love Burt. Hell, he represents half of them!" Sunderland crowed to Jean.

Still, something told Jean that her husband's continued association with Sklar would bring him trouble one day. And now this!

She leaves the waiting room to call Greta.

"Jeanie, darling! You're an absolute angel to call. How is Sun?"

"He's going to pull through, Greta. I'm sure of it," Jean replies, not because she knows anything from the doctors, but because positive thinking has always been her forte.

"Thank God! Do you want me to come to the hospital?"

"No, sweetie. I'm okay. Besides, you still have your dinner party, right?" Jean says, unsure.

"Yes. And all our thoughts and prayers will be with you, my dear, brave friend. We'll drink a toast to Sun's full recovery," Greta says, figuring it's best not to mention that their mutual friend Magma the Magpie will be there to spice up the evening with her eyewitness account of the crime.

Jean hangs up, touched by Greta's offer to come to the hospital. Still, she can't help wondering if there are places on earth where dinner parties are canceled when the guest of honor gets shot.

Chapter Seven

Greta Lauber's guests arrive at her apartment in varying states of shock and dismay. Greta greets them all with her usual upbeat charm: "I just spoke to Jean at the hospital. She says Sun's going to pull through!"

Greta feels like an archangel bringing tidings of comfort, if not joy. People are clearly disturbed that one of their own has been shot by one of their own. Everyone needs a drink, and not just those decorous flutes of pink Cristal champagne which are a Lauber party staple. Tonight, everyone who isn't in recovery wants the hard stuff. Greta breaks out the coveted seventeen-year-old double wood Balvenie scotch which was the preferred drink of her late husband, Jake Lauber, the distinguished publisher.

As the guests mingle in the living room, all anyone can talk about is the shooting and how Maud managed to get away. Many of them knew Maud when she lived in New York. They remember her bookshop with fondness. She was quite social and well liked before she went around town like some Park Avenue Cassandra, warning people that Burt Sklar was a crook. Maud's been nuts for years. But *this* nuts? Who knew?

Several people at this very dinner party are clients of Sklar. Sklar looks after them by taking care of all their finances—doing their taxes, paying their bills, overseeing their investments and real estate interests, setting up trusts for their kids, etc. He's a nanny accountant, a mensch money manager, constantly reassuring his brood that they are in great financial shape.

"Don't worry, you can afford it," is a Sklar catchphrase.

He likes telling rich people they're richer. They like hearing it.

As the group rehashes the crime, Greta glances at her watch for the tenth time. It's eight-thirty. Everyone is there except Magma. Magma knows that Greta runs her dinners like clockwork: Invited for seven forty-five. Sit down at eight-thirty. That way everybody's out by ten or ten-thirty. No one wants a late weeknight. It also helps her chef, whose delicious concoctions depend on perfect timing.

Greta invites her old friend Magma to every single one of her dinners, even though it's always a major pain in the ass to find an extra man for a single, older woman. Tonight, Greta's dredged up an eligible for Magma—no easy feat in a town where unmarried heterosexual men are rarer than legal parking spaces. He's a writer named Brent Hobbs. Greta sat next to Hobbs at a recent charity event. The forty-ish Hobbs made a small splash some years ago with a book on the mortgage crisis called *Complicity*. He has since descended into the blogosphere with a site called *HobbsNobbing*, where he spices up financial news with gossip.

Greta went out on a limb calling Hobbs out of the blue. But Sunderland once mentioned Hobbs' book on the country's near economic collapse was one that, "got it right," and she always likes to surprise her guest of honor in some interesting way. Thus she invited him. Plus, Greta knows that great hostesses have to be vampires, ever in search of new blood to keep their parties lively.

Greta figured Magma, too, would relish the prospect of meeting a smart, heterosexual, younger man—Magma being a widow with lusty appetites. Yet how has her friend repaid her? By being late. At eight-thirty-five Greta instructs Martyn to tell the chef they will sit down.

He gives her a solemn nod. Words are not necessary. He understands his employer perfectly. They will start without Mrs.

Hartz. Martyn has been her butler for over twenty years. Friends and parties come and go. He stays.

As guests are being served the first course in the candlelit dining room, Magma makes a breathy entrance.

"*Hello, everybody!* So sorry to be late. But I was at The Four Seasons today. I saw the whole thing! I'm an absolute *wreck!*" Magma says, raking a hand through her thick, dyed-blond hair.

Greta doesn't think her friend looks a wreck. In fact, Magma's glowing with excitement. Her round face is flushed, her kohl-rimmed blue eyes are sparkling, and she's wearing a dress that leaves little of her ample cleavage to the imagination. Tonight she looks more like her sexy, youthful self than ever.

Greta and Magma have known each other for ages. They met back in the day while working at *Glamour*. Magma wrote features for the magazine and Greta was the assistant beauty editor. They hit it off immediately and stayed in touch through the years, speaking the shorthand of true friends. They've gone through good times and bad, confiding in one another about their lives and families. They are godmothers of each other's children. Both women are widows now. But Greta is a rich widow, while Magma must scrape by on her late husband's service benefits, plus what she gets for the articles she writes for women's magazines. But there's very little money in that. Who wants beauty and fashion tips from an older widow?

Magma is seated next to Brent Hobbs, who seems even more taken with her ample bosom than with the caviar blinis. Their flirtatious conversation is quickly interrupted by guests demanding to hear Magma's account of the shooting. Sensing she is the star of the evening, Magma holds forth, describing Maud's journey to Sunderland's table step by long-winded step until—*gasp!*—*bang!*

"My old and dear friend! *Shot!* I saw him being carried out on a stretcher!" She bursts into tears.

The first time Magma bursts into tears the guests are moved by her dramatic ordeal. The second time she breaks down, during the entrée, they are less sympathetic. Her third outburst, during the salad course, is met with stony stares. By the time the Grand Marnier soufflé arrives, people wish to hell Magma had gone to some other fucking restaurant. They resent their hostess for allowing a conversational terrorist to hijack the evening and take it down with her in flames. Magma keeps saying, "It all happened so fast." Yet her retelling has taken a decade.

The weary, despondent guests leave right after dinner—all except Magma and Brent Hobbs, who is now drunkenly diving into Magma's cleavage with the same gusto he dived into the *boeuf-a-la-mode*. Greta's polite hostess façade crumbles.

"If you two want a bed, the guest room's upstairs—second door on the left. I'm done!" she announces, knowing Sun isn't the only casualty of this ghastly day.

Chapter Eight

Poker has its own moral universe. Lying is called bluffing. Deception is the norm. I entered that amoral sphere without actually realizing it until it was too late. At first, poker was simply good theatre: Every hand a scene, every player an actor. Time flowed differently at the tables. Playing poker was the only way I was able to forget my problems for long stretches of time. I didn't understand how profoundly the game was changing me until the change was complete.

I've played poker with everyone from a Supreme Court Justice to the guy who delivers takeout from a greasy spoon in D.C. I've learned tricks and strategies from people who make their living at the game, and, in some cases, at even dicier careers as well. For example, when I told people Burt Sklar was a swindler, a guy I played with offered to "take care" of him for me if I just said the word. I didn't take him up on his kind offer mainly because the theft of money simply wasn't a strong enough motive for me to exact such a terrible revenge. I didn't know then what I know now. Then, I just felt sorry for myself.

I used to come home to my tiny apartment after a long day doing grunt work, and surf the web, obsessing over how I ever let a con man like Burt Sklar into our lives. One evening, just by chance, I discovered *Pokerstars*, a site where you could play poker online for fake chips. Remembering those comforting old times when I played cards with my dear grandmother, I logged on and started playing No Limit Texas Hold'em—definitely not my granny's poker.

But here's the thing: On the Internet I wasn't Maud Warner, an old bag in curlers and fuzzy slippers sitting in front of my computer with a bag of potato chips and a Coke. On the Internet, I was "BluffaloBill237," a disaffected, unemployed construction worker, who was mad, bad, and dangerous to play with. I amassed so many fake chips I figured this game was definitely for me. It wasn't long before I started playing for real money. I was very lucky at first and made enough in cash games and in tournaments to quit my dumb office job and play poker all day.

I hid behind this male persona until one cool Friday morning in April when I logged on to Pokerstars as usual to play a tourney. To my horror, the entire site was shut down. April 15, 2011, known to poker players as "Black Friday," is the day that lives in poker infamy. Citing banking and gambling law violations, the United States Department of Justice had issued an indictment against the three biggest online poker sites in the country. Playing online poker for real money in America was effectively over.

I went into withdrawal. I needed poker like an addict needs a fix. Then I ran into an acquaintance who told me he could get me into a home game run by a pal of his named Billy Jakes. I was so desperate I agreed to try it, even though I was scared as hell to play live poker where people could see me as I really am: An older woman.

The first time I played at his house—the Poker Palace, as it was nicknamed—Billy saw that I was nervous and was very patient as I fumbled my chips and occasionally bet out of turn. After the game, he took me aside and told me he had watched me play. He said I had great card sense but I didn't know what the hell I was doing. He said he could give me a couple of lessons in No Limit Hold'em, if I wanted. I accepted with pleasure.

Billy became my mentor and a good friend. Pretty soon we

were driving to casinos together, playing cash games and tour-naments. During those long drives, we learned a lot about each other's lives. Billy was a stand-up guy I could trust. I knew he'd come to my rescue now.

I look up from my table and see Billy staring at me across the poker room. There's deep consternation in his boyish face. I acknowledge him with a slight nod. We'll meet outside. There are cameras everywhere. It's important we're not seen walking together. I play another hand, then rise and load my chips in two full racks. It's been a profitable night.

An irascible player I'd nicknamed Yosemite Slimebucket in my mind pipes up: "Not leavin', are you, girly? The night is young,"

"But I'm not. So long…" I want to add "Suckers!" but now is not the time.

I cash in my chips at the cage. Billy is waiting for me in his car on the service road outside the casino.

"Thanks for coming, Billy." I buckle up in the passenger seat.

"I must be crazy," he says.

"What's the news?"

"*You're* the news, Maudie!"

"No, I mean, Sunderland. Is he dead?"

Billy looks at me askance. "*Jesus*! Do you *want* him to be? He's in intensive care. What the hell were you were thinking?"

"An eye for an eye…?" I say like it's a question.

Poor Billy's waiting for me to elaborate.

"That's *it*?" he says at last. "That's all you're gonna say about shooting a guy in cold blood? Did you even mean to shoot *Sunderland*? I thought Sklar's the one you hate so much."

I pause for a moment. "Let me ask you something, Billy: Who's your worst enemy at the poker table?"

"*What*? What's that got to do with *anything*?"

"Just answer the question, Billy. *Who*?"

Billy sighs in exasperation. "I dunno…the asshole who always raises your big blind."

"*Yourself,*" I correct him. "*You* are your own worst enemy—in poker and in life."

"What the hell does *that* mean?"

"It means that if you don't know yourself very well, you'll always lose. Believe it or not, that is the single most valuable lesson I ever learned from poker."

Billy is shaking his head. "Oh really? Well, then, who the hell are *you*, Maud Warner? The woman who's been my closest friend and confidant for the last five years? Or the lunatic who just shot the Pope of Finance in a restaurant?"

"Can't I be both?"

I turn away and stare out the window at the neon-pricked night whizzing by. It's good to be free and not cooped up in some cell, as I expected. We drive in silence the rest of the way to Washington. Forty minutes later, we pull up in front of Billy's two-story brick house on a tree-lined, residential street off Nebraska Avenue. Billy sneaks me in through the Poker Palace entrance.

I walk through the converted garage feeling nostalgic for the times I played there. The brick walls are decorated with poker memorabilia, including large framed photos of famous old-time poker players like Doyle Brunson and Stu Unger. Baseball caps from various casinos hang on hooks. A neon sign on the mantelpiece shimmers with four aces. There's an open kitchen with a stove, sink, refrigerator, and microwave oven, plus a long refectory table for setting up food. A water cooler nestles in one corner. A large plasma TV hangs on a wall. I run my fingers lightly over one of two casino-quality felt-lined poker tables, thinking of all the fun I had there before I got so hooked on the game I needed to play a lot more than once a month. Like a true addict, I needed the fix of a game that ran every day—a dangerous, illegal game, which is as far from the Poker Palace as Chateau Lafitte is from rotgut.

The phone is ringing as we enter the main house.

"Betcha this is Gloria from Madrid... '*Lo?*" he says, answering in a fake sleepy voice.

I hear Gloria's excited voice shrieking through the line. Billy makes faces at me as he tries to calm his wife down. He finally hangs up the phone.

"*Hola*. They know all about you in Spain," he deadpans.

"What else did she say?"

"Basically, that if I heard from you, I was to give you her love. And turn you in."

"I don't blame her."

Billy heaves a beleaguered sigh. "The guest room's upstairs. Glo gets back in two weeks. You've gotta be gone by then."

Billy gives me an old nightgown of Gloria's to sleep in and some toiletries. I'm pretty beat. Still, it's so good to be free, sleeping in a nice cozy bed instead of on a slab at Rikers. My own private tournament has begun. Having unexpectedly escaped, I have time to monitor the situation, to see if everyone has as strong a stomach as I do. Will they play their hands like champions? I'm counting on it.

I told them many times, "No matter what happens…don't fold."

Chapter Nine

Jean Sunderland awakes from a fitful sleep in the drab hospital waiting room. She glances at her watch. It's past two in the morning. She gets up to stretch her legs. She walks slowly up and down the hospital corridor, reminding herself that she's a strong woman.

Jean had a big life before she ever met Sun. As the young creative director of Streeter/Greene, Jean was viewed as a successful woman who didn't need a man to fulfill her. She appeared supremely happy with her life. All the women's magazines held her up as an icon for The New Independent Woman. Like the advertising woman she was, she knew that image is all—except when you go home to an empty house. Success cools the more you cling to it for warmth.

Much as she hated to admit it, there were times when she'd have traded her brilliant career for a wonderful man who would take care of her. She knew how pathetic it was to feel this way, particularly for a woman who'd made her reputation on being a staunch advocate for women's rights. But she couldn't help herself. Jean understood the Prince Charming fairy tale to her core—which is why she was so good at selling it to others.

When Sun Sunderland came courting her, she felt blessed. He rescued her from the deep loneliness which had shadowed her for as long as she could remember. She embarked on what she now thought of as her *real life* at last, brimming with fun and friends and experiences, with a man she adored and admired. Separately they were each very successful. Together they were a power couple. The Sunderlands. A brand.

Back in the waiting room, Jean sees she's not alone. A dark-haired young woman in large insect eye sunglasses, wearing a short patent leather raincoat and matching boots, sits cross-legged, tapping her long red nails on the sides of her chair. She seems both bored and anxious. Jean sits down a decorous distance away. They respect each other's space by not speaking.

Jean checks her iPhone. There are too many e-mails and messages to count. She feels overwhelmed. She shuts off the phone, debating whether to go downstairs and get some coffee. Just then, a young resident comes in. Jean perks up. He glances around.

"Which one of you is Mrs. Sunderland?"

Jean and the young woman bolt up simultaneously, answering in unison: "*I am!*"

Jean says gently, "He's asking for *me*, dear. *I'm* Mrs. Sunderland."

"So am I."

"*Excuse* me?" Jean says with an appalled little laugh.

Who is this woman? A reporter? A kook? *Who?*

The young woman lowers her sunglasses and stares at Jean for a brief moment. Glimpsing bloodshot, mascara-smeared eyes, Jean knows there's a real story here, one she's not going to like.

"I'm sorry you had to find out this way," the young woman says softly.

"*Are you mad?*" Jean cries.

The young woman turns to the doctor. "Take us both in, please."

The doctor doesn't know where to look. Med school doesn't adequately prepare you for the psychological dramas of the profession. Only TV soap operas do that. All this poor guy knows is that a critically ill patient is asking for his wife, and there seems to be two of them in the waiting room.

"Look, we don't have a lot of time here," he says. "Both of you come with me. You ladies can sort it out later."

The two women follow him down the corridor into the ICU. Several minutes later, Jean Sunderland emerges in tears.

Alone.

Chapter Ten

Greta is sound asleep when her phone rings. She fumbles for it, murmuring a sleepy, "'Lo?"

"Greta, it's me. I'm downstairs. Can I come up?"

Greta recognizes Jean's distraught voice. She perks up immediately. "Of course, darling! I'm right here. Tell the doorman it's fine."

Greta throws on the pink cashmere robe that's always laid out on her divan. As she waits for the elevator, she prepares herself to hear that Sun is dead. Why else would Jean seek solace at this ungodly hour in the morning? When Jean steps off the elevator, Greta throws her arms around her dear friend.

"Jeanie! Sweetheart! I'm so, so sorry!"

Jean stares at Greta with rat-red eyes. Greta has never seen Jean look quite so upset and bedraggled—not even three summers ago in Southampton when Jean got caught in a riptide and almost drowned. Greta leads Jean into the bedroom and sits down with her on the divan.

"Talk to me, Jeanie," Greta says, wrapping a consoling arm around her friend.

Jean doesn't answer. Finally, with the solemnity of an undertaker, Greta ventures, "He's dead, isn't he?"

"Worse," Jean says.

"*Oh no...!* Paralyzed? A coma?"

Jean heaves a weary sigh. "I need a drink. Have you got any scotch?"

"Of course, darling."

Greta scurries to the library bar and fetches the Balvenie. She pours Jean a glass. Jean swills it down in gulps, like it's iced tea on a sweltering day. Greta doesn't say a word as she watches her friend slowly relax into the divan. She senses Jean is gathering her thoughts. Greta is very good at waiting for people to say what's on their minds. That's why she's such a great friend: She knows when to shut up.

At last, Jean speaks. "Tell me something, Greta. Have you ever heard any rumors about Sun?"

"Rumors?" Greta is perplexed.

"Since he's been married to me. Have you ever heard he's had any other…attachments?"

"*Are you serious?* Absolutely not! Why?"

"I just found out he's a bigamist."

Jean says this so matter-of-factly, Greta thinks she's misheard. "What…?"

"A *bigamist*. As in, he has *another wife.*"

Greta draws back. "Sweetie, I think you're in shock."

"Goddam right I am," she says, holding out her glass. "Another please."

Jean sips the warming liquor as she tells Greta the story. Greta is riveted as Jean describes the moment in the waiting room when the doctor came in asking for Mrs. Sunderland and she and "this patent leather floozy," as Jean describes her, both sprang to their feet.

"I thought she was some kind of kook. But I was just too exhausted to argue. So we both followed the doctor into intensive care where Sun was lying flat on his back like some sort of hideous sea creature with all these tubes and wires going in and out of him. This bitch in her hideous sunglasses and I were standing on either side of his bed. I bent down and whispered, 'Sun, darling,

it's me, Jean.' He blinked a couple of times, then turned away…
Towards *her*. At which point, she took off her sunglasses, bent
down, and gave him a kiss. On the mouth! Then he turned back
to me and managed to utter two words…"

Jean pauses. Her eyes well up with tears as she relives the
moment.

"Which were…?" Greta prompts, on the edge of her seat.

"*Mrs. Keppel.*"

Greta frowns. "*Mrs. Keppel?* What's *that* supposed to mean?"

"Oh I knew *exactly* what he meant. And he *knew* I knew,"
Jean says with a mordant little chuckle.

"*What? Tell me.*"

"Sun fancies himself a great history buff, as you may recall
from some of his endless digressions at dinner parties. He's
obsessed with monarchy—especially the Edwardian era. No surprise. He's always wanted to be a king so he could behead people.
Anyway, when Edward the Seventh was dying, the horny old toad
told Queen Alexandra he wanted to be with his mistress—the
love of his life. At that moment, all the pomp and circumstance
fell away because he was about to meet his maker. King or no
king, I guess human beings just want to be with the one person
they truly love when they're on the way out. Queen Alexandra
graciously and unselfishly granted her husband's last request.
Long story short? Horntoad Eddie croaked with his mistress by
his side, not his wife. Her name was Mrs. Alice Keppel. It's one
of Sun's favorite stories so I knew what he meant. And now I
know why. That creature calling herself Mrs. Sunderland is the
love of his life—not yours truly!"

"That is kind of romantic…I mean about King Edward,"
Greta quickly adds.

"Oh, yeah? Well, guess what? *I ain't Queen Alexandra!* Oh,
Greta, I feel like such a goddam fool!"

Jean weeps. Greta hands tissues to her anguished friend. This
serious incident has brought serious betrayal to light.

"So you're saying Sun is a bigamist? Maybe she's just calling herself Mrs. Sunderland…"

Jean shakes her head. "No…he *married* her. She showed me her driver's license! That's when I left the room." She breaks down again.

Greta's heard juicy secrets, but never anything as juicy as this. Or as shocking. She's so appalled she joins Jean in a stiff glass of scotch, even though it's four in the morning and they're not in Palm Beach.

"I can't believe it. *Sun!* Of all people! A *bigamist!* And for you to find out in this ghastly way! I mean, finding out in *any* way is bad. But while he's *dying*. You can't help feeling sorry for him *and* loathing him at the same time. Talk about an emotional *tour de force*."

"Right now I just loathe him," Jean says, wiping her eyes.

"I don't blame you, darling. It's a blow. What are you going to do?"

"Kill him if he lives."

"Seriously. What if he dies?"

"I don't give a shit. It won't be Sun dying. It'll be a complete stranger—some felonious creep I was living with like one of those poor deluded wives who only finds out her husband's a serial killer when she discovers a severed head under the bed. I hope he does die, the bastard!"

Greta winces. "You need to call your lawyer, sweetie. You need professional advice."

"I never had a clue. *Not one clue!* I mean, he was away on business a lot…He'd call up and say he had to spend more time in Washington…He's all involved in fundraising and politics down there so I never questioned it."

"Is that where she lives?"

"*How the hell do I know?*" Jean snaps. "I assume so since that's where he spends the most time."

"Do you know her name? Anything about her?"

"Her name is Danya Sunderland, according to the license. *Christ almighty!* I can't believe this is happening!"

"Is it possible they're not *legally* married?" Greta says, aiming for a bright side.

"I don't care! It's the *betrayal*, don't you see? Hell, I'm going to sue the bastard for everything he's got! I'm gonna hit him where it hurts the most—in the *money*."

Greta pats her friend's shoulder in an effort to be consoling. "Listen, Jeanie, I know you're upset…"

"Ya *think?*" Jean cries angrily.

"I know, dear, I know…but we need to think this through for a moment."

Greta uses the word "we" because when one of her friends is in trouble, she takes it personally.

"I've thought it through, believe me. I'm going to drag his rotten, stinking name that he gave to someone else through the sewers of New York! Her, too! You just watch me!"

"Calm down, Jeanie, calm down," Greta says in her most soothing, friend-indeed voice. "I understand how you must feel. But you don't want to look bad."

Jean's jaw drops. "Sun's a goddam *bigamist!* How do *I* look bad here?!"

"I know, I know…but he's just been shot. He may die. No matter what he's done, you may want to hold off letting the world in on it, just for the moment. It's a lot for people to process."

"For *people* to process? How about for *me*, his *wife?!*" Jean downs another glass of scotch.

"Please listen to me, Jeanie. The consequences of this could go far beyond your marriage."

"Whassat supposeta mean?" Jean slurs her words as the effects of the liquor begin to take hold.

"Sun's got that company with Sklar in which I and many of our friends have invested. If he's arrested for *bigamy*…? What's that going to do to his spotless reputation? Sun's image will be shattered—not to mention the company's."

"I don't give a shit."

"Jeanie, bigamy's *illegal*. Not to alarm you, darling, but you have to wonder what other illegal things he may be up to? Let's face it: A man who betrays his wife might well betray his investors. At least that's what people will think. Trust me, there are fortunes at stake here. And you know how some of our friends fear being swindled more than death."

"I wanna see the bastard fry! *Fricassee!*"

"I know. But you don't want to fricasee *with* him, do you, sweetie? You don't want to go broke. I assume your finances are all tied up with his, aren't they?"

"I have no idea," Jean says, sniffing back tears.

Greta's eyes widen. "What do you mean you have no idea?"

"Sun handles all the financial stuff. He always has."

Greta is stunned and appalled. "Jeanie, don't you know what you have and where you have it?"

"Not really. I gave my money to Sun when we got married and let him take care of it. He's the Pope of Finance, isn't he?"

"Jeanie, you were a successful business woman, for God's sakes!"

"I was on the *creative* side of advertising. Business wasn't a priority. When I married Sun, I was truly happy for the first time in my life. *I didn't think about money!*"

"One should always think about money, no matter how happy one is," Greta says like a prim etiquette instructor. "I mean, look at poor old Lois Warner. Maybe Burt Sklar really did steal her fortune, like Maud says. And that would be because she never thought about money, and left everything up to him."

"*Sklar*," Jean scowls. "I bet he knows about this. I betcha anything he's been in on it from the beginning."

"He *is* Sun's best friend."

"Yes. And he was the one who always called me to say that Sun was stuck in meetings down in D.C., or that Sun had to fly off somewhere and couldn't contact me. I never *dreamed* that odious creep was lying. He *must* know about her. He's got to!" Jean gasps with a sudden revelation. "*Greta!*"

"*What?*"

"I just figured it out! That's the *real* reason Sun would never give Sklar up as a friend. It's not just that they were pals back in the day. Sklar *knew* about the bigamy and he was helping Sun cover it up. *Of course!* It all makes perfect sense now!"

"Jeanie, listen to me, as someone who loves you. You've got to protect yourself here. You need to tread very, *very* carefully. You can't let anyone know about this. Not yet."

Greta is thinking clearly about this delicate situation. She understands that as much as Jean wants revenge, her fortunes are intertwined with her husband's, both financially and socially. She knows that before Jean acts, she needs to get sound legal advice on what to do. Sun's downfall could result in her dear friend's ruination as well.

It takes some doing, but Greta finally convinces Jean to call her lawyer before she does anything else. She then tucks her exhausted, distraught, and drunken friend into bed in the guest room. As Greta closes the door, she pauses, wondering what other dangers are lurking beneath the surface of her privileged little world.

Chapter Eleven

Burt Sklar sits behind the steel and glass desk in his office, absently twirling a pen between his fingers as he gazes out the window. The Park Avenue cityscape looks like a smoky mirage on this hazy, gray day. That suits him fine. He's in no mood for sunny weather. First and foremost, he hasn't heard from the one person on earth he longs to hear from. Second, Maud Warner's on the run. The crazy bitch has managed to evade all of law enforcement.

Sklar had always typed Maud as one of life's lucky dabblers—a spoiled, prep school brat, insulated by money, who grew up viewing the real world from the safe distance of never actually having to earn a living. Sklar was sure that if it hadn't been for her rich stepfather, the plain, bookish Maud would probably have wound up working in a bookshop—never owning one. However, in light of recent events, Sklar knows he's sorely misjudged her.

He can still picture Maud at the funeral of her stepfather some years back. She stood on the stage, speaking in a barely audible, grief-stricken voice. She looked so thin and pale and exhausted that no one thought she'd get through it. Was that scarecrow wreck of a girl the same person who had just marched up like a seasoned infantryman and taken a shot at him? What the hell happened to this disappointed loser not worth bothering about that changed her into a would-be assassin?

The intercom buzzes. Sklar's secretary announces that a Detective Chen is there and would like to talk to him about the shooting. Sklar remembers Chen from The Four Seasons. He didn't laugh when Sklar made that crack about being safer in Syria. Now's the time to get on the detective's good side. It's always good to have allies in the police department. One never knows when the law might be a problem.

Straightening up in his chair, Sklar clears his throat, and gets into character. He's taught himself a little trick when he wants to impress people. He pretends he's in a movie and thinks of a star he can emulate. Today, he will be Gregory Peck in *To Kill A Mockingbird.* Atticus Finch was a real stand-up guy, an old-time hero, facing injustice and violence with calm, courageous resolve. There's nothing cruel or false about Gregory Peck as Atticus Finch. The man is compassionate strength itself. Sklar holds that image in his mind as his secretary shows Chen into his office.

The round-faced Chen is older and slightly heftier than Sklar remembers. But he still has that annoyingly humorless attitude Sklar couldn't liven up with a joke. Sklar thinks Chen's inscrutable, all right, with none of the wry charm of the cliché cinematic detective, Charlie Chan, as played by the Swedish American actor, Warner Oland.

"Detective Chen. Good to see you again, sir," Sklar says, rising to shake hands. "Please have a seat."

Chen sits on one of two leather and steel swivel chairs across the desk. Sklar leans forward with an air of deep concern.

"How's my best friend Sun? Any word?"

"Not that I've heard."

"Please God, he pulls through." Sklar bows his head for a brief dramatic moment.

"So, Mr. Sklar—"

"Call me Burt."

"I'm here to talk to you about Maud Warner."

Sklar relaxes back in his chair. "I figured," he says with resignation. "I take it she hasn't been caught yet?"

"Not yet."

"You'll get her."

"I'm sure we will."

"Poor old Maudie…" Sklar sighs.

"You say that like you feel sorry for her?"

"*Truthfully*…? I do. Very much so."

Chen furrows his brow. "That's interesting, considering a lot of people think you were the one she was aiming at."

"Oh, I *know* she was. But I still feel sorry for her. She's been through a lot."

Would Atticus badmouth Scout even if she took a shot at him? Never! Not Atticus. Not Gregory Peck. And not himself playing Gregory Peck playing Atticus Finch.

"*Candidly*…? Maudie may not be in her right mind, Detective."

"Oh…? What makes you say that?"

"Her brother, Alan, died, fairly recently. She's all alone in the world now. A very sad situation. People can go really nuts without any support. You're blessed in this life if you have a family."

Sklar pegs Chen as a family man himself and figures it can't hurt to pledge allegiance to that vanilla flag. But Chen doesn't salute.

"Tell me a little about your history with Ms. Warner."

Sklar stretches out his arms to encompass the room. "*Aye-yi-yi!* Where to begin! Okay, so I've known Maudie and her family for, oh, over twenty years now. I was her stepfather's accountant. Sidney Warner. Wonderful man. Genius in business. We were very, very close. Sidney made me the executor of his estate. As per his wishes, I took care of his widow, Lois, and her children, Maud and Alan."

"Maud was the eldest?"

"Yeah. But she wasn't Sidney's biological child. Her mother was married before. Her real father died. Sidney adopted Maudie when he married Lois. Lois despised Maudie's real father, and never really trusted Maud as a result. She always used to tell me how much Maud reminded her of her first husband."

"But Mrs. Warner trusted you?"

"Absolutely. But lemme explain something, Detective. Lois Warner was a very beautiful, very charming, very *willful* woman. She made a lot of terrible investments against my advice. By the time she died, there was very little left. Maudie had to blame someone. Unfortunately, she blamed me."

As Sklar speaks in carefully measured words, he thinks about Lois, a drama queen who felt she'd given up a promising acting career for her family and was bitterly disappointed with her choice. He remembers her endless phone calls which drove him nuts. All the woman ever did was complain—about her kids, her staff, her failed career, her decorator, her doctors, her aches, her pains, and all the random violence in the world. Although, as a once-great beauty, she considered aging to be the ultimate terrorist attack.

"When's the last time you saw Maud Warner?" Chen asks.

"Not counting The Four Seasons, right?" Sklar says, trying a little joke. Chen remains stony-faced. Insufferably inscrutable, Sklar thinks.

"A few months ago," Sklar goes on. "I can check my calendar. She came here with her brother. I hadn't seen her in a while. She looked godawful."

"What was the purpose of her visit?"

"Money. Her brother Alan owed a lot of money to loan sharks. Alan was kind of a screwed up kid. An addict. Maudie asked me if I'd help him out."

"And did you?"

"Yup. Fool that I am."

"So you gave her money for her brother?"

"I did."

"How much?"

"I forget. A few thousand bucks, maybe. Nothing huge."

"In cash?"

"Yeah. I keep quite a bit of cash in the office. Celebrity clients in from out of town need to cash a check, can't be bothered to go to a bank. You know how it is with some of them, I bet?" Sklar chuckles.

"I'll take your word for it," Chen says flatly. "Given your history with Ms. Warner, I'm surprised you gave her money."

"*Honestly…*? Sun and I were doing a big deal for our company at that time. The last thing we needed was any bad publicity. Maudie's gone around saying libelous, ridiculous things about me for years—not that anyone believes her. But you know yourself, Detective, there's always some envious creep out there looking for a lie to spread around. I thought if I helped her out, she'd play nice. Then she goes and takes a shot at me! Talk about no good deed, right?"

"So you believe she was aiming at you?"

"Absolutely. No question. She had no reason to dislike Sun."

"But her aim was bad?"

"Obviously…"

So far no one has come forward to say they saw Sklar pull Sunderland in front of him. But Chen is getting into dicey territory so Sklar casually shifts the focus of the inquiry.

"Lemme ask you something, Detective. Can you believe anyone like Maud—you know, older lady, well brought up, privileged background, well-educated—could do something this utterly bonkers?"

"Actually, from my experience, I believe anyone's capable of anything at any time. Do you have any idea where she might be?"

"Believe me, if I did, I'd tell you. *Truthfully…*? I'm worried she might come back. She didn't complete the mission, right?" He laughs, then stops abruptly when Chen fails to see the humor.

Sklar's folksy charm offensive doesn't seem to be working with the detective. He's relieved when his cell phone vibrates. He takes it out of his pocket and answers the call.

"Hold on a minute…" he says to the caller. "I'm sorry, Detective, but I really should take this unless we're not done here—"

"Take your call, Mr. Sklar," Chen says, rising.

"Thanks so much, Detective Chen. Anything I can do. Please keep me posted! Call me Burt!"

Sklar makes sure Chen is well away down the hall before he shuts the door and returns to the call. He clears his throat and speaks in a soft, loving voice.

"Dany…How'ya doin', sweetheart?"

"I'm still at the hospital. I saw Jean. Oh Burt, she *knows!*"

Chapter Twelve

Chen goes directly from Sklar's office to the Sunderlands' elegant double wide limestone townhouse on East Seventy-third Street. A maid leads him up a sweeping marble staircase to the living room on the second floor.

"Mrs. Sunderland will be right with you," the maid says.

Left alone, Detective Chen browses around a spacious living room, nearly stifled by plush, tasseled furniture covered in pastel silks and velvets. The walls are dotted with beautiful paintings, but none more impressive than the massive orange and yellow Rothko presiding over the fireplace mantel like a glorious sunset. As he strolls over to look out the French doors at the manicured back garden, he notices a dangerously frayed lamp cord under a gilded console. The tattered old cord looks particularly menacing in the midst of such opulence, a stealthy danger that could burn the whole place down. He thinks about another dangerous secret that great wealth may be hiding. He knows he must tread cautiously because the secrets of the rich are like mercury—poke at them and they will scatter in all directions, becoming impossible to verify.

"Detective Chen?" says a voice from the entrance.

He turns. An attractive, neatly coiffed blond woman in her mid-fifties, wearing a cobalt blue dress and a strand of pearls the size of quail eggs, is cruising toward him with her charm-braceleted hand outstretched. Behind her is an older, distinguished-looking man with thick, fastidiously combed pewter-colored hair and a sharp, coinlike profile. He's sporting a pinstripe suit, starched white shirt, vest, red and blue club tie, and a clenched attitude. He strikes Chen as vintage Ivy League.

"Hello, I'm Jean Sunderland," the woman says with vigor, shaking Chen's hand so firmly the charm bracelet jingles. "This is my lawyer, Squire Huff."

Maintaining his dour expression, Huff extends a stiff arm to Chen. Chen finds it interesting that Jean Sunderland wants her lawyer present.

Jean politely asks Chen if he would like something to drink. He politely declines. Formalities over, she gestures toward a seating area. Chen sinks down deep into the plush velvet couch, finding himself nearly at eye level with the finely sculpted bronze stag head at one corner of a glass coffee table. Jean and Huff sit on the matching yellow silk upholstered bergère chairs across from him, staring down at him like he's dangerous game.

"First, let me say how very sorry I am about your husband, Mrs. Sunderland," Chen begins.

"Thank you."

"You have a beautiful home."

"Thank you. We like it."

Huff interjects impatiently. "Do you have any more news for us, Detective?"

"No, I'm afraid not," Chen says.

"I'm keeping my fingers crossed," Jean says.

The vague smirk in her tone makes Chen wonder if she means her fingers are crossed for her husband's recovery, or his demise. Then, as if realizing the way she came across, Jean quickly adds, "You're sure he's doing well, right?"

"Far as I know," Chen says.

"Why in heaven's name haven't you people caught that lunatic Maud Warner yet?" Huff asks accusingly.

Chen ignores him. "Tell me, Mrs. Sunderland, did you and your husband know Maud Warner personally?"

"Yes. Maud was a social acquaintance. I was always on very friendly terms with her. I used to order books from her bookshop and have lunch with her occasionally. I liked her a lot."

"Do you know of any reason why she'd want to shoot your husband?"

Jean's hand flies up in protest. "She didn't mean to shoot my *husband!* She obviously meant to shoot Burt Sklar. She has a very bad history with Mr. Sklar."

"I understand that's what people think," Chen says.

"That's what people *know*, Detective. She's loathed Burt for years and made no bones about it. She went around saying very inflammatory things about him. I think she even ambushed him a few times. But I'm sure you've heard all this already."

"When's the last time you saw Ms. Warner?"

"Oh, Lord...let me think...not for *ages*. Sun and Burt are best friends, so naturally I had to keep my distance from her. I did feel sorry for her, though."

"Do you think there was there any truth to what she said about Mr. Sklar?"

"I have no idea. I mean, her mother *was* a very rich lady who died practically penniless, from what I heard. But I don't know if it was Burt's fault. He always claimed that Mrs. Warner was a spendthrift. Who knows?" Jean shrugs.

"So Mr. Sklar and your husband are very close," Chen says.

Jean nods. "As I said, best friends. Sun's known Burt for years. They knew each other way back when they were both married to their first wives. They both got divorced around the same time. It was a bond between them. Burt was also Sun's accountant. A few years ago, they formed a company together."

"That would be SSBS Investments?"

"Correct."

"What did you think when they went into business together?"

"I wasn't really consulted about it."

"Why not?"

Jean musters a tight smile. "You look like an intelligent man, Detective. You must have gathered I'm not Burt's greatest fan."

"How come?"

"I don't know…I guess I just never took to Burt the way some people do. Plus, he and my husband share a long history together that I'm not part of. A wife always likes to feel she's the closest one to her husband. Don't you agree?"

"Are you close to your husband?"

"Of course," she says softly.

There's an awkward silence while Chen decides how best to frame his next question.

"When did you last see him, Mrs. Sunderland?"

Jean glances at Huff. "At the hospital."

"Yesterday?" Chen presses.

"Yes," Jean says curtly.

Huff interjects. "Mrs. Sunderland's been extremely preoccupied with family and business matters as a result of this terrible tragedy."

Chen levels a hard gaze at Jean. "Why haven't you been back to see your husband, Mrs. Sunderland?"

"*Dee-tect-ive…*" Huff begins with a weary sigh. "Wouldn't it be a more profitable use of your time to track down Maud Warner? Why are Mrs. Sunderland's whereabouts of any interest to you?"

"I'm investigating a crime, sir. Everything's of interest to me—including the young woman who's been at your husband's side the whole time he's been in intensive care. Do you happen to know who she is, Mrs. Sunderland?"

Jean looks to Huff for guidance. He gives her a reluctant nod. Jean clears her throat. "I know who she's *claiming* to be."

"Who is she claiming to be?" Chen asks, as if he knows full well.

"I think I'll decline to answer on the grounds that it might incriminate my husband," Jean says with sour smile.

"Well, fortunately, the attending doctor was not as reticent as you are, Mrs. Sunderland. Tell me, did you have any idea that your husband had another wife?"

The phone rings. Saved by the bell!

Jean bolts up from her chair. "Excuse me."

She walks over to the gilded black lacquer Louis XVI desk in a far corner of the room. Chen watches her closely as she picks up the phone.

"This is she," she says.

As she listens to the caller, she flinches, clenching the receiver tighter.

"Thank you." She hangs up.

Jean squeezes her eyes shut and stands motionless for a long moment before turning back to Chen and Huff.

"He's dead," she announces without emotion.

Chapter Thirteen

I'm asleep when Billy knocks and pokes his head in the door. I glance at my watch. It's two in the afternoon.

"You asleep?"

"I was."

"Sunderland died. It's on the web."

Billy stands there waiting—I dare say *praying*—for my reaction. I get the strong sense he needs me to be upset and show remorse for having murdered a fellow human being in cold blood. To be honest, I know I *should* be upset and remorseful. When I planned all this, I was ready to take that consequence, if it arose. But that's where poker has been so incredibly helpful.

When I first started playing poker, I used to get very upset if I made a bad mistake, or if the cards were cruel and I got beat holding the best hand. I'd go "on tilt" for days blaming myself or fate if I lost. A loss would obsess me and taint the new game I was in until one day I had a simple revelation. There is no point in dwelling on dashed hopes or what might have been. I knew I had to clear my mind, learn from my mistakes, make peace with fate's little merry pranks, and forge ahead. The great truth of poker—and of life—can be summed up in two words: "Next hand."

Practicing this mindset was easier said than done, however. My emotions were more difficult to govern than a flock of butterflies.

I gradually learned to throw a net over them, to gather and control them, then let go of them completely. At some point, I'm not exactly sure when, I found I could be relatively emotionless—not only in poker, but in life.

When I stopped blaming the cards in poker, I stopped blaming fate in life. When I stopped punishing myself for my mistakes in poker, I stopped punishing myself for past mistakes in life— including the one that has landed me here today in my newfound role as a killer. That mistake was bringing Burt Sklar into my family.

● ● ● ● ●

I vividly remember that stormy spring day over two decades ago like it was yesterday. A man came into Edgar's, my hole-in-the-wall mystery bookshop on Eighty-second and Third, patting the rain off his head with a handkerchief. He was wearing thick-soled black shoes, and a wilted gray suit to match what I first thought was a wilted gray personality. I figured he'd just ducked in out of the weather with no intention of buying anything. But when he asked me if, by any chance, I had a copy of *The Golden Spiders*, a vintage Nero Wolfe which was hard to find, I took notice. Luckily, I had a old paperback in fairly good condition.

He paid cash and introduced himself.

"I'm Burt Sklar."

"Maud Warner."

We shook hands, then got into a lively conversation about mysteries which endeared him to me right away. He was very upbeat about indie bookshops like mine, despite the fact I knew we were fast becoming an endangered species. I loved his optimism. He cheered me up by giving me hope, especially on that dank day of a dull week with no customers. Later I came to realize that one of Sklar's main talents was convincing people their lives were going to be great. He understood that most people believe what they *need* to believe, despite all evidence to the contrary.

Voicing heartfelt wishes is a tool con men use to jimmie their way into people's trust.

Sklar kept coming back to buy books and schmooze. When he told me he was an accountant I laughed and told him how hopeless I was with numbers. He offered to help out if he could. I can still see him sitting in my back office, his long fingers flitting over the calculator like a mad spider. He organized the bills and invoices and orders littering my desk. I offered to pay him. He refused. I gave him books instead. It all seemed so...*fortuitous*.

Years later, I went to a book party and met a guy who worked at Waterman & Cashin, Sklar's old accounting firm. I asked him if he knew Burt.

"Burt Sklar? Hell, yeah. He stole the Warnco account right out from under us and started his own firm! My boss was furious."

"Do you know how he got the account?"

The man shrugged. "I guess he knew someone who knew someone who knew Sidney Warner, right? Isn't that the way it always works in this town?"

Boom.

Sklar hadn't just innocently walked into my bookshop that stormy day and cultivated my friendship because he was *a real nice guy*. He was using me to get to my very wealthy stepfather. He was the pro at the poker table and I was his first fish in the game.

So now poor Billy is standing in the doorway, hoping I'll break down with the news that Sunderland's dead. But the truth is, I'm not upset. Nor am I happy. I've prepared myself well. I'm still in the hand. I have on my poker face. I don't say a word.

Gradually, the hope in Billy's eyes curdles into fear.

"Where's the gun?" he blurts out.

I laugh, knowing he's remembering what I often said to him about Sklar: "What a person does to one, he will do to another." I think Billy's worried I may be crazy enough to shoot him too.

"Don't worry, Billy. I dropped the gun at the restaurant so they're sure to find it."

He doesn't seem relieved. On the contrary.

"You may want to think about turning yourself in," he says, bowing out of the room.

It's all I can do not to cackle, "All in good time, my Billy," like the witch in *The Wizard of Oz*.

All in good time...

Chapter Fourteen

Sun Sunderland's funeral at the Church of Saint Ignatius Loyola on Eighty-fourth and Park Avenue is *the* place to be on this hazy October day. Like all funerals of prominent people, there's an A-list party atmosphere. This is a chance for the lesser-known to rub elbows with the well-known and make valuable contacts through grief. Amid the tributes and the tears, there will be surreptitious exchanges of e-mails, phone numbers, and irreverent whispers.

Question: What do you get for dessert at The Four Seasons…? Answer: Shot!

Funeral networkers know that a joke, however macabre, can forge a bond during a grim occasion.

The mourners move slowly up the steps where two attractive young women in tight black sheaths check names off the lists on their black leather clipboards. Nearby stands a guard built like a fire hydrant who looks uncomfortable in his too-tight black suit. No one's getting past this bruiser without an invitation. He is Cerberus guarding the gates of hell, or heaven, depending on the deceased's destination. Absolutely no press is allowed.

People will be rewarded for interrupting their busy lives with a very good show. Jean has arranged the "entertainment" with Greta's help. It hasn't been smooth sailing. Jean really wasn't in the mood to mourn her bigamist husband. When Greta suggested majestic floral arrangements and international musical entertainment, Jean said: "*Are you kidding?* After what that bastard's done to me, he's lucky I don't have his body thrown into a wood chipper to the tune of an old kazoo!"

Greta understood and sympathized with her friend's point of view. It was the galloping fury of a woman who's been cataclysmically betrayed by the man she has loved and catered to for over twenty years. But Greta knows all too well that in New York you can't afford to let personal feelings get in the way of appearances.

"I know you're angry, Jeanie. But you have to trust me on this. Right now, Sun's a media martyr who's been shot down in the prime of life by a lunatic. The world expects you to give him a magnificent send-off. No one knows about this other thing yet. And it's absolutely imperative that you act as if you don't know. As I've said, we're not sure what else he's done behind your back. Let's face it, bigamy may be just the tip of the iceberg."

Reluctantly, Jean takes Greta's wise advice. Greta helps her organize a regal send-off for the Great Man, replete with towering topiaries, a world-class choir, distinguished speakers, and a special guest appearance by the great Tony Bennett, Sun's favorite singer. Untraditional though it is, Greta assures Jean that the incomparable Bennett will stir this jaded crowd to tears and make an indelible impression.

The four front pews of the church are reserved for family and friends. Jean sits in the first row between Greta and Squire Huff. Also in the pew are Michael Sunderland, Sun's son from his first marriage, along with his wife and four-year-old son. There was always friction between Sun and his only child because young Michael sided with his mother during the divorce.

Sunderland was a strict parent, determined that his son should regard him as a strong man, not some wimp whose wife had left him for a woman. Whenever Michael visited them, his father challenged him, both physically and mentally. If Michael met with his father's approval, he was rewarded with a financial bonus.

Love and money were forever intertwined in the Sunderland household, where there never seemed to be enough of either.

Jean liked her stepson, but they were not close. She and Michael tiptoed around one another like polite houseguests. Jean understood the young man's allegiance was always to his mother. He once hinted to Jean that his mother left his father for darker reasons than his father would ever admit. Now, as Jean sits in the pew, she can only imagine what those darker reasons were. She longs to tell Michael his father is a bigamist scumbag. But she refrains, knowing it's just a matter of time before the whole world finds out.

Among the notables in the congregation are Vance Packer, the newly elected Manhattan District Attorney, and his wife, Heathia. Packer is a tall, thin, patrician man, who hails from a long line of dedicated public servants who staunchly believed that God and country must come before personal ambition. He is a member of the faded WASP elite—a man who attended Groton, Harvard University, and Harvard Law School and prays that his background will not be held against him. He has worked hard to eradicate the "privileged son-of-a-bitch white guy" image that now haunts those of his ilk. Before entering politics, he rolled up his shirtsleeves (literally) and worked with the poor as a *pro bono* lawyer for the Urban Justice Project.

Today he's standing front and center in his most characteristic pose: Arms crossed, head slightly bent like President Kennedy's official White House portrait, with a gloomy expression on his aging boy face. In public, Packer always tends to look like he's at a funeral, giving the impression of a man of extreme gravitas. In private, he's more animated, but still careful. He's not a person to ignore public opinion, nor does he rush to judgment.

The Packers are social acquaintances of the Sunderlands, which is to say that they know each other chiefly from the glittery galas and pricey political events around town, not because they hang out with each other like real pals. Packer knows this brazen crime is the first great test of his first term in office. He's under enormous pressure to bring the fugitive Maud Warner to justice.

Vance Packer was brought up with the Mauds of the world: Prep school debutantes swathed in privilege who treated their good fortune with disdain because they had scant appreciation for how lucky they were. Having attained from birth the status so desperately sought by others, they had no idea what to do with it. He's seen too many rich kids with no guidance get caught up in the riptides of addiction and neurosis. Their wasteful lives were both a caution and a source of anger to him.

Packer is also keenly aware that all New York is watching closely to make sure justice is done in this case. He knows that if an African American or Hispanic male had walked into The Four Seasons, suspicious eyes would have followed him to the Sunderland table. Odds are they would have tackled the guy before he even drew the gun. But the Maud Warners of the world—older, white, well-dressed women of privilege—are perceived to be no threat. Maud waltzed out of there because no one could fathom it was she who'd pulled the trigger. Her crime and improbable escape are a publicity nightmare for Packer's office and the NYPD.

Once she's been apprehended, Packer has vowed to show the world that former debutantes like Warner are not above the law. On the contrary. The hammer's going to come down even harder on her. Lady Justice may be blind, but the public is an all-seeing, all-hearing, all-Facebooking, all-tweeting mob, ready to pounce on him for being too lenient. People have even dared approach him in the church to say he better make an example of her—"if you ever catch her, that is." Their snarky remarks rankle him more than he cares to admit.

Meanwhile, with every law enforcement agency in the country looking for Maud, Packer's mind is less on the service and more on Detective John Chen. He's dispatched Chen, armed with search warrants and a list of contacts, to D.C. to get the goods on Maud.

"Find out everything you can about Ms. Warner. And I mean *everything*—from the day she was born. No—make that from the day she was *in utero*. We want to be prepared when we catch her," Packer instructed Chen.

And yet...Packer has an uneasy feeling about this case. There are whispers about the victim. Maybe Sunderland isn't the great man of probity everyone thinks he is. For instance, Chen has told him that Sun's wife, Jean, didn't come to the hospital to keep a vigil over her husband, and that another, younger woman was constantly at his side—a woman calling herself Mrs. Sunderland. Packer doesn't want to hear it.

"Sun Sunderland's not on trial here. Find Warner," Packer commanded.

Chapter Fifteen

Though Burt Sklar is one of the first people to arrive at the church, he's one of the last people to enter the doors. He stays outside, meeting and greeting his fellow mourners with a solemn air, not only to make absolutely sure they all know he's in attendance, but mainly to be filmed by the news crews.

Sklar was desperate to be included among the roster of distinguished speakers paying tribute to Sunderland, knowing how good for social life and business that would be. Sklar has always been dependent on reflected light. However, when he offered to give his "best friend" a eulogy, Jean turned him down flat, thus depriving him of his big moment in the funereal sun.

Sklar enters the church and heads down the aisle to the front to the pews reserved for "friends and family." He's intercepted by an usher who gently steers him to an aisle seat near the back, the funeral equivalent of Siberia. Seething, he sits down and bows his head in ostentatious grief. As he stews about this fresh insult, he's startled by a tap on his shoulder. He looks up and sees Magma Hartz, who is being ushered down front. Magma leans down and whispers, "Oh, Burt, you poor dear man. This must be so difficult for you—I mean, knowing that bullet was meant for *you*. I was *there*, you know. Saw it all. Thank God you survived." The usher moves the Magpie on.

Sklar tenses, wondering exactly what she saw. Did anyone see him use Sunderland as a shield? In this day and age of cell phones, he knows it's possible that someone might even have recorded the event. But wouldn't they have come forward by now? Unless maybe they're going to save it to blackmail him. No…he's just being paranoid, he thinks. And though he feels that paranoids are the only ones who notice anything these days, he pushes the idea out of his mind. Worry is not his forte. Optimism is.

As the service progresses, Jean is well aware she's the focus of attention. She sits with a sad expression on her face, like a theater-goer pretending to be moved by a play she despises. During the eulogies, she finds it a teeth-gritting challenge to hear over and over what a great and good and honorable man her husband was. To keep from screaming, she imagines what they'd be saying if they knew the truth about the loathsome rat. She wonders if anything—*any goddam thing*—Sun ever said to her was true, most of all the words: "I love you." Jean is worrying about the onslaught of legal woes she will soon face, not to mention the cataclysmic public scandal that will erupt when the whole sordid affair comes to light.

As Tony Bennett sings a haunting version of "I'll Be Seeing You in All the Old Familiar Places," there are audible sobs in the crowd. Greta reaches out to comfort her friend. A tearless Jean squeezes Greta's hand so hard her nails bite into Greta's palm.

Two and a half hours later, the church doors open. Swells of organ music echo out onto the street. The Honorable Sun Sunderland has been laid to rest with all the pomp and pageantry expected to accompany great men to their graves. The grand service has helped people forget the bizarre circumstances of his death—for the moment. Mourners filing out of the church are hit by the glare of cold sunlight and scatter, eager to resume their busy lives.

No one pays attention to the veiled woman standing off to one side, waiting for Burt Sklar.

Chapter Sixteen

Burt Sklar exits the church and spots the veiled woman, a slim figure in a patent leather raincoat, glinting like a black sequin among pebbles. He gives her a discreet nod of caution and walks on ahead. Sklar leads her to an old-fashioned luncheonette on Lexington Avenue, figuring it's the last place any of the pampered mourners would deign to dine. They sit in a booth at the back.

"So how was it?" the woman says, removing her veil.

"The bitch seated me in the boondocks."

"And you're surprised? She's gotta figure you know about me."

"Yeah, well…she'll be sorry…" Sklar reaches across the pink Formica table and takes both her hands in his. "How'ya doin', Dany baby?"

"Oh, just great! I've been in a fuckin' hospital for the past four days watching him die, wishing he would, then hoping he wouldn't, then wishing he would. Fun times!"

"Fun times are coming, baby, I promise you. Let's order. I'm starving."

"How is it you can always *eat?*" she says, disgusted.

"I'm a growing boy."

Sklar orders sandwiches and coffee for them both. Danya chews on the end of a straw and stares at Sklar.

"So what happens now?"

"Now the fun begins."

"For who?"

"For *whom*," Sklar corrects her.

"Oh, yeah? Maybe for *yoom*! Not for me!" she snaps. "I don't have shit to show for all these wonderful years of sex, lies, and terror. No savings. No real cash. No house of my own. I'm getting too old to strip. What's gonna happen to me, Burt? That sadistic fucker better have left me something. But not in the will. She won't let me have diddly-squat it if it's in the will."

Sklar looks at her without saying anything.

"*What, Burt*...? I fuckin' hate it when you stare at me like that. It creeps me out. I can't figure out if you're a lap dog or a serial killer."

"Can I ask you a question, sweetheart?"

"*No*. I mean you're gonna ask it anyway so just fuckin' ask it! *What*?!"

"Calm down, baby. I know you're upset...The night we all met—?"

"*Jesus H*! Don't remind me!"

"Didn't you know I was interested in you?"

"Um, let's see...Well, I guess if I had an IQ below the national fuckin' speed limit, I might have missed it. Of *course* I fuckin' knew. Why do you always ask me this question?"

"But you preferred Sun."

"Why are we going into this now? *Again*!"

"Because Sun's gone now. So I want you to help me understand a little more about why you preferred him over me."

"Geez, Burt...Like I've told you a thousand times, I never had a dad...Well, I mean I *did* have a dad—a bad dad—abusive son-of-a-bitch that he was. I thought Sun was gonna be a *good* dad. But he turned out to be the *bad* dad I already had and worse—as you fuckin' know very well. Go figure!"

"You once said that if Sun hadn't been there, you and I might have—"

Danya throws up her hands in exasperation. "Jesus H! I need a cigarette! Can I smoke in here?"

"No."

"Fuckin' health Nazis rule the world. I'm going outside. I'll be back."

"Want me to come with you?"

"Not unless you wanna help me pee too. Where's the john around here?"

Sklar points to a door at the back of the shop. He watches her walk away, savoring the sight of her perfect ass and the wiggle in her step.

He recalls the first time he ever clapped eyes on Danya Dickert at King Arthur's, the upscale gentleman's club in D.C. where he took Sun one night for some guy relaxation after a conference-heavy day. They were sitting at a front table, enjoying the show, when a raven-haired, lithe-limbed, busty beauty in a diamond thong and white lace bra, pranced onto the stage, snaked herself around a silver pole, dipping and twirling her way into his fantasies. Sklar stuck a hundred-dollar bill in her white satin garter and she gave him a heart-melting smile. He was planning to come back to the club alone to meet her when Sunderland turned to him and issued a command, "Burt, go tell the manager we'd like that girl to join us."

Sklar did as he was told, as usual. Soon afterwards, the young woman bounced up to their table with the perky confidence of a cheerleader.

"Hi! I'm Danya!" she chirped.

Both men stood up. Sun pulled out a chair for her, obviously surprising her with his gallantry.

"Will you do us the honor of joining us?" Sun said.

Do us the honor? Who's he kidding with the fake courtliness? Sklar wondered.

Sklar knew firsthand that his friend had no respect for strippers or any woman who worked in the sex industry. Yet it was his contempt for them that fueled his desire. After their mutual divorces back in the day, he and Sunderland had frequented strip clubs and upscale brothels together in an attempt to exorcise their failed marriages. One drunken evening, Sunderland had confessed to Sklar that he could only achieve ultimate sexual satisfaction with women he felt superior to, and dominated in dangerous, sadistic ways. He needed special women to put up with his proclivities. These were not women he could ever bring into his world or love in an affectionate way. Though he had loved his wife, he had never desired her in the way he desired women for whom he had no respect. He tearfully told Sklar he was resigned to never truly falling in love. Through the years, Sklar had helped his friend lead a risky double life, up to and including Sunderland's remarriage to Jean.

Danya sat down and talked with the men until her next set. She declined a bottle of champagne, which was unexpected since Sklar figured she got a cut of the tab. Instead, she sipped a Shirley Temple. Sklar surmised that the golden hue of her skin meant she was from mixed race parentage. He sat staring at her, trying to figure out the stew of genes that had produced such a stunning beauty.

Danya's upbeat conversation was as aimless as a sunny cruise heading nowhere. She was gorgeous, playful, a little raunchy at times, and very relaxing to be around—a woman who made men feel sexually powerful and intellectually unchallenged. Yet, underneath all her peppy sweetness and light, Sklar sensed a darker reality. She struck him as wounded game, ill-used by men and vulnerable to abuse. Just Sun's type. In short, Danya was the exact opposite of Jean, that smart, elegant icicle Sun had married to further his social ambitions.

Sklar turned on all his charm for Danya, sure he would impress her with his lively conversation and jokes. Yet for some unfathomable reason, Danya preferred Sunderland to him. He still can't quite get that through his head. By the end of the night, the heat between the two of them was like a sauna. Sun's avuncular gravitas had obviously appealed to her more than his own gym rat vigor.

Sklar had no choice but to stand by and let this flirtation run its course, like all the others. Up to now, Sunderland had managed to keep his dicey sexual needs in check so they never interfered with his big important life. However, when Sun kept on inventing excuses to come to D.C., Sklar knew this relationship was different. Danya and Sunderland were in love, and it broke his heart. But he would wait.

Danya arrives back just as the food is delivered.

"I thought you quit smoking," Sklar says.

"I thought so too."

Sklar digs in as Danya leans back on the banquette, her arms crossed, wincing as Sklar devours an egg salad sandwich, chewing too heartily.

"You oughta try one of these. Delish."

"I asked you a question, Burt. What's gonna happen to me?"

Sklar washes down the last bite of his sandwich with a large swig of Coke. He wipes his mouth, pushes his plate away, and assumes a businesslike attitude.

"Okay, let's talk," he says.

"I'm waiting."

"Do you understand that under the present circumstances you have no rights to Sun's estate?"

"Didn't I just say that?"

"Sun understood this very well. And that's why you and your humble servant here are now inextricably intertwined."

"English please."

Sklar pauses for effect and clears his throat. "You and I are now partners of a kind."

She narrows her eyes. "Partners of *what* kind exactly?"

"During his lifetime, I helped Sun set up an arrangement for you—for all three of us, actually."

"What arrangement?"

"He knew you'd have no legal rights to his estate. So he wanted to make sure that if anything ever happened to him, his love for you would be reflected in, let's say, a *concrete* way."

"Okay…That's nice…Can you be more specific?"

"*Truthfully*…? The most important thing now is that you trust me, Dany."

"What's new? I've always trusted you, Burt. Who's always handled everything since the beginning? You!"

"True. But now, you have to do absolutely everything I tell you to do *when* I tell you to do it. You have to obey my orders."

Her jaw drops. "What the *fuck*?! You sound like Sun before he used to tie me up."

"This is not a sex thing, baby. This is a legal matter. You may be forced to fight for what's rightfully yours."

"If it's rightfully mine, why do I have to fight for it?"

"That's life, baby. You have to fight for things. That's why you have to trust me."

Danya shakes her head in exasperation. "You know, Burt, things were great when me and Sun first started out. But then after the marriage and the miscarriage, things got really bad. You were *there*. You saw the bruises. And that time you took me to the hospital…? Remember? I don't know why I didn't just leave. I really don't. But he could always talk me back like it was never gonna happen again. Plus, he told me he'd kill me if I left, so…" Her voice trails off.

"I'm sorry, Dany. You know I understand."

"You think he really would have killed me?"

"No. But he's gone now. And I'm gonna take care of you."

"Yeah, but you sound just like him telling me I have to *obey* you and all this shit. What's this about anyway?"

"I can't go into details now. But I will tell you this: You're going to be a very, very rich woman if you just do exactly as I say."

"But—"

He cuts her off. "Just trust me, Dany. I'm sending you back to D.C. in a limo. Go home and wait to hear from me. And for Christ's sakes don't talk to *anyone*."

"As if I had anyone to talk to. I wasn't allowed to have any real friends."

"I'm your real friend, baby." He reaches for her hand across the table.

"I hope so," she says, as he clasps her hand tight.

"No one knows anything yet."

"No one except *Jean*," Danya scoffs.

"I'll deal with Jean," Sklar says. "Eat your sandwich. It's a long drive."

Chapter Seventeen

FYI: Tolstoy had it wrong when he said all happy families are alike. Trust me, all *un*happy families are alike. I ought to know because any time miserable grown-ups get together we sound like miserable kids, complaining about our rotten parents and childhoods, or lack thereof. Happy families have individual memories. Unhappy families have collective amnesia. Just as a poker pro knows there's no weaker target than a fish, a con man knows there's no weaker target than an unhappy family. When I met Burt Sklar, our family was misery on a stick, ready to be gobbled up by a hungry predator.

Mummy and I had a fractious relationship because she hated my real father even more than she hated the presence of a growing daughter reminding her of her age. My stepfather, Sidney Warner, had a rapidly advancing case of Parkinson's disease which, understandably, made him depressed and cranky. He refused to use a wheelchair and often stood in doorways for hours, unable to move, refusing all help. My younger half brother, Alan, was transitioning from marijuana to more potent drugs, a fact he managed to hide from everyone but me—though he denied it. On any given day, our house had more drama than a Broadway season. It was into this mightily dysfunctional household that I introduced Burt Sklar to my stepfather because "Siddy," as I called him, needed a new accountant.

The afternoon I brought Sklar over to the apartment for the first time, Siddy was having a relatively good day. He managed to walk to the library without stopping for fifteen minutes every other step. He even made a joke about his "pesky Parkinson's." I'd prepped Sklar about Siddy, and Sklar got the ball rolling with an admiring comment about Siddy's collection of first editions, displayed in floor-to-ceiling brass bookcases. I poured the coffee set up on a silver tray, then sat off to one side as the men began their conversation.

Sklar's entire demeanor changed with Siddy. With me, Sklar had always been avuncular and relaxed, a benign authority figure, and an easy talker. But with Siddy, Sklar assumed the air of a disciple at the feet of a great man. He only spoke to ask Siddy questions.

For all his success and wealth, Sidney Warner was a shy soul. Sklar instinctively sensed that Siddy was aching to tell his story to someone who would listen and truly appreciate his rags-to-riches tale. I knew from experience that no one listened better than Sklar. With Sklar's expert prodding, Siddy regaled Sklar with his life story: How he'd grown up dirt poor in Brooklyn where his father sold cigars and his mother took in washing; how he'd studied to be a pharmacist, but instead went into the sugar business where a man's handshake was more powerful than a contract, then the toy business where he saw Japanese ingenuity firsthand, and finally, the electronics business, where he hit the mother lode.

After a while, he started telling Sklar the more intimate stories of his single life in Paris in the fifties—a life of models, artists, writers, exhibitions, great food, and wonderful conversation. I'd heard all these stories before, but Siddy rarely shared them with others. He clearly liked Sklar a lot.

Their thirty-minute appointment stretched to two hours, at the end of which Siddy asked Sklar if he'd be interested in becoming our family accountant.

"There's just one little hitch," Siddy said. "My wife, Lois, has to approve."

The next day when Sklar stopped by my bookshop to thank me, I told him frankly, "Siddy's worried my mother might not like you."

"How come?"

"My mother doesn't like anyone."

Sklar asked me to tell him the one story about my mother that really encapsulated her. I didn't hesitate. I told him about Chock Full O' Nuts.

Mummy called me up one day in a panic and asked me if I'd heard about a gruesome freak accident that had occurred earlier that morning. A gust of wind had blown a stop sign through the plate glass window at the Chock Full O' Nuts coffee shop on Madison Avenue and decapitated a waitress. It was all over the news and I'd heard about it. But I let her think she was the first to tell me because Mummy loved nothing better than informing people of disaster.

"How horrible!" I exclaimed.

"Maud, I was *there!*"

Now I was alarmed. "*Oh, my God, Mummy!* You *saw* it?"

"No. But I was there during Christmas shopping, sitting at that very counter, having a sandwich! And it was very windy that day."

I paused because I didn't really want to say what was on my mind. But the Imp of the Perverse made me blurt it out.

"Mummy, Christmas was months ago."

"Oh, for heaven's sakes, Maud! Don't you understand…? It was windy that day! *That could have been me!*" She hung up, outraged by my lack of sympathy.

I told my brother, Alan, about Mummy's crazy call. From that day on Alan and I alerted each other to our mother's insane mood swings and distortions of facts with the code words: "Chock Full O' Nuts, *incoming…*"

Sklar got a laugh over that story, as anyone who ever heard it did. However, Mummy's desire to cast herself as a constant victim, to get attention by placing herself at the center of every tragedy, no matter how far removed, turned out to be valuable information for Sklar. I know he filed away that story, along with other things I told him, like a spy amassing a dossier on a country he intended to invade.

Knowing Mummy would probably loathe Sklar on sight, I armed him with a secret weapon.

Alan and I were there when Siddy introduced my mother to Sklar. Mummy looked him up and down like he was a homeless person who'd just wandered in off the street. Sklar stepped forward to shake her hand with the eagerness of a hopeful fraternity pledge. She evaded his grasp and said, "Won't you sit down?" in a theatrical English accent.

Alan whispered to me: "Oh-oh, she's in dowager duchess mode. You know what *that* means."

"Yeah. She hates him. But I gave him a secret weapon," I whispered back.

Mummy saw everything around her as a reflection of herself in some way, from furniture to people. I knew what she was thinking: This dreary man, in his ill-fitting gray suit, sad tie, and thick-soled shoes, is "common," an adjective Mummy used to described people who were not worth consideration. Sklar was common to the core.

Sklar sat facing my mother across the Chinese lacquer coffee table in the library where refreshments were once again set out on a silver tray. Siddy, Alan, and I all sat on the couch. I poured everyone a cup of coffee from the silver coffeepot—everyone except Mummy, who helped herself to her special *tisane de verveine* from her favorite Sevres porcelain teapot. In the silence, the pouring liquids sounded like Niagara Falls. Sklar then reached into his pocket and pulled out a pretty miniature-size book and offered it to my mother. I nudged Alan and surreptitiously pointed at the book.

"What's this?" Mummy said, hesitating before accepting it. "A limited edition of Shakespeare's sonnets with illustrations by Dante Gabriel Rossetti. I understand you love Shakespeare as much as I do. I thought you might like to have it."

Mummy's face softened in appreciation. She loved presents. She loved Shakespeare. She loved Rossetti. Most of all she loved the fact that Sklar knew of her deep affection for the Bard's work, as if her likes and dislikes were subjects of universal interest. It never occurred to her that I'd supplied him with the book so he could win her favor. In that one simple gesture, my mother's resistance to Burt Sklar melted like spring snow, as I knew it would. As Mummy relaxed in Sklar's presence, Siddy left for work. Alan excused himself because he knew what was coming. I stuck around to watch Sklar and Mummy interact.

For the next hour, Mummy recited entire sonnets to Sklar by heart. He applauded her efforts with effusive claps. She was a wonderful actress with a melodic voice. It gave me a pang to think she felt cheated out of her career for a family life that was so obviously disappointing for her. When she ran out of sonnets, she regaled Burt with tales of her difficult youth, a subject of which she never tired. Once Mummy got going, she was on an Olympic luge, careening down the travails of her childhood as fast as the words would take her.

She told Burt the one story she told everyone she ever met, including manicurists and taxi drivers—namely, that her father, a prosperous import-export merchant, had been swindled out of all his money by his cousin who persuaded him to sign a Durable Power of Attorney. The cousin promised he would take care of the family if anything happened to my grandfather. Instead, the cousin embezzled all the family's money.

I listened to Mummy describe for the umteenth time how she was yanked out of Brentwood Convent on Long Island when she was only sixteen years old because the family could no longer afford to keep her there. Blessed with great beauty, she got a job in the Garment District modeling hats. From there, she tried her hand at acting but got nowhere until she bribed her way into a part in an off-Broadway play by telling the producer she could get him all the costumes free. She used her contacts in the garment industry to make good on her promise. But the producer went back on his word and fired her before the play opened. She got her revenge by landing the part of Ophelia in a more prestigious production. These were the formative events of my mother's youth, tattooed on her psyche forever, enabling her to elevate victimhood to an art form.

"So don't you ever dare ask me to sign a Durable Power of Attorney!" she said, wagging a playfully scolding finger at Sklar, who laughed.

I left the room when Mummy started trashing my real father, whom she still hated with a homicidal passion, despite the fact he was dead.

When I came back that evening to find out how she liked Sklar, I was shocked to find he was still there. He and Mummy were in the library right where I'd left them. Mummy was sitting next to him, sobbing on his shoulder.

When I came in, she looked up at me and said, "Maudie, I love this man. He's like a father to me!"

This was odd, not only because Burt was thirty years her junior, but because Mummy had often hinted that her father had abused her as a child and that's why she was sent away to a convent at the age of eight. It should have been a clue that she was about to relive her early victimhood.

With my mother's wholehearted approval, Siddy made Sklar our family accountant. After Siddy died, Sklar took over the family finances. Eventually, Sklar swindled my mother out of all her money, just like her father before her had been swindled out of all his money by an accountant. I think about the patterns which govern families without their recognizing them until it's too late. I wonder if there were ever any murderers in my family. Or have I the dubious distinction of being the first?

Chapter Eighteen

Jean Sunderland has read the document in front of her twice.

"I still don't understand what this means," she says softly, fearful that she understands all too well.

Burt Sklar is seated across from her at the long, polished mahogany conference table. Sitting beside him is his lawyer, Mona Lickel, a prim, gray-haired woman with smug eyes and red lips thin as knife slashes.

"*Truthfully*, Jean…? I know how difficult this is for you on a helluva lotta levels," Sklar says.

Jean suppresses the urge to scream at Sklar, a man whom she's always detested. She glances at her lawyer, Squire Huff, who is seated beside her wearing the grim face of a wartime sentinel.

"Thank you, Burt, for your understanding. But I'm unclear… That is, I can't quite grasp…*Oh the hell with it! What in God's name does this thing mean?*" she cries, waving the piece of paper in front of her.

Sklar clears his throat. "Jean, I believe that document is self-explanatory," he says with a condescending air.

Jean looks at the document again, although some of the print appears blurry to her enraged eyes. The heading reads:

"DURABLE GENERAL POWER OF ATTORNEY, NEW YORK STATUTORY SHORT FORM." Underneath in smaller print is an explanation: "*The powers you grant below continue to be effective should you become disabled or incompetent.* CAUTION: THIS IS AN IMPORTANT DOCUMENT. *It gives the person whom you designate (your "Agent") broad powers to handle your property during your lifetime, which may include powers to mortgage, sell, or otherwise dispose of any real or personal property without advance notice to you or approval by you..."*

Jean pauses.

"This document names *you* as Sun's agent to, let me see, '*Act in my name, place, and stead, in any way which I myself could do, if I were personally present...*' Don't tell me Sun signed this *willingly!*" she cries.

"*Truthfully,* Jean...? He did. And as you can see, it's been duly notarized by Ms. Lickel here." Sklar nods to the lawyer.

"You also witnessed this document?" Huff asks.

"I did. Along with Ms. Margaret Henson," Lickel says.

"And where is Ms. Henson?" Huff asks.

"Unfortunately, Ms. Henson passed away two years ago," Lickel says.

"How convenient," Huff sniffs.

The sumptuous wood-paneled conference room in the venerable old white-shoe firm of Huff and Gaines is now a battlefield where the gentlemanly Huff is dangerously outmatched by wily rebel forces.

"So am I to understand that my husband handed all his financial affairs over to you over three years ago without my knowledge?" Jean says to Sklar.

"That's a slight oversimplification. But that's what it boils down to, yes," Sklar says.

Jean shakes her head in disbelief, thumbing through another folder.

"According to these bank accounts and records, there's hardly any money left in the estate!" Jean says.

"I don't call five million dollars hardly any money, Jean," Sklar says.

"It is when he was worth close to a billion! What the hell happened to the rest of it?"

Sklar is about to answer when Mona Lickel intervenes. "Mr. Sunderland instructed Mr. Sklar to set up what is known as a 'tontine.' Substantial investments were made in various entities controlled by three people. In such an arrangement the surviving partners always benefit the most."

"The three people being—?" Jean says warily because she already knows the answer.

"Mr. Sunderland, Mr. Sklar, and Mrs. Danya Dickert Sunderland," Lickel says matter-of-factly.

Bigamy, the lusty elephant in the room, has reared its ugly head. Unable to control herself, Jean leaps up from the table, screaming at Sklar, "*You bastard! You're not getting away with this!*"

Squire Huff follows his client to a corner of the conference room to try and calm her down. Sklar and Lickel exchange sly glances at one another as Huff confers with Jean for a long moment. Though still distraught, Jean returns to the table and speaks in a more measured tone.

"What about my house?" she asks.

"The house in New York and the estate in Southampton have both been mortgaged and will be sold—unless, of course, you want to buy them," Lickel says.

"*Buy* them? I *own* them!"

"Unfortunately, that was never the case. They were both in Mr. Sunderland's name," Lickel says.

"Yeah, Jean. Sun had me mortgage them years ago to take advantage of the markets. I'm surprised he never told you," Sklar says.

Jean is so beside herself she grabs a bound copy of Sunderland's Last Will and Testament and flings it across the conference table at Sklar.

"*And this ridiculous will...*! He makes *you* the executor? I'm his *wife*, for God's sakes! At one point *I* was his executor. When the hell did *that* change exactly?" she cries.

"Four years ago, as per the codicil," Lickel says with no emotion.

Jean slumps back in her chair, robotically shaking her head.

"You've arranged everything very neatly, haven't you, Burt? As his wife I'm entitled to half his estate. But there's not much of an estate left, is there? Thanks to you."

Squire Huff now tries to take control. "Mr. Sklar—*Sklaah* (as he pronounces it in his mid-Atlantic accent)—rest assured that my client is going to contest every single document pertaining to Mr. Sunderland's finances."

Sklar ignores Huff. "I'm not keeping anything from you, Jeanie. Scout's honor." Sklar raises his fingers in a boy scout salute.

"Mr. Sklar, you will kindly address *me* from now on," Huff says.

Sklar leans forward and clasps his hands together with the expression of a concerned clergyman. "Listen guys, I know how painful this is for you on any number of levels. But let me assure you…everything I've done concerning this will and, indeed, concerning all of my best friend Sun's affairs has been done entirely at his direction—"

"*Which doesn't mean it's honest!*" Jean interrupts.

"Which means it's *legal*," Mona Lickel shoots back using her "exorcist voice," as Sklar calls it—the deep-toned, satanic rasp which is so effective in negotiations because it scares the shit out of people coming from this soberly tailored, tightly permed grandmotherly figure. Huff looks unnerved.

Sklar goes on. "Look Jean, Sun was my best friend, as you know—even though you didn't let me speak at his funeral and seated me in Siberia. He was a great man. A flawed man, to be sure, but a great man. He felt he'd amply provided for you and his son during his lifetime. And not to rub salt in the wound, he fell in love late in life. He had a bad heart and he wanted to make sure that if anything happened to him, the woman he loved would be amply provided for."

"You call getting it *all* amply provided for?" Jean says bitterly. "There's still the art, Jean, dear," Huff says in an audible whisper.

Lickel holds up her index finger to indicate not so fast. "Sorry. There's a problem there."

"What problem is *that*?" Jean says through gritted teeth.

Sklar takes over again. "*Honestly…*? I told Sun this was a bad idea at the time. But he deemed it prudent to pledge all the art to a donor's room in the Museum of Modern Art, thus ensuring his legacy and avoiding estate taxes at the same time. I hate to tellya, but the art's pretty much gone."

"That's just not possible. *He would have told me*!" Jean says, immediately realizing how ludicrous she sounds.

What are the odds a man who commits bigamy and gives Burt Sklar his Durable Power of Attorney would be honest with his wife about *anything*?

"He *gave* me some of some of those paintings. *They're mine*!"

"Can you prove it?" Lickel asks.

"I don't have to prove it. They were presents! Birthday presents, anniversary presents. We built that collection *together*."

"But he paid for them so we have no way of knowing," Lickel says. "Bills of sale in Sunderland's name were provided to the museum when the pictures were pledged. We have them all, if you'd care to examine them."

"Oh, we will, Mr. *Sklaah*," Huff says. "We will, indeed, be looking into everything."

There's something almost comic about the polished, clubbable Huff, an ivy league lawyer in a Porcellian Club tie and bespoke suit and vest, trying to intimidate Sklar, the hip, black clad, ninja accountant.

Knowing her side is dangerously out-matched, Jean heaves a deep sigh of resignation. "Fine. I guess we'll just have to settle all this in court."

Sklar raises a conciliatory hand. "*Candidly…*? I'm sure something can be worked out."

"*Worked out? How?*" Jean snarls.

"No one wants a long and public legal battle here—with the possible exception of the lawyers, right guys?" Sklar jokes, nodding at Huff and Lickel. "I'm sure we can arrive at some sort of compensation for you."

"Compensation? For twenty years of marriage and unimaginable humiliation? I wonder how much that will be? Tell me, Burt, did you and Sun joke about how easy I was to dupe?"

"*Truthfully*, Jean…? I feel very bad for you."

"Well, here's how *I* feel, Burt. You engineered this disgusting, illegal marriage. I wouldn't be surprised if you and that slut were in this together right from the beginning. For all I know, you introduced her to Sun in order to carry out this…this…*theft*. Sun may be a bigamist, but I still don't believe he knew about any of this other stuff. This is exactly what you did to poor old Lois Warner, saying she'd signed a Durable Power of Attorney over to you. I should have believed Maud. We all should have!" Jean rises abruptly. "Let's go, Squire!"

A bumbling Huff hurriedly stuffs papers in his briefcase and follows Jean. "You'll be hearing from us, Mr. Sklar! I promise you!"

"Can't wait," Sklar says.

At the door, Jean turns, levels a hard gaze at Sklar, and says, "I wish to hell Maud Warner had shot you both!"

Chapter Nineteen

Greta Lauber is giving a small luncheon when Jean arrives uninvited.

"I'm so sorry to barge in on you like this, Greta. But I just got through a meeting with Sklar and that Medusa lawyer of his. You're the only one I can talk to." Sensing Greta's unease, Jean draws back. "Am I interrupting something? I can leave."

"No, Jeanie! It's not what you think. It's that, well…Come join us."

Greta ushers Jean into the dining room where Magma Hartz and Lydia Fairley are enjoying their first course. The minute Jean sees Lydia, she knows something's up. Lydia Fairley is a tall, slim, indigo-eyed blonde who may look like one of the chic "ladies who lunch" but is, in fact, the tough, brilliant lawyer society folk turn to whenever their haute cocoons get rocked by scandal. She's Clarence Darrow in couture.

Greta pulls up a chair for Jean at the small round table in front of French doors leading to the terrace. She presses an invisible buzzer. Martyn enters, sets another place, and brings Jean the appetizer: ginger squash soup, served in a paper-thin porcelain bowl shaped like an acorn husk. It's all very decorous and genteel. Yet a conspiratorial silence hangs over the room like smoke.

"Are you *sure* I'm not interrupting?" Jean asks.

Never one to beat around the bush, Lydia says: "Okay,

Jeanie...You may as well know it. I'm going to defend Maud Warner when they catch her."

Jean now understands the tension in the air. The women watch Jean digest the news that Greta, her best friend, is hosting a lunch for Lydia, another good pal, who plans to defend her husband's killer.

"Do let me know if I can be of any help," Jean says nonchalantly as she samples the soup.

"You're not upset?" Magma says, as if wishing Jean were.

"May I have some wine, please?" Jean asks.

Greta pours Jean a glass of white wine from the crystal carafe. Jean savors a few sips, then holds the glass up to the light, admiring the pale gold liquid.

"Like you, Greta, we only served the very best wines at our parties, remember? Sun was so intent on impressing our guests. I never drank a drop of those thousand-dollar bottles because I knew that alcohol and a hectic social life don't mix—not if I wanted to look good for the photographers and *especially* for my beloved husband, who put such store in appearances. Do you know what I wish I'd done with all that fine wine now...? Poured it into a vat and drowned his fat ass in it!" She drains the glass.

The women exchange uncomfortable glances. "I take it your meeting with Sklar didn't go well," Greta says.

"That would be an understatement. Sklar's engineered it so he and the slut have stolen most of Sun's money. I don't even own my house!"

Greta is shocked. "*Oh, my God, Jean! What happened?*"

"What slut?" Magma says.

"You haven't told them, Greta?"

"Of course not," Greta says proudly.

"Told us *what*?! What *slut*?!" Magma cries.

"Well, ladies, turns out my beloved husband had another wife. The great Sun Sunderland was a bigamist."

Magma gasps as her hand flies to cover her mouth. Lydia furrows her brow in amused disbelief.

"How unexpected," Lydia says wryly.

Magma is so flustered she can hardly think. "*Unexpected?* It's not *possible!* It's the most sinister thing I've ever heard! Is she anyone we *know?*"

"No, dear. Unless you know any twenty-something strippers."

"She's a *stripper?*" Magma cries.

"She was. Now she'll probably buy the club."

Greta has been sitting in stunned silence, trying to digest this news. "Wait, Jean. You're his *wife.* You have rights to his estate. Where's your lawyer?"

"Where's the *estate* is the real question. There's almost nothing left."

"Wait a minute! Sun was enormously rich!" Greta says.

"*Was* being the operative word. There's almost no money left in the estate now because Sklar claims Sun gave him his Durable Power of Attorney to—shall we say—*rearrange* the money."

"What's a Durable Power of Attorney?" Magma asks.

Jean heaves a weary sigh. "You explain it, Lydia. I need another drink."

Lydia shifts into lawyer gear. "A Durable Power of Attorney is the most serious document a person can sign. People only assign them when they're terminally ill or going off to war or about to do something where there's a chance they'll die. Whoever you give this power to will have complete control over your financial life. They can act *for* you in any way they choose: sell assets, move money around, mortgage property. You have to really trust the person you give it to because, in effect, they *are* you," Lydia explains.

"And you're saying that Sun gave this power to *Sklar?*" Greta asks incredulously.

"Exactly. Sklar also set up something called a *tontine* with himself, Sun, and the slut as beneficiaries."

"What's a tontine?" Magma says.

"A partnership where survivors take all. How original. Sleazy, but original," Lydia says.

"Sleazy is right," Jean agrees. "And now that Sun died, it's gone into effect with two surviving partners. Sklar's been moving Sun's money into various offshore entities and LLCs controlled by the tontine for years. It's sleazy, as you say. But unless we can prove that Power of Attorney's a forgery, it's legal."

Lydia is nodding her head knowingly. "That's exactly what Maud says he did to her mother."

"I should have listened to her," Jean says.

"Jeanie, do you think Sun knew what Sklar was doing?" Greta asks.

"Who knows? Clearly, he was *distracted*," Jean says angrily. "I'm certainly taking the position that he never would have signed such a thing. But Sklar was covering up the bigamy for him. So who knows what that rat made him do? I'm pretty sure that's why he went into business with Sklar in the first place."

"I'm going to fire Burt this instant!" Magma says.

"You better hope it's not too late," Jean says.

Magma bolts up from the table. "I need to call my lawyer!"

"Magma! Wait! We have to talk about Maud's demeanor in the restaurant!" Lydia calls after her.

"Later," Magma says, running out.

Greta shakes her head. "This will be all over town in an hour."

"Not *that* long," Jean says with a smirk. She sips her fourth glass of wine. "So, Lydia, you're gonna defend Maud, eh? Maybe they won't catch her."

"I hope they don't. She's a heroine," Greta says.

"Oh, they'll catch her. And I plan to help her."

The three women sit in quiet contemplation as Martyn clears the table for the main course. After a time, Greta turns to Lydia.

"You're the legal eagle here, Lyds. Please tell us Sklar can't get away with this."

"Do you have a good lawyer?" Lydia says to Jean.

"Screw lawyers. I need a cartel killer."

"Well, disputing the Durable Power of Attorney is a good

delaying tactic. However, in thinking about it, I do have another suggestion," Lydia says.

"*Tell* me," Jean says eagerly.

"Go public."

Chapter Twenty

I have to say, it feels a little surreal to be sitting here with Billy in D.C. about to watch the Wanda Balter Special with Jean Sunderland as her guest, considering I'm the reason for the show. Seconds before the program begins, Billy flings me a guarded glance. Over the past few days, our relationship has grown less chummy. We mostly play heads up poker, which doesn't require a lot of conversation.

Sometimes we reminisce about the old days when we used to travel to poker tournaments together and talk about our lives. He said if ever I needed a friend, he'd be there for me. I confided to him that I'd sometimes thought of killing Burt Sklar. I doubt he ever dreamed I'd actually go through with it. That may be the reason he slinks around me like a wary dog. He let me into his house out of the goodness of his heart for old times' sake. Now he doesn't know how to get rid of me. He locks his door at night. I don't blame him.

Wanda Balter's aging face is an Impressionist blur on camera. I'm thinking they must use a vat of Vaseline to make the legendary newswoman look this good at her age. Either that, or ruthless ambition actually is the Fountain of Youth. Balter speaks directly to the camera, addressing her audience like she's talking to a group of friends.

"It's been twelve days since billionaire statesman Sun Sunderland was sensationally shot while he was lunching with his close friend Burt Sklar at The Four Seasons Restaurant in New York City. Sadly, he died of a heart attack the next day. His stellar funeral was attended by dignitaries and celebrities from around the world. The shooter, a fifty-six-year-old socialite named Maud Warner, is still on the run. I'm here tonight with Sun Sunderland's widow, Jean, who is giving her first interview since the tragedy."

Jean is sitting in a chair in front of the fireplace, with the gorgeous orange Rothko as a backdrop. She's wearing a long-sleeved blue dress and pearls. Her hands are clasped on her lap, as if in prayer. Her carefully coiffed blond hair glows like a halo. With her stoic countenance and dignified bearing, she is every inch the saintly, bereaved widow.

"Jean, thank you so much for allowing us to be with you here in your beautiful home tonight," Balter says in a cloying voice.

Jean tilts her head forward in a solemn acknowledgment. Balter leans in and furrows her brow with that air of intrusive concern which has made her famous at eliciting intimate revelations.

"Jean, where were you when you heard the news that your beloved husband had been shot?"

"I was in a board meeting at the Museum of Modern Art."

"Can you describe that moment?"

As Jean relives her nightmare with admirable restraint, talking about the shock of it all and her anxious trip to the hospital, I feel Billy's eyes on me. I just know he's waiting for me to show some sign of sympathy for this poor woman I've made a widow. I pretend not to know he's looking and just keep staring at the set, poker-faced.

Balter is taking her time, as usual. She briefly describes the crime, and me, and Burt Sklar, and the whole scene in the restaurant, plus my miraculous escape. Once again, I hear myself referred to as "Mad Maud," that tired old sobriquet I've had to stomach for years. Then Balter slowly leans more forward, zeroing in hard on Jean. Balter fans all know she's about to deliver one of her signature zingers.

"So, Jean…What would you say has been the *most* difficult moment for you during this whole ordeal?" As Jean appears to be thinking, Balter gives her a prompt: "Is it perhaps knowing that your dear husband *wasn't* Maud Warner's intended target? That she most likely was aiming to shoot her old nemesis, Burt Sklar, and that Sun might be alive today had she not accidentally missed?"

As Balter's audience knows from close to two generations of watching her, this somewhat tactless question is meant to pierce Jean's impressive poise and get her to break down on camera and bemoan the injustice of fate. Jean pauses for a long, thoughtful moment, then speaks in a halting but clear voice.

"Well…no, actually, um, I think by far the most difficult moment was finding out that the man I loved…the man to whom I've devoted my life for more than twenty years was…"

Balter leans in further. "*Was…?*"

"A bigamist," Jean says firmly.

"I'm sorry. *What?*" Balter grimaces, like she misheard.

"Sun was secretly married to another woman for years. I think that's called a bigamist."

Blindsided by this explosive revelation, Balter looks like she's been slapped in the face. Her jaw drops into a comically startled expression and for the first time in her long career, she's at an embarrassing loss for words. But her reaction is nothing compared to poor Billy's.

"WHAAAAAAT?" he screams at the set. "*Sun Sunderland, a bigamist? Maudie, did-did-did you hear what she just said?*"

I shush him. "*Listen!*"

Balter plays for time by clearing her throat and sitting up very straight.

"Well…so, Jean, you're saying that Sun Sunderland, the Pope of Finance, was a *bigamist?*"

"Correct."

"And when did you find this out?" Balter asks, now seeming truly interested as opposed to scripted.

"In the hospital. At his bedside. When he thought he was dying."

"*Whew*!" Balter gasps unwittingly, then recovers. "Okay, then! Please describe *that* moment to our viewers!"

I listen to Jean describe the scene in the hospital like she's like she's talking about the weather. She's doing great. She's wearing blue. I'm proud of her.

"And you had absolutely no inkling?" Balter says, her face contorted into a permanent incredulous expression.

"Obviously not."

"Do you know who this woman *is*?"

"I do now, yes."

"*Who is she*?" Balter says with glee.

"I'd rather not say. There's a lawsuit pending. But I'm sure the media will find out very shortly. You always do."

The program concludes with a breathless wrap-up by Balter who is giddy with the knowledge she's added another delicious scoop to her resume.

Billy turns off the set and collapses back on the couch with a grand sigh. "*Wow*…I'm in total shock. Aren't you?"

I shrug. "Not really."

He narrows his eyes suspiciously. "You didn't know about this, did you, Maudie?"

"Why? Would it matter?"

"Are you *kidding*? People are gonna be effin' *outraged* that your victim isn't the great man everyone thought he was. Hell, *I'm* outraged! Fuck it! Sunderland's just another prime example of the high level hypocrisy that goes on in this country without anyone knowing about it until it's exposed! The guy's a billionaire, so he thought he could get away with any goddam thing he wanted."

"Including murder?" I venture.

"Yeah, sure! Who knows with these people? But you don't seem that surprised. Please tell me the truth, Maudie. Did you know Sunderland was a bigamist? Look at me. Did you?"

I look at Billy with the face that's launched a thousand folds at the poker table. No one can ever believe that this old bat is capable of a three-barrel bluff.

"No, Billy, I did *not* know Sunderland was a bigamist. Happy now?"

He studies my face, my body language, the pulse in my neck— all the little "tells" that poker players focus on to try and figure out if an opponent is lying, and if they should fold or call.

"Okay. I believe you," he says at last.

He folded.

I'd bluffed him.

I *knew*.

Chapter Twenty-one

The day after Balter's interview, Danya is "outed" as Sun Sunderland's mystery bigamist wife. Burt Sklar has driven down to D.C. to whisk her back to New York before the reporters find out where she lives. They are in Danya's bedroom, where Danya is packing and Sklar is sorting through a banker's box of photographs. The TV is tuned to CNN so they can follow the news. When the anchor mentions Sunderland's name, both Danya and Sklar immediately stop what they're doing and focus on the set.

"Danya Dickert Sunderland is a twenty-eight-year-old former stripper from D.C..."

As the anchor speaks, a photo of Danya dancing at King Arthur's appears on screen. Danya shrieks in horror and runs to turn off the set.

"Shit! Where'd they dig up that horrible shot of me!?"

"Calm down, baby. You looked gorgeous."

Danya whirls around, leveling a furious gaze at Sklar. "*Gorgeous*?! I was on a pole with daisies on my boobs and a jungle vine halfway up my ass. You call that *gorgeous*? This whole thing's a fuckin' *nightmare!*"

Danya picks up her beloved cat and cuddles the creature for comfort. Sklar bridles at the sight of the hairless Sphinx. He's always loathed the wrinkled, veal-skinned beast who reminds him of a fetus. He tries to hide his repulsion by smiling too broadly.

"Aw...you and Mooncat are so cute together. But we really need to get going, baby. Soon they're gonna find out where you live down here."

Danya looks plaintively at Sklar as she continues stroking the cat. "The whole fuckin' world thinks I'm some two-bit stripper who was only after Sun for his money."

"They may think that now. But soon they're gonna think you're a poor, innocent young woman who was taken advantage of by a rich and powerful man who you loved...and *feared*. That's how we're gonna spin it."

"You'd have to be a genius to spin that one, Burt."

"That's what I am, baby—a genius! *Truthfully*...? PR's the only thing in this world that counts. The truth is bullshit. It's what people want to believe that matters. Jean thinks *she's* a sympathetic victim? Just wait'll they get a load of these!" Sklar says, closing the lid on the box of photographs documenting Danya and Sunderland's kinky sex life together, plus her injuries.

"You think we'll ever use those?" Danya says.

"I'm gonna use whatever it takes to achieve our goal. *Candidly*...? We've got Jean over a barrel and she knows it. All this other stuff is window dressing."

"Bigamy is a crime. You know my history. Hell, I could get arrested here!"

"That will never happen," Sklar says, waving a decisive hand. "Now keep packing. I'll take Mooncat over to your neighbor's."

"I still don't understand why he can't come with us!" Danya says.

"For the hundreth time: My building doesn't allow pets."

She gives the cat a hug and kiss, then reluctantly hands him over to Sklar, who grits his teeth at the feel of the animal's suede-like skin.

"Mooncat's going bye-bye," Sklar says, playfully waving the cat's paw at Danya.

In more ways than one, he thinks.

When Sklar returns, he loads Danya's luggage into the trunk of the car—all except the box of photographs which he lays on the backseat so he can keep an eye on them.

"Just out of curiousity, baby… How come you didn't destroy those pictures like Sun told you to?"

"Insurance," she says, slamming the car door.

Sklar nods his approval. "Smart girl."

Danya thinks: *Burt, you have no idea.*

Chapter Twenty-two

Maud Warner's continued evasion of law enforcement is a major embarrassment for both the NYPD and the Manhattan District Attorney's office. Vance Packer is feeling the heat. He and Detective John Chen are in Packer's office going over some logistics of this troublesome case.

"So you finally got the warrants for D.C., right?" Packer says.

"We're heading down there tomorrow," Chen says.

Packer takes a couple of Advil for his headache. "You saw Jean Sunderland's interview. Can you believe she's been married to a bigamist for *years* and she just finds out about it when he's *dying*...? You're married, right, Detective?"

"Sixteen years."

"So let me ask you something. You think it's possible for a wife not to know somewhere deep down that her husband's leading this major double life?"

Chen chuckles. "My wife suspects I'm leading a major double life if I'm in the shower too long."

Packer is deep in thought. "Here's what I want to know. When did a guy like Sunderland have *time* for all this? I don't have time for one wife, let alone two."

"I guess the heart wants what it wants..."

"Oy! Don't remind me of *that* case, please. You understand we're getting killed in the press on account of this new revelation, right? Did you happen to watch CNN this morning?"

"No."

"So they're talking about Sunderland and what a shock it is to find out this great man was a bigamist. They're showing pictures of his funeral and I see *myself* coming down the steps of the church. I swear to God I almost threw the glass of orange juice at the set. Anyway, there's not one shred of sympathy for our victim anymore. And worse, they're now calling Maud Warner a folk heroine. Folk heroine, my foot! She's a murderer! It's all because Sunderland's such a scumbag and we can't catch her!"

"She's the D.B. Cooper of little old ladies," Chen smiles.

"Jesus, I hope not! They never *did* catch D.B. Cooper. Face it, John, we have a very, very unsympathetic victim here."

"True," Chen agrees. "A billionaire bigamist is one rung below serial killer in the unsympathetic department."

"Exactly. How the heck do I get a jury to convict Grandma Moses for killing Ted Bundy?" Packer says ruefully.

"Let's catch her first."

Chapter Twenty-three

Billy's wife is getting home from Spain tomorrow. It's time for me to leave. I think I've overstayed my welcome. Billy won't even play heads up with me anymore. I think he thinks I'm nuts. After I make a phone call to my next port of call, I get dressed in the thrift shop clothes Billy bought for me, plus a ratty blond wig, floppy hat, and sunglasses. Billy drives me to a deserted side street and lets me out near Wisconsin Avenue. He leaves me with a friendly caution.

"I hope you know what you're doing, Maudie. This isn't poker."

"Oh, yes it is, Billy. You watch."

I thank him for everything and walk to the nearby McDonald's. I sit in a corner and keep my head bowed low nursing a Coke and some fries. I have several hours to kill. I watch a family of five having a meal of Big Macs and milkshakes. I can't help thinking they look a helluva lot happier than my own family did dining at "21" on filet mignon and Chateau Lafitte. Alan used to joke that our family meals were Inquisitions where we got burned eating steak. He coped with the constant shouting and criticisms by coming to the table high. I just tuned out and excused myself before dessert.

I have to admit that after Sklar came into the picture, meal-times became bearable, pleasant even. Mummy and Siddy seemed happier together. Siddy credited Sklar for easing tensions in the household.

"Your mother has someone to complain to other than me," Siddy said.

Sklar encouraged Mummy's confidences. She got into the habit of dropping by his office unannounced to show him the new clothes she'd bought, or a new hairstyle. Sklar gave her the attention she felt she wasn't getting at home. Then Siddy suddenly died of a heart attack. His death was a great blow to our family. At the funeral, my mother wept on Sklar's shoulder, not Alan's or mine. In poker that's called a "tell."

"If it weren't for Burt, I'd have followed your father into the grave," Mummy said.

A wealthy widow is a predator's dream. In my mother—a needy, narcissistic aging beauty with an addict son she adored and a daughter she viewed as direct competition—Sklar, the patient pro, had his aces at last.

I get more fries and another Coke, waiting for evening to descend.

Chapter Twenty-four

Armed with the necessary search warrants, Detective Chen and his forensic team take the Acela to Washington to collect evidence from Maud Warner's apartment in one of the colorful old row houses of Georgetown. Chen pokes around the cramped one-bedroom apartment while his team collects evidence and takes videos.

The place is cluttered with faded chintz furniture and knick-knacks—a brass hourglass, a pair of white china dogs, a horse weathervane, needlepoint pillows, a yellowing wicker chair that reminds Chen of old bones. There are books everywhere—in bookshelves, on tables, in piles on the floor. The apartment reeks of a shabby gentility, as if Warner had tried to import as much of her old life as would fit, only to wind up creating the atmosphere of a thrift shop.

He wanders into a bedroom barely big enough for its single bed. The fraying, hand-embroidered sheets are relics of long gone luxury. A pillow on the bed is embroidered with a gun, the ace of spades, and the words, *"Know when to hold'em... Up."* He picks up a photograph on the night table to take a closer look. It's a black-and-white candid of a young boy and a teenage girl in wet bathing suits, laughing together on a beach. The photo captures the joyous camaraderie between the two. Chen removes the photo from the tarnished silver frame. "Me & Alan, East Hampton," is written in faded ink on the back.

In the bathroom medicine cabinet Chen finds several pill bottles, including a prescription for Zyprexa, an anti-psychotic drug. The prescription is a month old but the bottle is full. Someone wasn't taking her meds, he thinks. He snaps a picture of it so the label is visible, then jots down the name of the doctor who prescribed them.

Taped to the refrigerator in the kitchen is a shooting range target with a hole in the bull's-eye. Chen finds similar targets showing she was a good shot stuffed into a cabinet.

As Chen is making notes, a technician hands him a newspaper clipping stapled to a sheet of paper from a memo pad headed: *From the desk of Burt Sklar.*

"This was on the desk with the computer," the techie says. "Thought you'd be interested."

Chen was indeed interested in an article sent to Maud by her nemesis, Burt Sklar. The scribbled note on the pad read: "*Poker player like you… E.E.D. defense expert. Enjoy! Burt.*" Cut out from *Washington Post* Style section, the article is a profile of a woman named Joyce Kiner Braden with the headline: "*D.C. Lawyer Wins Big In Poker Tournaments and In Court.*" Chen makes a note to call her.

The team finishes documenting the apartment. They bag the computer hard drive and head back to New York. Chen stays behind and grabs a cab to the West Wing of the National Gallery, where he has an appointment to meet Bunny Westerly. A woman in New York had told him Westerly and Maud were close.

Chen is in the Garden Courtyard of the museum, admiring its towering marble columns and trickling fountain, surrounded by lush green plants, when the tranquil atmosphere is pierced by a chirpy voice.

"Detective Chen?"

He turns around. A tall, thin woman with sparkly brown eyes and slightly disheveled brown hair is striding toward him with girlish energy. Her breezy, self-assured air is like an invisible armor of privilege.

"Ms. Westerly?"

"Call me Bunny!"

"Thank you for agreeing to see me."

"Are you *kidding*? I couldn't *wait* to see you! Maudie's one of my oldest and dearest friends in the entire world. I just can't believe it, y'know? It's like, *whaaaat*? Oh, my God! Never in a million...! Wow."

They sit down near the fountain.

"Tell me how you know Ms. Warner?"

"Um, so...Maudie and I roomed together our junior and senior years in boarding school. I used to go visit her a lot in New York. The Warners had this huge apartment, like about ten times the size of our house in Hartford. The living room was roped off on account of the paintings. We weren't allowed in there. But Maudie snuck me in one time so I could touch the Picasso and the Matisse with my finger. I never do that here, by the way," she giggles. "Anyhow, they were so rich. I couldn't believe it when Maudie told me her mother died broke."

"So you two kept in touch?"

"So, like, yeah...on and off. We went to different colleges. I got married and moved to Washington. Maudie got married to this stuffy banker who lived in Greenwich. When she split up with him, she moved back to New York and opened her bookstore. I saw her whenever I went up there."

"Did she ever talk to you about Burt Sklar?"

"Oh, my God, yeah. I mean she really liked him a lot in the beginning. And she introduced him to her stepfather and everything. But then after he died, she started getting suspicious that Mr. Sklar was stealing from her mom. She also thought he was manipulating her brother, Alan."

"How so?"

"I think, um, like giving him money on the sly and keeping him addicted to drugs. Maudie said that Mr. Sklar wanted to keep Alan as a friend so Alan wouldn't side with her."

"When did Ms. Warner move down here?"

"Pretty soon after her mom died. She called me up and said she couldn't afford to live in New York anymore. I was, like, shocked because I thought they were so rich. Anyway, I told her to come down here. It's cheaper and a helluva lot more friendly—if you're not in politics, that is. A pal of mine who's a real estate agent found her this cute little apartment in Georgetown. Not quite what she was used to, but safe."

"Was she seeing anyone in particular?"

"Like dating? Not that I know of."

"The superintendent of her building says she often stayed out all night. Is it possible she has a relationship she didn't tell you about? Someone she might turn to if she was on the run?"

Westerly laughs. "She's staying out all night because she's playing poker!"

"She plays *poker*?" Chen says, thinking about the article Sklar sent her on Joyce Kiner Braden.

"Oh, my God, she's an total *addict*. She's really funny about it. She calls herself a poker slut! At her age! Go figure."

"Interesting..."

"Yeah. She told me she got so depressed the day they shut down Internet poker she actually thought about moving to *Las Vegas*. I mean that's *really* depressed."

"April 15th, 2011. Black Friday. A lot of people got really depressed that day," Chen nods. "Where does she play around here?"

"So there's this casino called Maryland Live. I know she plays there a lot. And then there's some guy she calls the Gypsy, who has this illegal game. She says it's dicey, but it's the only place to play every day. I don't really get it. Poker's definitely not my world, as you can see," she says gesturing to the paintings.

"So, I have to ask... Have you heard from her?"

Westerly guffaws. "*No!* My husband works for the State Department. I'd tell you if I had. Scout's honor."

"You've been very helpful, Ms. Westerly. Thank you."

As Westerly escorts Chen out of the museum, she says, "One thing I can't figure out. Why'd she shoot Sunderland, not Sklar?"

"People assume she missed," Chen says.

"Are you kidding? She's a great shot. We nicknamed her Maudie Oakley in school because she was a champion skeet shooter."

"Shooting people is a little different."

"I dunno…I guess she was out of practice. Trust me, in the old days, if Maudie was aiming at someone, no way she would have missed. *No way.*"

Chen thinks back to the shooting range targets in the apartment. She definitely wasn't out of practice. He's beginning to get a clearer picture of Maud Warner. But the more he finds out about her, the more mysterious she becomes.

Chapter Twenty-five

Chen is ushered into Joyce Kiner Braden's office. Braden stands up to greet him with a big smile that is both disarming and oddly threatening at the same time.

"So have you caught my poker sista yet, Detective Chen?"

Chen notes that Ms. Braden's newspaper picture didn't do her justice. She's a vivacious redhead with violet eyes magnified by jeweled butterfly glasses. A tweed suit hugs her hourglass figure like a corset. She's wearing a gold bracelet that looks like a handcuff and gold earrings the size of ingots.

"So you two know each other?" Chen says, taking a seat.

"We do."

"I read the article about you in the *Washington Post*. I liked your quote about poker and the law."

"This one?" Braden says, turning a plaque on her desk toward Chen.

Chen reads the inscription aloud: "'*There's no law in poker, but plenty of poker in the law.*' That one, yeah."

"It's very true. There's plenty of poker in a lot of things."

"The article says you specialize in the Extreme Emotional Distress defense."

"Specialize is a big word. But yes, I've used that defense successfully on a few occasions."

"You talk about it in the article. You say it's hard to prove."

She narrows her eyes. "What's this all about, Detective?"

"How did you meet Ms. Warner?" Chen says.

"At a poker tournament in Atlantic City."

"Did she approach you?"

"I don't remember. We were two older women playing poker in a sea of testosterone. Naturally, we bonded."

"Did you ever discuss your cases with her?"

"We mainly talked about poker."

Chen senses that Braden is choosing her words carefully so as not to lie, but also not to give him any ammunition.

"Is it possible Ms. Warner sought you out on purpose?"

Braden swivels from side to side in her chair, eyeing Chen.

"You want to know what I think you're *really* asking me?"

"What's that?"

"*Oh, come on…*" Braden says, shaking her head in amused irritation. "We're talking about the woman who walked into a crowded restaurant and shot a man at point-blank range. Unless her plan is to spend the rest of her life in prison, she's going to try for an E.E.D. defense, right? A defense with which, as you know, I'm quite familiar."

Chen isn't surprised she's hit the nail on the head, only that she's so frank about it.

"The thought crossed my mind," Chen admits. "Would you defend her?"

"I'd have to know a lot more. The E.E.D. defense is no slam dunk. It's very difficult to prove. If it weren't, a whole lot of people would be getting away with murder."

"Do you think she might contact you?"

"She might. Do you think she might contact *you?*" Braden says, needling him. She glances at her watch. "I'm afraid you'll have to excuse me, Detective. I have a meeting."

She escorts Chen to the door.

"Thanks for your time," Chen says, then stops. "One more question?"

"Make it short."

"Is Ms. Warner a good poker player?"

"She's pretty good for someone who started late in life, like me."

"Can she bluff?"

Braden lets out whoop. "That's like asking a tennis player if they can serve! If you can't bluff, you shouldn't play poker."

"Can you bluff an E.E.D. defense?"

Braden taps her watch. "Next hand, Detective. Say hello to Vance Packer for me. Wish him good luck!" she adds with a wink in her voice.

Chapter Twenty-six

I'm huddled against a building, trying to keep warm on this cold night. A few yards away a homeless man is curled up on a blanket with a dirty white mop of a dog sleeping beside him. I camped near him because of the dog. I love dogs. I've had dogs all my life. I should have known about Sklar when my old schnauzer, Mr. Spencer, bit him. Dogs are smarter than people.

It's past three so the Gypsy's game is definitely over. I rise quietly so as not to disturb my neighbors. I walk around the corner, checking out my surroundings before venturing into that dark alley where the stench of danger outweighs the stench of garbage from the restaurants out front.

I remember the first time I ever came here with Billy. As he led me up three long flights of a rickety, rusting fire escape toward the metal door at the top, he made me promise I'd never go here by myself. It was far too dangerous. I gave him my word, but you can't trust a poker player. That glowing yellow light atop the Gypsy's door eventually became as seductive to me as the green light on Daisy's dock was to Gatsby. I couldn't stay away. I became a regular.

I knock on the door. An eye shadows the peephole. The door opens. Pratt, the night dealer at the Gypsy's, a thirty-year-old guy I think of as my "poker son," looks at me in astonishment. "Whoa. It *is* you, Maudzilla. You dye your hair, girl?"

"Blonds have more fun. It's a wig, honey. Everyone gone, I hope?"

"Yup. There was a detective here tonight, asking about you…"

"I wanna hear. But first I gotta pee. Sorry."

I dash off to the bathroom, a truly foul enclosure reminiscent of the latrine dirt pits in Third World countries where I used to go trekking. Tonight, however, it's a heavenly oasis. When I emerge, Pratt is putting the chips in racks. The red chips are so filthy they look brown.

"What do homeless people do when they have to go to the bathroom?" I ask.

"That alley down there…? Just be careful where you step."

"Is there any food left?"

"Pizza's all gone. Sorry."

"It's never *all* gone."

I dig out some half-eaten pizza crusts from the industrial-size garbage can, brimming with dirty paper plates, soda cans, and beer bottles.

"Maudzilla dumpster diving!? Icicles are forming in hell," Pratt laughs.

I stretch out on the ripped, springless couch, scarfing down leftover pizza crusts. I think about my poker journey which began on the Internet, then went live at Billy's Poker Palace, and pretty much ended here in this dismal loft, operated by an elusive character known as The Gypsy because he often sports a red bandanna and an earring. No Poker Palace amenities here. The poker table, under a single hanging lamp, is the only bright spot in a vast room reeking of Thai cuisine from the restaurant directly below. The wall-mounted TV has a lousy picture, much to the fury of players who bet on sports. Whereas my tablemates at Billy's were a cross-section of Washington's elite, here at the Gypsy's, I played with a more colorful, diverse crowd, including felons and felons-in-waiting, guys I knew only by nicknames like Night Fox, Zombie, Joker, Cowboy, Big O, Professor, Beast, and The Great North American AJ, aka Sasquatch Man.

This is back alley poker—a filthy, dingy, depressing space with players who make their living at the game. The Gypsy's is as far a cry from Billy's Poker Palace as fois gras is from Spam. Yet I feel more at home here than I did at Billy's, or even in my own house growing up. I've gone to the underworld. I'm comfy here.

"So tell me about the detective," I say, gobbling a pizza crust.

"Asian guy around forty. The Gypsy got a call from someone and let him come. An accommodation so they don't shut us down."

"What'd he want?"

"*You*, dummy! You're a fugitive, remember?"

"So did he think I was just gonna be here playing poker so he could arrest me, or what?"

"You *are* here. So how crazy is it for him to think you might *be* here? He was just asking about you. What people thought of you. When's the last time we saw you. Did you ever talk about Sklar? I think he was just trying to get a feel for who you are."

"I give up. Who am I?"

"Fuck knows! That's some crazy-ass shit you pulled in that restaurant, Maudzilla. I'm not even gonna ask why you did what you did. I gotta wonder if *you* even know."

"Pratt, just to be clear: I know *exactly* what I did and why I did it."

"I call…Why?"

"I thought you weren't gonna ask."

"I lied. Why?"

"Because it had to be done. That's why."

"Gee, thanks! That clears it all up."

"And FYI: It's not over. Are you still with me?"

"I gotta do the bank and get the chips locked away. Then we'll get going. Okay?"

"Okay."

I knew I could count on Pratt.

Chapter Twenty-seven

Sklar stares at himself in the cheval mirror in his bedroom, trying to decide who he will be for this gala evening at The Met. He knows all eyes will be on him. Jean Sunderland's accusations are now common knowledge. Many of his clients have called to express their concerns about the situation which eerily reflect Maud Warner's similar claims against him years ago. He's assured them all that there are two sides to this story, just as there were in Lois Warner's case, and that everything he, personally, has done is aboveboard. Still, he knows that the odor of Sun's bigamy is wafting around him like foul air, so he definitely needs to strike the right note this evening. He's pleased with the way he looks in the Tom Ford tuxedo he bought for the occasion. It makes him look killer elegant.

He's got it: *Bond...James Bond.*

Cloaked in this persona, Sklar walks down the hall to the guest room where Danya is staying. So far, she's seemed singularly unimpressed with all his efforts to please her. He was excited to show her his two-bedroom aerie he decorated with her in mind. She hardly noticed the sweeping views of Central Park, the yacht-quality woodwork, the stainless-steel fittings, or the custom-made furniture covered in gray microsuede. She said the (fake) Cy Twombly hanging frameless over the steel-rimmed fireplace looked like, "a bunch of scribbles." She didn't even appreciate the guest room he'd furnished just for her in shades of pink and beige.

Like an adolescent boy with a mega crush, Sklar can't believe he could be so passionate about Danya if she didn't feel the same way about him. In the years they'd spent together, he'd convinced himself that it was only her perverse loyalty to Sunderland that prevented her from expressing her love for him in any way. But now Sunderland's gone. Danya's been living in his apartment for two days. Tonight he's Bond...James Bond. James Bond would definitely make a move here.

Sklar knocks softly on Danya's door, not waiting for an answer before barging in. She's in sweats, lounging on the bed, reading *Cosmopolitan*.

"Burt!" she cries, startled.

"How do I look?"

"Swell," she says, going back to her magazine.

"Come with me. I want to show you something."

She reluctantly tosses the magazine aside and follows him into the den.

"I wish I could take you to the party tonight, baby. I'd love to show you off. But before I go, I want you to hear something."

Sklar presses a button on a remote control. Roberta Flack's famous love song, "The first time ever I saw your face," fills the air.

Sklar moves to take her in his arms. She feels she has no choice but to comply. They dance to the love song. She feels his erection as he sings along: "'*The first time ever I saw your face, I thought the sun rose in your eyes, And the moon and the stars were the gifts you gave to the dark and the endless skies, my love...*'"

His breath smells like low tide in the Chesapeake Bay. For Danya, this moment is even scarier than that time in high school when Mr. Potts, her portly, pockmarked math teacher promised not to fail her if she pulled up her blouse and let him fondle her breasts. She ran away then and would love to run away now. Except she's terrified of Sklar, knowing what he's capable of.

"You know I'm in love with you, Dany. I have been for years," Sklar whispers.

He's been wanting to tell her that for as long as he's known her. He was going to do it over the celebratory dinner he had planned for them when all the papers were signed. But the time seems right now because he's Bond...James Bond.

Danya artfully extricates herself from Sklar's arms. They stand facing one another as Danya tries to think of a gentle way to let him down.

"Look, Burt, I'm, like, you know, flattered and all that. But now's just not the right time for me."

"Will it ever be the right time?"

"Who the fuck knows? I'm not ruling it out. But I just got out of the relationship from hell. I need a breather."

"Okay. I'm not going anywhere. I just want you to understand how deeply I feel about you."

Danya watches warily as he unlocks the bottom drawer of his desk and removes a bunch of letters secured by a rubber band. He drops the packet down on the coffee table in front of her.

"Read these when I'm gone," he says. "Make sure you notice the dates."

The minute Sklar leaves for the party, Danya starts opening the letters. They are all love letters from Sklar to her, some of them written years ago when she first met him and Sunderland. These letters *prove* he was obsessed with her, and would have done anything to have her. She knows a certain person will be very happy to know these letters exist. They are an unexpected bonus in the grand scheme of things. These love letters are pure gold, and a lot more.

Chapter Twenty-eight

Magma Hartz loathes the term "cougar." Do they name men who prefer dating younger women after predatory animals? No! It's only women to whom they give sharp teeth and claws if they dare to break a societal taboo. That being said, Magma does feel slightly couger-esque when it comes to Brent Hobbs, the cute writer she met at Greta's house the night of Sun's shooting. She Googled Hobbs after he took her home that evening. She was surprised to find out that she is fourteen years older than Hobbs—not that he needs to know that. Magma's lied about her age since forever. Only Greta knows the truth and she ain't talkin' because that would reveal her own age. Age may be "only a number," as the optimists say, but like money in an offshore account, the bigger the number the more secret it should be.

Despite their heavy necking on Greta's couch, Hobbs never called her. So Magma bit the bullet and called him first, inviting him to escort her to a black tie dinner at the Metropolitan Museum's great party venue, the Temple of Dendur. He sounded thrilled to accept. She's spent quite a lot of time getting ready for this date. Wearing a short black cocktail dress with a plunging neckline displaying the ample, if slightly crinkled, cleavage which got Hobbs' attention, Magma looks as sexy as a woman of an uncertain age can.

When she opens the door for Hobbs, he draws back and gives her a raunchy once-over.

"*Wow!*" he exclaims like he really means it.

Hobbs looks very "writerly," Magma thinks—a little soft around the gut, like a man who sits a lot and enjoys his grog and vittles. His tussled brown hair could use a comb and a cut. His tuxedo is old and his dress shirt a wee bit frayed around the collar. His cuff links are cutesy typewriter keys of his initials: One B, one H. His clip-on tie is crooked. His black needlepoint dress slippers—one embroidered with a red pen, the other with a red sword—give the tired ensemble a touch of humor. Despite the lack of chic, Hobbs seems entirely comfortable in his own literary skin.

As Hobbs helps her on with her coat, he leans in and gives her bare neck a lingering kiss with some tongue involved. Magma feels a thrill. There's chemistry between them. She likes that. Hobbs grabs her hand and leads her out the door. His grip is strong. She likes that too.

The ancient Temple of Dendur is aglow in red and orange lights. Guests milling around its perimeter look excessively ruddy.

"You think the Temple of Dendur was Egypt's first tanning parlor?" Hobbs cracks.

"Oh, Brent, you *do* make me laugh!" Magma nuzzles his shoulder.

They stroll through the crowd. On the arm of this clever, younger guy with his irreverent air, Magma feels like a goddess. She's always preferred macho to money when it came to men. She'd rather be with a cute young guy than a billionaire her own age. Magma proudly introduces him to everyone she knows. Brent spots a couple of the titans he writes about in his blog and points them out to Magma, supplying her with juicy tidbits about their private lives and private planes.

"How do you know so much about these people? I've known most of them for years and I don't know half what you know," Magma says in wonder.

"I have my sources," Hobbs says.

"I'm surprised you didn't find out about Sun. What a sordid story *that* is! Jean's a great friend of mine, as you know."

"Success breeds discontent. You'd be surprised how many of these people want to be something other than what they are. A lot of them lead double lives. Maybe not as flagrant as bigamy, but dangerous nonetheless."

"And yet they all look so happy!"

"One of the first things I ever learned as a reporter: Don't trust smiles in life or in photographs," Hobbs says.

As they head for the bar, Magma spots Burt Sklar heading toward them.

"Turn around!" she orders Hobbs, grabbing his arm. "I don't want anything to do with that man."

Magma is in Jean's camp now, firmly convinced Sklar knew all about Sun's bigamy and abetted him in the cover-up. Too late. Sklar accosts them.

"Magma! How'ya doin', sweetheart?" Sklar says, as if he's oblivious to the fact she's just fired him.

"Don't talk to me, Burt. I think what you've done to poor Jean is absolutely *disgraceful!*" Magma says.

"You made that very clear on the phone, Magma. And as I told you, I'm only carrying out Sun's wishes."

"Following orders…just like the Nazis. I need a drink. You coming, Brent?"

Sklar notices Hobbs. "*Hobbsy!* I didn't recognize you. Long time, no see."

"You *know* each other?" Magma asks incredulously.

"I'm a big fan of his work, aren't I, Hobbsy?" Sklar says.

Burt Sklar is one of Brent Hobbs' prime sources. They've had an arrangement for years. Sklar gives Hobbs inside gossip. Hobbs boosts Sklar's friends and clients in his blog.

"Are you coming, Brent?" Magma says impatiently.

"Give me a minute, baby," Hobbs says.

"I'll be at the bar!" Though she loves when he calls her baby, she walks off in a huff.

"Well, well, well…fancy seeing you here, Hobbsy!" Sklar says.

Translation: *What's a humble scribe like you doing in the exalted Temple of Dendur at a gala costing twenty-five hundred dollars a head?*

"How come you don't return my calls?" Hobbs asks.

"I've been a little preoccupied, as you may have heard."

"That's obviously why I was calling. Not nice, Burt. I'll remember," Hobbs says, holding up his index finger.

"Touchy, aren't we…?"

"*You fuckin' bet!* You're part of the biggest story of the decade and you don't return my calls? How many favors have I done you, Burt?"

"It hasn't exactly been a one-way street, Hobbsy. But, as it happens, I was going to call you because I have a little something that might interest you."

"I'm listening," Hobbs says.

Sklar steers Hobbs off into a quiet corner and pauses for effect. "Danya Dickert Sunderland," he says.

"What about her?"

"How'd you like to interview her?"

Hobbs's eyes widen. "Are you *kidding*?!"

"Would I kid a scribe in the presence of Osiris?"

"Here…take my right arm now," Hobbs says, excited.

"She's a great girl, Brent—nothing like the slut they're portraying her as in the press. Jean's thrown a lot of mud on her. I'm trusting you to wash it off."

"Just say when."

"Tomorrow at ten. My apartment. Bring a friendly pen."

"Burt…have I ever let you down?"

"You better not, seeing as I'm handing you the biggest scoop of your career," Sklar says. They shake on it.

Hobbs can't believe his good fortune. He feels like a prospector who's just struck gold. He finds Magma at the bar. She's still irritated.

"I don't know why you want anything to do with that odious man. You know he's ruining my friend Jean's life," she says.

"It's business, baby. I deal with people who ruin other people's lives on a daily basis."

Hobbs doesn't tell her he's about to land an exclusive interview with the second Mrs. Sunderland. He knows enough about Magma to know she's more dangerous than Twitter.

Dinner is announced by a series of tinkling temple bells. The fiery lights dim to ember wattage as the guests take their seats at round tables of ten dotting the space. Though striking at first glance, the centerpieces are much too big. Diners begin grumbling that they didn't pay twenty-five hundred bucks to stare at a pyramid made of leaves.

"Isn't it amazing how life goes on? Sun's dead and it's just like he never existed," Magma says to Hobbs.

"Tell that to the pharaohs," Hobbs says absently, thinking about the scoop he's just landed.

Chapter Twenty-nine

Danya cracks open her door and peers out into the corridor, making sure Sklar isn't lurking there. She was freaked out when he got home from the party, tiptoed into her room, and stood over her bed for a minute while she pretended to be asleep. He finally left. But it felt like the longest minute of her life. She puts on a robe and walks barefoot to the kitchen so as not to make any noise. She's startled to see Sklar there making coffee. He's in gray silk pajamas with the top unbuttoned.

"Hey, baby girl! You're up bright and early."

"Hey." She hugs the robe tight around her.

Sklar holds up the coffee bag. "Mocha java, your fav."

"Thanks."

"So… Did you read my letters?"

"Some."

"And…?"

"And, like, if you're so in love with me, Burt, how come you didn't stop him?"

"Stop him…?"

"From *hurting* me! How come you didn't?"

"*Truthfully*…? I had bigger plans for us."

"For *us*? You saw me the morning after he almost killed me with that fuckin' strangle thing he liked to do. You took me to the emergency room when he dislocated my arm. There might have been no *us* if he'd fuckin' killed me."

"You're exaggerating, sweetheart."

"Yeah? Well, I nearly got exaggerated to death. *Screw you!*"

Sklar looks sheepish. "Okay, I'm sorry. Just believe me when I say it's all been worth it. You'll thank me very shortly. We have a meeting with the lawyers this afternoon."

"Don't tell me I have to sign more shit."

"Yes. Problem?"

"What exactly are these papers I've been signing all these years? You guys would never tell me."

"You're gonna find out this afternoon in my lawyer's office, okay? But in the meantime, I have some more very good news for us."

"Catch me, I'm falling," she deadpans, buttering a piece of toast.

Sklar ignores her sarcasm. "I ran into Brent Hobbs last night at the gala. Know who he is?"

"Nope."

"He writes a gossipy business blog called *HobbsNobbing*. He's an old pal. I trust him." Sklar thinks it wiser to portray Hobbs as a friend rather than a guy with whom he swaps favors in a shady arrangement.

Danya sits down at the opposite end of the steel kitchen table and munches on the toast.

"Jeez, Dany, so far away? I feel like we're in that great breakfast scene in *Citizen Kane* where they sit a mile from each other and eventually quit talking. Remember that scene?"

"I don't know what the fuck you're talking about, Burt."

"*Citizen Kane*. You don't know it?" She shakes her head. "Most influential movie of the twentieth century. We'll watch it tonight on the big TV in the den. Would you like that, sweetheart?"

"Whatever."

"So, anyway, Hobbs is coming over here this morning to meet you."

"Why?"

"You're going to give him an exclusive interview."

"No, I'm not."

"Yes, you are. Don't argue. This is the guy who's gonna to spin the story *our* way. You're gonna talk to Brent and charm the hell out of him. Then you're gonna meet me at the lawyer's office and sign some papers. We're almost there, baby. I'm just doing my best to protect you."

Danya rolls her eyes and lets out a guffaw. "*Protect* me? Are you fuckin' *kidding?*... The whole world thinks I'm some gold-digging bimbo slut. I'm being sued. I could be arrested for bigamy. I have no money, no credit cards, no place to live. I can't get hold of the neighbor who's taking care of Mooncat! I still have scars from all that stuff with Sun that you did nothing to stop... *You haven't protected me from shit, Burt. I miss my cat!*" Danya buries her head in her hands and weeps.

Sklar pulls up a chair beside her and puts a comforting arm around her. At first she resists. But gradually she melts into his shoulder, crying softly. He strokes her hair. He loves the look of her, the softness of her, the smell of her. The man who's made a career out of talking people into doing whatever he wants them to do is inexplicably tongue-tied.

Danya looks up with glistening eyes. "Can I ask you a question?"

"Anything, baby."

"What are these papers I've been signing, Burt? Why do I have to sign more?"

Sklar draws back. "What's the matter? You don't trust me all of a sudden?"

"I just want to know what they're about."

"They're about making both of us very, very rich. That's what they're about."

"I think I need to know more before I sign anything else."

Sklar grips her arm tight. "Now you listen to me, Dany. You're gonna sign those papers *today*. You don't have a choice." His grip tightens.

"*Okay, okay*! You're *hurting* me!"

His releases her as if he, himself, is frightened of what he might do.

"Sorry, baby. But this is important."

Danya rubs her arm. "You know, for a minute there I thought you were Sun back from the grave."

"You need to realize there's a helluva lot at stake here. My lawyer will explain everything to you at the office. I need your promise that you and I are together in this thing. Otherwise, we both lose and it will all have been for nothing."

"What will?"

"Just go get dressed, like a good girl!" he says, spurring her on with a pat on the rear. "Brent will be here soon. Wear something sexy so he'll fall in love with you like everyone else!"

Chapter Thirty

I'm finishing up the breakfast of coffee and doughnuts Pratt so kindly left for me. Aside from the *kaffeeklatsch* of chattering birds, it's nice and peaceful here in Odenton. Pratt's small cabin on a ragged patch of land surrounded by scrubby woods is quaintly furnished with rag rugs, calico curtains, and cheap cherrywood furniture. The worm-eaten antique butter churn, a parting gift from a girlfriend he dumped, strikes me as quite the inventive revenge. This cabin is a far cry from my parents' so called "cottage" in East Hampton—a twenty-room gray-shingled house, set back on ten acres of emerald green lawn dotted with towering shade trees. The carefully landscaped grounds included a swimming pool, tennis court, greenhouse, plus vegetable and rose gardens. Though different in size and scope, these abodes do have one major thing in common: Drugs.

Pratt is a drug dealer. Alan was a drug user. With the smell of marijuana now wafting through the house, I can't help thinking of Alan, who got into drugs at a young age and never really grew up as a result. I go over my brother's history often. It's like a poison fairy tale I keep hoping will have a happy ending. But Alan's death is the second biggest reason I'm here.

My mother always refused to admit her baby boy had a drug problem. But deep in her heart she knew. Knowing she couldn't discipline Alan herself, she turned to Sklar. He suggested Mummy set up a trust fund for Alan over which he, Sklar, would have control. Sklar promised to supervise my brother, get him a job, and make sure he was clean. Sklar convinced Mummy he would watch over Alan with the same care and attention he was watching over her money.

Then came the day Alan was arrested for trying to buy heroin on the Lower East Side. He couldn't get hold of Sklar so he called me to come bail him out of jail.

"Swear you won't tell Mom," Alan pleaded with me as we left the court.

I refused. I explained to Mummy exactly what had happened. She was so upset, she finally listened to me. I told her to quit relying on Sklar and get Alan professional help.

"Alan's got to go to rehab," I said. She agreed.

I arranged for an "intervention." Alan came to Mummy's apartment, where she and I and a counselor confronted him about his drug use. After a grueling session of accusations and denials, Alan finally agreed to go to Hazelden, a well-known drug treatment center. Arrangements were made. He was scheduled to leave for Minnesota at the end of the week. As an added bonus, I'd also persuaded Mummy to let someone else have a look at her finances.

Sklar called me the next day.

"Maudie, I just got back from L.A. and called your mother. She sounds upset with me. She told me to call you. What's up?"

"I had to bail Alan out of jail for buying heroin. He admitted to me that he hasn't had a job in months and that you've been giving him money without the supervision you promised our mother."

"*Candidly*, Maud, that's simply not true," Sklar said.

"Well, true or not, Alan's going to Hazelden at the end of the week. And Mummy's agreed it's time to let another pair of eyes look into her financial affairs. I'm arranging that now."

After a brief pause, Sklar said: "*Honestly...*? If that's what your mother wants, then that's what will happen. I'm happy to talk to anyone you like and show them anything they want."

Sklar spoke to me without rancor or any sign of panic. I gotta say I was impressed by his reaction, but wary nonetheless.

The day before Alan was scheduled to go to Hazelden, Mummy summoned me to her apartment for tea. When I arrived, I found Mummy in the library with Sklar. Their conversation stopped when I entered.

"Sit down, Maud," Mummy commanded, pointing to the couch. "Burt has something to tell you."

I sat on the tufted chintz ottoman across from Sklar and Mummy, who were seated on chairs, peering down at me like judges at a witch trial. Kindling lit, I smelled smoke. Panic buzzed in my gut. Sklar's pious demeanor was scary. He looked like Cotton Mather in Armani.

"*Truthfully*, Maudie…? There's been a terrible misunderstanding." I crossed my arms in defiance. He went on. "Your brother was *not* buying drugs. Alan was caught up in a sweep. And through absolutely no fault of his own, he got arrested."

"That's not what he told me," I said.

"*Truthfully*…? Alan was afraid you wouldn't bail him out if it didn't seem really important."

I threw my hands up in exasperation. "What does that even mean?"

"*It means your brother doesn't have a drug problem!*" Mummy cried. "And we're going to get this ridiculous record expunged forever! Right, Burt?"

"That's absolutely correct, Lois," Sklar said with a solemn nod.

I took a shaky breath. "If Alan doesn't get help now, he could wind up dead."

Mummy turned to Sklar in exasperation. "Sharper than a serpent's tooth! I told you she'd be like this, Burt!"

"Mummy, *please*! Once he has the tools to fight this disease, he'll conquer it. But he *needs* to go to rehab. It's all set up now. What's the harm? It's only a few weeks."

"The harm is in stigmatizing your brother just because you're jealous of him. Alan told me *himself* he doesn't have a drug problem. It was all a ghastly misunderstanding. And I believe him."

Now I was furious. "*Really?* Just when did you talk to him about this?"

Sklar and Mummy exchanged knowing looks.

"Alan was here for lunch. He just left," Sklar said.

"*Perfect.*" I shook my head in disgust.

"Your brother doesn't want to go to that awful place because he's not an addict and he's afraid of being surrounded by addicts," Mummy said.

"Mummy, listen to me…Alan *is* an addict. Addicts *lie*. He's lying to you and very possibly to himself. He was arrested by an undercover cop! He admitted everything to me."

Mummy shook her head. "No! Alan's afraid of you, Maud. He's been afraid of you since he was little and you teased him and played mean tricks on him because you were jealous. You're your father's daughter, all right."

I shot back. "I know, I know, I'm the spawn of Satan because my real father treated you like the devil. But I've got news for you, the only devil in the picture is sitting right beside you."

Mummy gasped. "What a *wicked* thing to say about Burt! And after all he's done for this family! You apologize to him *this instant!*"

"She doesn't mean it, Lois, dear," Sklar said.

"I *do* mean it!"

"Well, Maud, I mean it when I say your brother's not going anywhere! Burt's going to continue looking after Alan. Aren't you, Burt?"

"I absolutely am. Count on it," Sklar said.

Sklar's hold on my mother was stronger than ever. As I left, he gave me a covert smirk, daring me to interfere any further.

I called Alan the second I got out of there.

"Alan, what the hell are you doing?"

"Not going to drug jail, for starters. Did Burt tell you he's getting my record expunged?"

"I don't care about your record. I care about your *life*. You need to go to rehab for your own sake."

"Maudie, I'm fine. Trust me."

"You're an addict. *That's not fine.*"

"I'm not an addict. I can stop whenever I want to. I just don't happen to want to stop at the moment."

"You understand, of course, that Sklar is using you to keep control of our mother, right? If you sided with me, Mummy would listen to us and he'd be out of the picture."

"You've got Burt all wrong. I know him better than you do. He's really an okay guy."

"Oh yeah? I wonder what you'll think when he steals all the money."

"Maudie, there's so much money there I'm pretty sure there'll always be plenty left."

"Don't bet on it."

Sklar called me that night. I didn't hang up because I was curious to hear what he'd say.

"Look, Maud, I'm sorry about this afternoon. It was tough on you because, as you well know, your dear mother has a problem with women. It's just bad luck you were born a girl. I'm calling to reassure you that I'm handling your brother. *Honestly…?* I also happen to be making your mom a ton of money. I promise you kids will both be enormously wealthy one day. Now, take my advice: Send your mom some flowers with a note. She loves you. I love you. Your brother's gonna be fine. Don't worry so much. You'll get an ulcer."

So here's the thing. I actually felt better after that conversation. I wanted to hear that my mother loved me, that Alan was going to be okay, and that Sklar was looking after the family fortune. So I quit bugging everybody and let the whole thing drop.

Sklar was like the guy at a poker table who assures you that you made a great fold. You feel good until you realize the son-of-a-bitch was bluffing the entire hand.

Chapter Thirty-one

Hungover from a night of booze and sex, Brent Hobbs arrives at Sklar's apartment a few minutes past ten. He succumbed to Magma's unsubtle invitation to spend the night with her, not just because she can be useful to him, but because she was hellbent on proving to him that she could outdo any younger woman when it came to satisfying him in bed. And whaddaya know? She was right! Magma was terrific in the sack—possibly not as terrific as that clinically depressed Russian model he interviewed for a piece he did on the oligarchs two years ago. But she came pretty damn close.

Sklar greets Hobbs as he steps off the elevator. The sleekness of Sklar's black designer duds makes Hobbs feel slightly self-conscious in his ancient tweed jacket, pilling cashmere sweater, stained corduroy trousers, and tattered loafers.

"Hey, Brent, howya doin'? Fun party, huh?" Sklar says, ushering Hobbs into the apartment.

Hobbs has been to Sklar's apartment on several occasions when the two men had information for each other they didn't dare discuss over the phone. Hobbs thinks of it as minimalist hell, but he envies the wealth it represents. He can't help comparing it to his own humble digs in a shabby, rent-controlled brownstone. He wants to make some real money and now's his big chance. The public can't get enough of this scandal. Sunderland's battered image is as shocking as a jackhammered face on Mount Rushmore. Hobbs knows if he plays his cards right, he'll hit bestseller trifecta: a billionaire, a bimbo, and bigamy.

Hobbs and Sklar sit in the living room and have coffee.

"Dany'll be out in a minute. So how do you know Magma?" Sklar asks.

"I met her at some dinner." Hobbs is purposely evasive. He never tells Sklar any more about his personal life than he has to.

"So are you guys an item?" Sklar probes.

"Not really."

"They call her Magma the Magpie, you know. She repeats everything she hears and makes up the rest. I wouldn't take anything she says too seriously."

"You mean like the fact she fired you?"

"I know she likes to tell people that. But, *truthfully*…? I had to let her go as a client."

"Really? How come?"

"Because she doesn't have enough money for my fees. I only took her as a favor to Jean. Can we speak frankly before Danya comes?"

"Sure." Hobbs takes out his notebook and pen.

"Off the record?"

Hobbs nods.

"*Truthfully*…? Dany's nervous about seeing you. The press hasn't treated her too kindly, as you know."

"I can see that would be a concern," Hobbs says, thinking of a recent *New York Post* cover featuring yet another grainy photo of Danya in a G-string, hanging off a pole, with the headline: BILLIONAIRE BIGAMIST'S BIMBO!

"I told her you're a good guy."

"Thanks. I appreciate it."

"Brent, is it fair to say I've been helpful to you in the past?"

"It's fair to say we've been helpful to each other," Hobbs says.

"*Candidly*…? I'm giving you the scoop of a lifetime here. You understand that, right? I'm counting on you to reciprocate."

Hobbs squints. "Reciprocate?"

"I'll spell it out for you, Brent. Jean Sunderland is a woman scorned who thinks that by trashing Danya in the public eye she's gonna delay the consequences of legal steps that were taken by me during her husband's lifetime at his own direction. Danya's the sweetest kid you're ever gonna meet. She's not some slutty gold digger. It's only fair the public hear her side of the story."

"Which is...?"

"That she's a innocent young woman who fell in love with a powerful man who fell in love with her and wanted to take care of her forever. Pure and simple."

Though Hobbs suspects there's nothing simple about this story and even less that's pure, he nods noncommittally. "I'm eager to meet her."

Sklar perks up. "And, right on cue, here she is now."

Danya is standing in the doorway, paused under an arc of light. Hobbs is struck by how young and fresh-faced she looks—nothing like her raunchy photos. Except for a hint of lip gloss, she's wearing no makeup. Her thick dark hair is pulled back in a ponytail. Her gray jumpsuit is a not altogether successful attempt to play down her voluptuous curves. Tall and tan and young and lovely...The Girl From Ipanema incarnate, Hobbs thinks.

"Dany, sweetheart! I was just talking about you. Come join us," Sklar says, waving her in.

Danya is hesitant. She eyes Hobbs warily as she sits down.

"Hello, Mrs. Sunderland. I'm very sorry for your loss," Hobbs says respectfully.

"Thanks." She's clearly surprised and appreciative he called her Mrs. Sunderland.

Hobbs studies the face that's launched a thousand headlines. She's not classically beautiful, but there's a striking sensuality about her. Her teenage face and luscious body are a striking combination. To Hobbs, she is the quintessential "*femme enfant*," the child woman who seems alluringly oblivious to her own charms even as she flaunts them. It's easy to see why an old guy like Sunderland—or any guy, for that matter—would fall for her on the spot.

Danya sips her coffee, peering at Hobbs over the rim of the mug. Their eyes meet. Her stare lingers. Hobbs wonders if she's flirting with him or sizing him up, deciding if she trusts him enough to talk. He knows from experience that most people yearn to tell their stories. The trick will be how to get her started.

"Danya... May I call you Danya?" Hobbs says.

She shrugs. "Sure."

"Please call me Brent." She nods like a biddable child. "So how did you and Mr. Sunderland meet?" Hobbs asks.

Sklar jumps in. "Dany was a young, impressionable kid, trying to become a professional photographer. She was all alone in the world. She's gorgeous so she got a job making the most money she could in order to pursue her dream. That job happened to be stripping. Are we supposed to condemn her for that? I mean, how sexist can you get?"

Danya bows her head. Hobbs can't tell if she's embarrassed, upset, or what. All he knows is that she's not going to open up to him as long as Sklar is there.

"Burt, I think it'd be more effective if Danya told her story in her own words," Hobbs says.

"I agree. Dany, tell him in your own words." Sklar leans back on the couch, crosses his arms, prepared to listen.

Danya doesn't say anything.

"Go on, baby," Sklar urges her. "Don't be afraid of Hobbs here. He's on your side...right, Hobbsy?" Sklar says with a wink.

Danya sits in silence with her head bowed. Hobbs twiddles his thumbs. Sklar's eyes dart back and forth between the two of them.

"You two just gonna sit there? How are we gonna get this thing done?" Sklar says. "Go on, baby. Tell Brent how Sun seduced you. She had no idea he was married. If Jean wants to play that angle, we'll sue her for defamation. Right, baby?"

Danya rises abruptly and walks out.

"That went well." Hobbs puts away his notebook.

"Wait," Sklar says.

Sklar finds Danya in the bedroom.

"What's going on, baby? Why won't you talk to Hobbs?"

"*Because you won't let me*! You keep interrupting."

"I'm just trying to get you to open up, that's all."

"I can't talk with you sitting there. You make me nervous."

Sklar is wounded. "I make you *nervous*? Dany, honey…I'm doing all this for you."

"I feel embarrassed talking to him in front of you."

"You're *kidding*. You know you can say anything you want in front of me. *Truthfully*, Dany…? I know more about you than you know about yourself."

"Then *you* give him the goddam interview!"

"Calm down, sweetheart. Calm down. It's important we get your story out there A.S.A.P. Brent's just the man to do it."

"How do I know that?"

"Trust me. I do plenty for this guy. He's wouldn't dare screw me. What's the matter? Don't you like him?"

"How the fuck would I know? I only know every time I open my mouth, *you* answer."

"Okay, okay…" Sklar says begrudgingly. "I'll go in the other room if it makes you happy."

They go back into the living room. Sklar leaves Hobbs and Danya alone to talk, but tries to eavesdrop on their conversation. At one point he hears them discussing digital cameras. At another, Danya is telling him about her beloved Mooncat. Sklar automatically tunes out whenever that little suede rat is mentioned. Sklar is relieved that Danya and Hobbs seem to be hitting it off, although his jealousy is triggered when he hears them laughing together. After an hour or so, he can't stand it anymore.

He walks in and says, "Okay, time to break you guys up. Dany and I have an important three o'clock meeting. You need to get ready, sweetheart. Hobbsy, you all set?"

"I think I've got what I need, thanks," Hobbs says, rising.

Hobbs gives Danya a courtly bow as he shakes her hand. "It's been a pleasure, Danya. Here's my card. If you think of anything else you might want to say, call me."

Chapter Thirty-two

"To blog or not to blog, that is the question…"

Hobbs is having a Hamlet moment.

He's back in his apartment, sitting at his computer, sipping a noonday Bloody Mary, obsessing over how to write up his interview with the enchanting, elusive Danya Dickert Sunderland. He needs to meet his self-imposed three o'clock deadline.

Hobbs knows that the age of journalistic integrity has pretty much gone the way of all typewriters. It's terrorist times out there. Hobbs once considered himself a "serious" writer, marching onto the publishing field in a red jacket with gold braid and a gleaming standard of integrity. He had contempt for those coonskin-capped frontiersmen of the Internet who jumped out of cyberspace posting any goddam thing they pleased, true or false. He knows now that people would rather read an entertaining lie than a boring truth. Who can maintain old standards in a war zone? He started his own blog. The public doesn't want *nice*; they want *vice*. The sewers of corruption and desire hidden beneath the lives of the great and powerful are what really interests them. That's why he deals with Burt Sklar, who feeds him salacious inside gossip in exchange for useful ink.

Hobbs and Sklar have made similar deals before. But this story is gargantuan compared with all the others. Sklar gives him access to a key player if he writes a puff piece about her. Hobbs gets a mega book deal. Sklar gains some traction for Danya's side of the story.

Quid pro bimbo.

Hobbs can see why Sunderland was so smitten with her. Still, he can't quite understand why a rich and powerful guy like Sunderland would commit *bigamy*? Why not just have an affair? Why did Sunderland risk everything to *marry* Danya? Did she threaten to leave him? Was he so enamored that he couldn't face losing her? What makes a well-known man like Sunderland commit such a reckless crime?

Just for the hell of it, Hobbs Googles "Famous Bigamists." A lot of Mormons come up, starting with Brigham Young. But Hobbs is more interested in the secular cases where people maintain secret second spouses until they die, or until someone outs them. He gets a chuckle out of what he finds.

Who knew the writer Anais Nin was a bigamist? Female bigamists are rare, yet the celebrated author of *Delta of Venus* maintained two marriages for *eleven years*, schlepping back and forth between her first husband, a banker in New York, and her second husband, an ex-actor with the Trollopian name of Pole, in California. Hobbs chuckles to think that when Nin wrote: "*Ordinary life shackles me, I escape, one way or another. No more walls!*" she could have been on a plane flying from one husband to the other.

Then there's that super high-flyer, Charles Lindbergh, who loved Nazis as well as three German women (two of them sisters) while he was married to Anne Morrow Lindbergh, his talented wife who wrote, *Gift From the Sea*. Lindbergh wasn't technically a bigamist, but he might as well have been, having maintained separate families on two continents. His wife never suspected a thing until he died and she found out her hero husband was actually the gift from hell.

As for the jaunty old journalist and television personality, Charles Kuralt... He met Patricia Elizabeth Shannon when he was "On the Road" and promptly took her off the road and into his bed. They shacked up for thirty years in Montana with her kids from a previous marriage. The world was shocked to find out about his double life only after he died and Shannon sued his estate. Love has its limits.

Now Sun Sunderland will be added to this list of consummate deceivers because of a comely stripper who stole his heart. Hobbs liked Danya when they talked. Despite her sexy vocation, she came across as a decent, not too bright beauty who fell in love with a powerful father figure who wanted to marry her. How could a girl in her position resist?

As Hobbs goes over his notes, he starts to wonder if he's been played by Danya. The fact that she didn't tell him any romantic stories about Sunderland bothers him now more than it did at the time. Usually when people are in love, they can't wait to harangue anyone who will listen with details about the relationship—particularly if the beloved has died and memories are all they have left.

Hobbs was a captive, interested audience. Yet, curiously enough, Danya didn't seem to want to talk about Sunderland. When he asked her how they met, she responded by asking him if he, himself, had ever experienced love at first sight, as though that answered his question. Now that he thinks of it, every time he asked her a question, she threw a question right back at him. He found himself talking more than he ever had in any interview he can remember. He now realizes Danya was interviewing *him*—not the other way around.

Why?

Did she really want to get to know him before she opened up to him? Or was she simply afraid of revealing herself? Maybe she didn't really love Sunderland after all. Or maybe she was just nervous because Sklar was lurking in the background. Or maybe, just maybe, there's a deeper story here—one she was reluctant or afraid to tell? Or, perhaps, one she's eager to tell—but only to the right person. One thing Hobbs is sure of: Something's roiling beneath the surface of this child woman. He can feel it.

But a bargain's a bargain, so Hobbs bangs out a short flattering piece about Danya, portraying her relationship with Sunderland as a Trilby-Svengali situation where innocent young Danya was hypnotized into doing everything the older, powerful Sunderland said. He throws in standard stuff about how difficult life was for her trying to make ends meet in order to pursue her dream of being a photographer. He sticks in that weird thing she begged him to say about her wearing her mom's blue satin dress at her illegal wedding because her mom was looking down from heaven. "Please don't forget to say it was *blue* satin," she pleaded with him.

He reads the article over, knowing it's a piece of sentimental crap, but one that will cement his position as the inside man on this juicy case. He's sure Sklar will be pleased and give him further access. He punches a key and sends the blog into cyberspace.

Hobbs is making himself a sandwich with what's left of two-day-old chicken salad, when the phone rings. He answers with his usual greeting: "Hobbs here."

"Brent, it's Danya. I need your help!"

Chapter Thirty-three

It's past three-thirty. Sklar's in his office conference room, along with Mona Lickel, two associates from her firm, and a notary public standing by. Lickel has gone over the documents she's prepared for Danya's and Sklar's signatures at least twice as they wait for Danya to arrive. Sklar has called Danya's cell phone and the land line in his apartment several times. No luck. His limo driver is still waiting for her downstairs. Sklar is cursing himself for not insisting they go together.

"You better hope she hasn't flown the coop," Lickel warns.

"She couldn't, even if she wanted to—which she *doesn't*," he says defensively.

Sklar's confident Danya didn't go anywhere because she has nothing but pocket change. He cancelled all her credit cards just in case she got some cockamamie idea she needed to get back to D.C. to see that fucking cat. He knows it's going to be a literal CAT-tastrophe when Danya finds out that skinless little freak is in cat heaven. He'll blame it on the neighbor.

"Burt, are you quite certain she understands she needs to sign these documents before we can proceed in any meaningful way?" Lickel says.

Sklar resents how dismissive Lickel is of Danya, and always has been.

"Yes, Mona. What makes you think I haven't made that clear to her?"

"The fact that it's three-thirty and she's not here," Lickel says dryly.

Mona Lickel has questioned this scheme right from the beginning—not only because she's resentful of all young and beautiful women in general, but also because she never trusted Danya to be as clueless as she seemed. Danya signed all the signature pages that Sklar put in front of her, supposedly without inquiring what they were. No one could be that naïve, Lickel thought, unless they were morons. Was it possible Danya did as she was told because she didn't want to appear to be a gold digger? Did she really have *no clue* she was forming a tontine with Sun Sunderland and Burt Sklar—survivor takes all?

Lickel, a spinster who graduated *magna cum laude* from Columbia Law School and became the first woman partner in her firm, loathes the fact that this bimbo is about to hit the jackpot simply because she had a billionaire wrapped around her G-string.

Of course, with Lickel's help, her old friend and client Burt Sklar will benefit equally well. The Durable Power of Attorney and the tontine were Sklar's ideas, and Lickel set them both up. He'll amply reward her when the time comes because she knows too much. But, at the rate things are going this afternoon, that time may not come as quickly as Sklar planned. Lickel knows better than anyone that Jean's lawsuit will delay them and delay puts them all at risk—the biggest one being Maud Warner.

When Maud Warner is captured she'll continue blabbing about how her mother was duped in the same way as Jean. Jean will use that. Sun's Durable Power of Attorney was executed legally—even if a key witness is now dead. However, if Jean continues to protest that her husband would never have knowingly signed such a document, the law might look askance on a coincidence which turned out to be so profitable for Sklar and for Sunderland's illegal wife.

Lickel has impressed upon Sklar that getting these companies properly set up as soon as possible will present Jean with a

Gordian Knot which will take years to undo. In the meantime, Sklar and Danya will maintain they have control over the companies and various offshore bank accounts. At the very least, this will make Jean amenable to a settlement.

Sklar slams down the phone. "The super says she's not in the apartment. She must be on her way. Sorry about the delay, folks. Not that you mind…right? Not at the fuckin' fortune you people charge me an hour, right?" he says testily.

Lickel looks at her watch. "I have a dinner engagement at eight. I'd hate to miss it."

Chapter Thirty-four

In his wildest journalistic dreams, Brent Hobbs never imagined he'd be sitting in his rat-hole living room trying to comfort a sobbing Danya Sunderland. From what Hobbs can glean from Danya's garbled, tearful telling, Sklar dropped her cat off with a neighbor and the cat is now dead. The vet suspected rat poison. A box of ashes is all that remains of her beloved pet.

"My Mooncat's dead! My Mooncat's dead! God is punishing me!" has been Danya's anguished refrain for over an hour. She can't stop blubbering.

When Hobbs finally calms her down with the aid of vodka and sympathy, he senses a sea change in her, like a new resolve has taken hold. No longer the seductive child woman or the bereft pet owner, Danya now strikes him as a pragmatic woman who's assessing her fate. She perches on his couch, her arms hugging her knees to her chest, and stares out at him like a turtle peering out from its shell. She pins him with a long, contemplative gaze.

"Okay…I lied," she declares after a time, her voice dropped to a lower register.

He was already pretty sure of that. But the unanticipated steeliness in her demeanor—so much the opposite of anything he ever imagined her to be—makes him think the truth will be one hell of a story. He doesn't say a word. He lets her proceed at her own pace.

"All that stuff I told you in the interview…? All that stuff you wrote about me being so innocent and Sun and me being so happy together…? All bullshit. I wasn't innocent. And I sure as hell wasn't happy."

Hobbs nods. "Go on…"

"I had no idea who the hell Sun was when we met. That part was true. But I found out pretty quickly. I lied when I told you I didn't know he was married. I knew because Burt told me that night. I knew Burt was interested in me. I think he thought that if I knew Sun was married it'd make a difference to me. It didn't. Sun and me, we fell in love. That part was also true. Thing is, it wasn't exactly the candy and flowers-type love I said it was. It was more like, y'know, cuffs and fetish-type love."

"Okaaaay…" Hobbs says evenly, trying not to give any hint of the excitement he feels knowing this scandal was about to go nuclear.

"I've always had this thing for older guys. Daddy complex. But pretty soon I found out Sun was like my real dad in more ways than one."

"What do you mean?"

"My dad was a sadistic bastard. Particularly to my mom…" She shudders. "He'd used to beat the living crap out of her, make her drink toilet water, shit like that…"

Hobbs winces. "Why didn't she leave him?"

"A poor black woman in the south with a kid to support…? Where the hell was she gonna go? She tried a couple of times. Especially when he started beating up on me. But he'd always sweet-talk her back. Me, too. My dad was a real sweet-talker. Just like Sun."

"Are you saying Sunderland abused you?"

She nods. "Oh, yeah. It didn't start out that way. I'm cool with bondage. But then it got pretty rough. I brought along some pictures with some other stuff."

"Can I see?"

Danya takes some photos out of a manila envelope and hands them to Hobbs.

"He liked to take pictures of me tied up. But I took a few selfies of me he didn't know about."

Hobbs leafs through several photographs of Danya in various states of bruising. She points out a particularly brutal shot of her face swollen almost beyond recognition.

Hobbs is horrified. "Christ…I'm so sorry, Danya. You should have left him."

She murmurs, "I couldn't."

"Why not? You're gorgeous, you're smart…"

Danya smirks. "I would have been dead gorgeous. He told me he'd fuckin' kill me if I tried to leave."

"I'm sure he didn't really mean it."

"How can you look at those pictures and tell me he didn't really mean it? He meant it, all right. But not 'cause he loved me. 'Cause I know too goddamn much."

"The bigamy?"

She laughs. "That's nothing compared to the other stuff."

Hobbs is on tenterhooks but trying not to show it. "What other stuff?"

"How 'bout murder?"

Hobbs eyes widen. "*Murder?*"

"He told me he committed a murder."

Hobbs stares at her. "He *told* you that?"

"Yup. Told me the whole thing."

Hobbs is dumbfounded. "Why? I mean why would he tell you that?"

"'Cause he was so fuckin' guilty about it. Sun was a Catholic, you know,"

"It's well known. That's why they called him the Pope of Finance."

"Part of him was real religious, even though he'd been divorced and everything and you're not supposed to do that. But this thing was, like, chewing up his insides. He was petrified he was gonna have a heart attack, he was so stressed about it."

"So he told you?"

"Yeah. He was gonna go do a confession with a priest. But he was, like, worried the guy might turn him in. He said he had to tell someone. So he told me. I'm the only one who knows about it—aside from the person who did it with him."

"Jesus. He had an accomplice?"

"Yup."

"Who was that?"

"Burt. Him and Burt did it together."

Hobbs draws back. "*Whoa…!* You're telling me that Sunderland told you that he and Sklar committed a *murder* together?"

"Yeah."

Hobbs raises a skeptical eyebrow. He's known Sklar for years. Though he thinks the guy is killer shady, he's never imagined him to be an actual killer.

"I see. Just who are they supposed to have murdered?"

"I'm not gonna tell you that."

"Sunderland didn't tell you?"

"He told me. I'm just not gonna tell you right now."

"Why not? You've gone this far."

Danya shakes her head. "You believe me, don't you?"

Hobbs considers. "I believe he *told* you. I'm just not that sure it's actually true."

"Why'd he tell me then?"

"To frighten you. Which he obviously did."

"You're a reporter. Don't you, like, *sense* if people are telling the truth or not? Sometimes your job kinda depends on that, right?"

"Right. We need to trust our instincts."

"Yeah, well, some of the jobs I've been on…? If I hadn't trusted my fuckin' *instincts*, I'd be dead right now. I *know* Sun was telling me the truth."

"Did he give you any details?"

"He said it happened a long time ago, and that even if it ever got out, the cops would never be able to prove it. He used to have nightmares and wake up in a sweat, screaming about it."

"Are you the only one who knows about this?"

"Burt knows 'cause he was *there*."

"Let me ask you something… Does Burt know *you* know?"

"*Hell, no*! I'm scared shitless of that guy. If he knew I knew, I don't know what he'd do! Well, actually I *do* know what he'd do! Kill me."

"You think Jean knows?"

"Are you *kidding*? Jean doesn't know shit. She loved being Mrs. Sunderland, all right. But she had no fuckin' idea who the guy really was. She married a position and a bank account. I married the creep himself. You know about how, like, some men have this—whaddya call it—Madonna whore thing? She was his Madonna. I was his whore. Now who do you think knew him better? And who do you think he'd confide in?"

Hobbs is stunned. He pauses for a long moment.

"Why now? Why are you telling me all this now?" he asks.

"'Cause right now I'm supposed to be at his lawyer's office signing more stuff. Burt says he's making us rich. But I got news for him. I ain't signing any more shit!"

Danya takes out her cell phone.

"Look…see? He's called me about a hundred fuckin' times since I got here." She flashes the Missed Call screen at Hobbs.

"Why me? Why tell me?" he asks.

"I liked you when I met you. And you remembered to put that thing in your blog about my mom's blue satin dress, like I asked you to. That was important. It meant I could trust you to keep your word."

"Then why won't you tell me who their victim was, Danya? There's no statute of limitations on murder."

"I have a headache. I need to go lie down."

Hobbs accepts that she's through talking. For now. He shows her into his bedroom.

"Sorry about the mess," he says, straightening up the bed.

Danya lies down and pulls the blanket above her head. As Hobbs picks up clothes strewn on the floor, he hears Danya's muffled voice say, "For Chrissakes, don't let Burt find out I'm here—unless you have a gun!"

Chapter Thirty-five

I remember the day my mother finally realized Burt Sklar was a crook—a date that lives in infamy for me. Mummy asked me to have lunch with her in the apartment. We'd hardly spoken since the whole drug debacle with Alan, so I saw this invitation as a possible chance for a reconciliation. We had lunch on trays in her bedroom, as usual, chatting about nothing in particular, until she said, "Maud, I think it's time you saw my will."

I was astonished. This was the very first time Mummy had offered to show me anything related to her estate.

She went on. "I'm showing it to you because I want you to know that if I die (*if*, never *when*), you and your brother are going to be very rich. I'm worth well over a hundred million dollars, thanks to Burt. You have to admit you've been wrong about him."

She handed me a thick folder, filled with legal-size documents, both bound and unbound. I looked over the will first.

"I see you made Burt the sole executor with an upfront fee of two million dollars."

"Of course. He was your stepfather's sole executor, too. He'll be very helpful to you and your brother when I'm gone. You don't have to read the whole thing now. It's yours to keep."

As I was putting the will back in the folder, a single sheet of paper fluttered to the floor, almost as if an angel had plucked it out of the pack for me to see. I picked it up, gave it a glance, then looked at my mother in disbelief.

"So you gave Burt your Durable Power of Attorney too...?"

She was taken aback. "Don't be ridiculous! You know very well I wouldn't give *God* my Durable Power of Attorney! Not after what happened to my father!"

"Then what's this?" I handed her the sheet of paper.

Mummy put on her glasses and read it over. "*I never signed this!*"

"Is that your signature?"

"Yes! But I never, *ever* signed a Durable Power of Attorney! You know my history!" She started to panic.

"Calm down, Mummy. Where were you when you signed this will?"

"Burt took me to Ms. Lickel's office. She's his lawyer. I signed it there."

"Did you read over everything you were signing?"

"Yes! I mean... *No!* Not *everything*. There were so many pages. Initials and everything. Ms. Lickel kept putting them in front of me to sign."

"Well, you signed this page too."

Mummy vehemently shook her head. "*No, no, no!* Burt knows I would *never, ever* sign this! There's been a mistake!"

I nodded. "Yeah. A big mistake. Some zealous paralegal made copies of *everything* you signed that day—not just the will. You were never meant to see this document."

"But...but I've told Burt so many times what happened to my father. I mean...oh, Maud, what does this *mean?*"

"It means that Burt's had *total* control over everything you own for over a year. And that doesn't even count the stuff you've been signing for years without knowing what the hell it was."

"*That's not true.* I've seen the statements. They come every month."

"Show me these statements."

"Burt told me never to show you anything relating to my finances."

"Screw Burt. Where are they?"

With a shaking hand, Mummy pointed to a chest.

"Bottom drawer," she said.

Next to a rainbow pile of neatly folded cashmere sweaters was a stack of statements from Sklar's office. They were all single pages showing a list of Mummy's holdings on one side with their corresponding values on the other side. The bottom line on almost every one was the same: One hundred and ten million dollars. They were the financial equivalent of a comic book.

"These are *all* he ever gave you? One page a month?" I said in disbelief.

"You see right there I'm worth a hundred and ten million dollars!"

"I see he put you into SSBS Investments. Forty-five million dollars. Isn't that Burt's company with Sun Sunderland?"

"Yes! Burt says it's a great opportunity! Sunderland is such an impressive man."

"I want you to authorize me to talk to Burt about these investments."

She hesitated. "He'll leave me if you get involved. He'll think I don't trust him."

"*Do* you trust him? He got you to sign a Durable Power of Attorney without knowing it."

The question hung in the air. I felt Mummy was softening toward me for the first time in many years.

"Oh, my God, Maudie. Am…I broke?"

"You very well could be."

"*Jesus, Mary, and Joseph!*" she cried. "I need to call Burt."

"He's just going to deny everything. Please let me handle this, for once."

"No! I'm calling Burt. He'll explain this to me. I know he will."

"Mummy *please*! I'm *begging* you."

Mummy held up her hand. "No! I'm going to talk to Burt. If I'm not satisfied with what he tells me, I'll let you get involved. Just leave me alone for the moment!"

Two days later, my mother was dead. The doctor said she died in her sleep of "natural causes." It made sense. She was old. But somehow, I always had my doubts because she died on a Thursday.

Sklar thinks he's winning the game he and I are in now. But being sure you're winning is precisely the time you lose. As I've learned from poker, nothing counts until The River.

Chapter Thirty-six

Magma is surprised and hurt she hasn't heard from Hobbs after their pharaonic night of sex. She read his blog about Danya Sunderland with twinges of jealousy. It sounded to Magma like he rather fancied the slut. Since rejection always makes Magma's lusty heart grow fonder, she decides to take action. She has the William Poll gourmet shop put together a smart little food basket of caviar, smoked salmon, and other goodies to soothe the savage writer. She stops off at a liquor store and buys a very good bottle of champagne.

As she walks to his apartment, lugging the little feast with her, she thinks how best to handle her surprise visit. She'll be honest and tell him it was a spur of the moment impulse just because she happened to be in the neighborhood. It's not as if she's a stalker. He has to be flattered about that, she thinks. She won't say she's read his blog. She'll pretend she doesn't know it even exists! That way it can't possibly look like she's jealous or anything.

Magma enters the cramped little vestibule of Hobbs' converted brownstone, praying he's home. She locates his name on the tenant roster and gives the black button beside it a long press.

"Who is it?" demands a voice over the intercom.

"Delivery!" Magma growls.

She's buzzed in. She trudges up four flights of stairs thinking what a sexy surprise it will be for Hobbs when he opens the door and sees her standing there with a picnic. She reaches the fourth-floor landing out of breath. She takes a moment to compose herself and check herself out in her compact mirror before ringing the doorbell of apartment 4B. Hobbs opens the door.

"Surprise!" Magma exclaims, beaming at him.

Hobbs' reaction is not all she hoped.

"*Magma*...! What the hell are you doing here?"

"Oh, I just happened to be in the neighborhood and I thought you might need some *sustenance*," she says, flirtatiously.

"Uh, well. You're very sweet but I'm working, baby. Now's not the best time. Can I call you later?"

She peers around him and spots a young woman lurking in the bedroom doorway.

"Is that...? Oh, my God it *is*! It's *her*! *I was right*!" she cries.

"Magma, baby, it's not what you think!"

"No, no! That's fine! Sorry I interrupted. *Here*!" She drops the picnic basket at Hobbs' feet. "You and that... that... *stripper* can choke on this when you're finished *working*!"

He chases her down the hall and grabs her by the arm.

"Calm down! Listen to me!" he commands.

Magma stands still in the limp posture of a wounded child.

"I should never have come," she says tearfully.

"No, listen, it was really sweet of you, baby. It was...I was gonna call you. But something happened."

"I can see that," she sniffs.

"Okay, look...If I tell you what's going on, do you *swear* to me you won't say a word to anyone? This is gonna be hard for you, baby, but you've gotta keep your mouth shut. Swear?"

"Swear," she says warily.

He ushers Magma into his apartment. Danya is sitting on the couch, smoking.

"Danya Sunderland meet Magma Hartz, a good friend of mine...and of *Jean's*."

"Hey," Danya says, saluting Magma with a slight wave of her cigarette.

Brent directs Magma to sit down. He joins Danya on the couch.

"Danya and I have been discussing a certain situation. Maybe it's providential you showed up," Hobbs says.

Magma stares at Danya, thinking how young and unthreatening she looks.

"You're a friend of Jean's?" Danya says.

"I am. A very *good* friend," Magma replies icily.

"Okay…so, like, I know you probably won't believe me, but, like, I'm really, really sorry about everything. I never meant to hurt Jean, okay?"

"Then why did you marry her husband?" Magma shoots back.

"*He* wanted to."

"So you *say*."

Danya stands up and looks accusingly at Hobbs. "*I told you no one would fuckin' believe me*! And if they don't believe me about *that*, they're sure as hell not gonna believe me about the *other thing* either!" She stalks off into the bedroom and slams the door.

"*Shit*," Hobbs mutters.

Magma crosses her arms censoriously. "Are you two having an affair?"

"*Jesus H. Christ.* Can't you see she's *scared?*"

"Of what, pray tell?"

"Of Sklar. And what he's gotten her into."

"You're just saying that because I caught you!"

"Come here…" Brent pats the couch.

Magma puts on a reluctant little show until Brent grabs her, pulls her down, and wraps his arms around her.

"Magma, baby, I love it that you're jealous. I really do. But we're in the middle of a critical situation here. I need you to behave like a real grown-up, not like a brat—even though you still look like a teenager…" he adds, pecking her on the mouth.

"You were so sympathetic to her in your blog," Magma says, petulantly, forgetting she wasn't going to mention she'd read it.

"I'm trying to help her."

"*Why?*"

"Because I believe, like she does, that she may be in considerable danger."

"*Rubbish!*" Magma says with a dismissive wave of her hand. "Jean's the only one in danger here. She believes those two set Sun up, right from the very beginning!"

Danya, who's been eavesdropping at the door, storms back into the room.

"*Bullshit!*" she cries out. "You can tell your friend Jean I never laid eyes on Burt *or* Sun before that night in the club. I had no fuckin' idea about all this money stuff until Sun died. I'm *scared shitless*, okay? *Petrified!*"

"Of *what?* Becoming a billionaire bimbo, perhaps?" Magma says.

"Of *Burt*, bitch! I'm scared he's gonna kill me!"

Magma looks at Hobbs in exasperated disbelief. "*Seriously...?*"

"Very seriously, Magma," Hobbs says firmly. "I'm trying to convince her to go to the D.A."

Danya guffaws. "Yeah, right! Look what just happened. *She* doesn't even believe me! Good luck with the D.A."

"That's because she doesn't know the whole story," Hobbs says.

"Who's *she?* The cat? I'm right here!" Magma says, irritated. She turns to Danya. "Believe me, I'm eager to hear the whole story. If you can convince me you can convince *anyone.*"

Chapter Thirty-seven

"I'm telling you, Greta, the slut is *credible*!" Magma cries.

Greta shakes her head. "So you just waltzed over to Hobbs' apartment in the middle of the afternoon without telling him you were coming, and she was there."

"Yes, exactly. Oh, I know what you're thinking. I tend to make myself too available. But am I glad I went! She's not at all what we thought!"

"What is she?"

"She's actually quite nice. And scared stiff of Sklar. Believe it or not, she's very upset about the whole thing with Jean."

"The whole thing being bigamy, grand larceny, and fraud?" Greta says, disgusted.

"Look, I was so furious I didn't want to believe a word she said at first. But after talking to her for over two hours, I *know* she's telling the truth. I'd stake my life on it. Just hear me out."

"I'm listening," Greta says wearily.

It seems to Magma that she has lived her entire life for this moment. Often referred to as the "truffle pig of gossip," Magma is famous for sniffing out the tastiest rumors buried deep in the dirt of any social scandal *du jour*. By offering up delicious, unsubstantiated facts at luncheons and dinner parties, the aging Magma has managed to remain relevant without the benefit of a big name or big bucks in avaricious New York. She considered it macabre good luck to have been at The Four Seasons when Sunderland was shot. She dined out on that for awhile. But she was just an observer then. Now she's an active participant, poised to play a pivotal role in what has now become the juiciest scandal in the country.

She pauses for effect, sipping her tea with a raised pinkie as she assumes an authoritative air. "First of all, I should tell you that Danya Sunderland is not the innocent that Brent portrayed her to be in his blog."

"How very surprising," Greta says.

Magma ignores her friend's sarcasm. "She admitted that to me right off the bat—which actually made me want to hear her out. She told me that Sun was into some seriously kinky stuff like S&M and bondage. Makes you wonder about our old friend, Jean, doesn't it? You think she's into that sort of thing?"

"Go *on*," Greta sighs.

Magma pauses to set her cup and saucer down on the table with deliberation.

"You know how in the blog Danya is quoted as saying the reason Sun risked committing bigamy is because he desperately wanted her to have a child that would bear his name? And how she went along with it because she was so in love with him?"

"I read all that rot, yes."

"None of that was true."

"No *kidding*!" Greta exclaims, barely able to contain her impatience.

"Do you want to know the real reason they got married?"

"No. I just want to sit here and look at you drink tea. Will you please get to the point?"

"Honestly, Greta, you don't have to be so snippy! Okay, so the real reason they got married is because Burt invented this scheme to get all Sun's money without Sun suspecting it!" Magma announces with pride.

Greta furrows her brow, totally perplexed. "*What*? How was he going to swing *that*?"

"I'm a little fuzzy on the details. But this is what Brent thinks happened: When Sun fell in love with Danya, he wanted her to be taken care of if anything ever happened to him. So he got Burt to set up that *tartine* thing Jean told us about."

"*Tontine*," Greta corrects her.

"Whatever. That thing where the people who live longer get the most money."

"I *know* what a tontine is, Magma. My father was a lawyer," Greta says imperiously.

"Okay, so Sun gives Burt his Limited Power of Attorney so he can set it up. The fact that Sun risked everything by actually *marrying* Danya shows that he was really serious about her. Burt was the only one who knew about the bigamy and he covered for Sun."

"That still doesn't explain how Burt got the money out of the estate," Greta says.

"Danya says that Sun was so beholden to Burt he stopped paying any attention to what Burt was doing. And Brent thinks that Burt got Sun to sign a *Durable* Power of Attorney instead of a *Limited* Power of Attorney. Or maybe Burt just forged Sun's signature. Whatever the case, Burt started transferring Sun's money into the assets of the tontine, which are mostly in these offshore accounts and private LLCs."

Greta leans in with interest. "Does this Danya person think Sun knew about this?"

"She says she doesn't know if he knew or not. But I doubt Sun knew the extent of it, don't you? This is exactly what Burt did with Maud's mother. Danya finds all this out *after* Sun dies. And she also finds out that Burt's been secretly in love with her for years!"

Greta is now listening intently. "So were Danya and Burt having an affair behind Sun's back?"

"*No!* That's what I'm telling you! Danya had no idea about *any* of this!"

"So she says," Greta sneers. "It sounds to me more like she and Burt planned the whole thing together. But, even so, how could either of them have known Sun was going to get *shot*? The plan only works if he dies."

"Well, it's Brent's theory that Burt was playing 'the long con'— to use his words. I mean, after all, Sun was almost forty years older than Danya. Plus he had a bad heart. The odds are he'd die first in any case. But, even if he didn't, Burt was holding the bigamy over his head."

Greta stares at Magma in disbelief. "I can't believe you and Brent are taking the bimbo's word for all this. I think she's conned the both of you."

"*No*! I *saw* her! She's absolutely *terrified* of Burt. She thinks he's capable of killing her. This is why I'm here."

Greta is losing all her patience. "I still don't understand."

Magma takes a nervous breath. "Danya wants to meet Jean. I told her you could arrange it."

Greta lets out an incredulous whoop. "*Don't be ridiculous*! First of all, I have no intention of arranging a meeting between Hitler and Churchill. Second of all, you're all out of your minds if you think that Jean would even *consider* it! She'll think it's a trick."

"No, just wait. Listen. Danya wants to meet Jean so they can go to the District Attorney *together*!"

Greta's jaw drops. Magma grins.

"The bimbo wants to go to the *District Attorney*?" Greta says, blinking in astonishment.

Magma nods sanctimoniously. Greta is flummoxed. Magma clearly has the moral authority here. This is the first time in their long friendship that Magma has the upper hand. Greta tries to save face.

"I know Jean better than anyone. She'll never agree."

"You're her best friend, Greta. *Ask* her."

Chapter Thirty-eight

Greta was surprised and a little disappointed when Jean agreed to meet with Danya after all—mainly because it gave Magma such smug satisfaction. However, when it was clear the meeting would take place, Greta graciously volunteered her apartment. That way she could be as supportive of Jean as possible, as well as in on all the action. Greta is with Jean in her bedroom now, helping her friend get ready for this second momentous meeting of the two Mrs. Sunderlands.

"Nervous?" Greta says.

"Of course. Wouldn't you be?" Jean replies.

"I think it's good you agreed to see her. You definitely want to hear what she has to say."

Jean absently fingers the gold and enamel unicorn pin on the lapel of her suit jacket.

"Sun gave this to me for our second anniversary."

"I remember." Greta says.

"I wonder if he ever really loved me," Jean says wistfully. "This may sound strange to you, Greta. But I think I'd feel better if Sun had always been a pussy hound."

"Why in God's name would that make you feel *better*, Jeanie?"

"Because Sun never looked at another woman until *she* came along. I *am* curious to talk to her, just to try and understand what the hell is so special about her."

"Jeanie…" Greta hesitates. "Can I tell you something I've never told you before?"

"Really? I thought we'd told each other everything at least a hundred times."

"Well, I never told you this. Mainly because when it happened, I could hardly believe it myself."

Jean furrows her brow. "*What?*"

Greta clears her throat. "Sun once made a pass at me."

Jean draws back in disbelief. "You're *kidding*."

"I wish."

"*When?*"

"Coincidentally, the night he gave you that pin. I sat next to him at your anniversary dinner at La Grenouille. He put his hand up my skirt during the *salmon en croute*."

Jean glares at Greta. "I don't believe it."

"Neither did I. But there was no mistaking his fingers crawling toward my crotch."

"*Jesus…*" Jean says, disgusted.

"I slapped him under the table. I asked him what the hell he thought he was doing, reminding him I was your *best friend*. He looked at me like a wounded dog and said, '*I know. But who else do you meet?*'"

Jean sinks down on the divan. "So *that's* why you never wanted to fly alone with him in our plane? I always wondered why you turned down all those rides to Southampton."

"Honey, I wasn't going anywhere *near* that man without you around," Greta says. "And, quite frankly, over the years, I heard rumors…"

"What rumors?"

"That his business trips weren't all business."

"You never told me."

"They were just rumors. You were happy. Why would I stir the pot? I'm not Magma."

"You think he ever propositioned *her?*"

"*Magma*? The Internet? He wouldn't have dared. Are you upset I told you?"

Jean shakes her head in grim amusement. "No. Relieved, actually. I'm just wondering how it's possible I had absolutely no inkling I was married to such a scumbag."

Greta shrugs. "Well, if it's any consolation, Gary Ridgway's wife had no idea he was the Green River serial killer."

"That's very comforting, Greta. Thanks a lot."

"I mean the point is, Jeanie, Sun was always a dog. You just never wanted to see it because you guys had such a big, important life together. Money masks a lot. Most often from the people who have it."

Jean takes a long breath. "What time is it?"

"Noon. They'll be here soon. I better go play hostess. You coming?"

"Give me a minute," Jean says.

Greta pauses in the doorway. "Just one more thought…I don't think Sun ever got over his first wife leaving him for another woman. Trust me, Jeanie, this stripper was an accident waiting to happen…Now get down there and fight for your rights, sweetie!"

When Greta leaves, Jean takes a long hard look at herself in the mirror. She removes the David Webb unicorn pin and tosses it into her purse, wondering how much it will bring at auction. It occurs to her that her marriage to Sun was just like that unicorn: A lovely myth based on wishful thinking.

Chapter Thirty-nine

Downstairs in the living room, Greta is helping Martyn serve coffee and homemade scones to Brent Hobbs and Squire Huff. Huff is in a snit. He's been against this meeting from the start. When Jean first told him about it, he was outraged.

"As your lawyer, I'm counseling you *not* to meet with this woman under any circumstances. We're in the middle of a lawsuit. You can't trust a damn thing she has to say so there's no point in talking to her. You're making a very grave mistake," Huff warned.

Jean quickly responded: "Magma assures me this creature has information that will help us against Sklar. Brent Hobbs has confirmed this. So I'm going to hear her out, no matter what you say, Squire. If you don't like it, resign."

Jean's imperiousness has put Huff in a foul mood. This isn't the first time his professional opinion has been ignored. He mourns the passing of the good old days when clients automatically took their lawyers' advice without question. He attributes this rebellion to the rise of gritty television shows that let the daylight in on the internal machinations and cut-throat billing practices of law firms. He sits silently stewing, wondering if it's time to retire to East Hampton and play golf.

Meanwhile, Hobbs is thrilled to be there for a number of reasons, but mainly on account of the book he's going to write.

Vicky Banks, his high-powered agent, is excited. She's informed him she can get him a high six-figure deal. Banks was disappointed when Hobbs' first book, *Complicity*, failed to become a bestseller despite the stellar reviews. She dismissed him as a "one book wonder." The only reason she kept Hobbs on her roster is because they go way back, specifically to a one-night stand Banks would rather forget, but which Hobbs hangs over her head like a Sword of Damocles when she doesn't return his calls. After his Danya blog, she perked up, especially when he told her he had the inside track. If only Vicky could only see him now, Hobbs thinks, as they all sit there waiting for these two archenemies to meet.

As Jean enters the living room, Hobbs bounds up to shake her hand.

"You're very brave, Jean. I know this can't be easy for you," he says.

"They should be here any moment, sweetie," Greta says.

"I just hope you and the Magpie haven't steered me wrong."

Jean pours herself a glass of scotch from the silver and glass trolley bar and sits down in a far corner of the room. Huff plants himself beside her.

"I'm not sure alcohol is the best palliative at this moment."

"It's marginally better than hemlock," Jean says.

"For the record, I'm still very much against this meeting," he warns.

Jean ignores him. "What time is it?"

Huff shoots the button cuff of his left hand to look at his watch—the warhorse Rolex given to him by his father when he graduated from Harvard umpteen years ago.

"Twelve-forty."

At that moment, Danya and Magma appear at the entrance—Danya in black, Magma in red. Hobbs thinks they look like soldier and prisoner on their way to the firing squad. Silence reigns as the two women slowly descend the shallow steps leading down to the living room. The tension in the room is electric.

When they reach the bottom, Danya freezes in apparent fear. Greta walks over to greet her guests.

"Greta, I'd like you to meet Danya Sunderland," Magma says. "Danya, this is your hostess, Greta Lauber."

"Hello, Danya," Greta says warmly, shaking Danya's limp hand.

"Hi," Danya whispers.

"Would you care for a drink or anything before…?"

Danya shakes her head. "I just wanna get this over with."

"Come with me," Greta says.

"*Courage*, dear." Magma releases Danya's arm and joins Hobbs on the couch.

She cuddles up next to Hobbs with an air of accomplishment. She and Hobbs are the proud architects of this momentous meeting. They will both benefit, no matter the outcome: Hobbs, professionally; Magma, socially.

Greta walks Danya across the room to the corner where Jean is finishing up her scotch in determined little sips. Huff springs to his feet like a guard dog.

"I'm Squire Huff, Mrs. Sunderland's lawyer," he barks.

Danya steps back in alarm. This frightened young woman is such a far cry from the predatory stripper of Huff's imagination, he can hardly believe his eyes. Can this timid, fresh-faced beauty be the same sexy stripper of tabloid fame? Or the "shiny insect" Jean has described to him? Jean stands up, motioning Huff to step aside.

Greta makes the introduction. "Danya, this is Jean Sunderland. Oh, but then I guess you two have already met," she says with an embarrassed little laugh.

Jean and Danya eye one another warily.

"Greta, dear, I wonder if we could have some have some privacy?" Jean says.

"Of course."

Much to everyone's disappointment, Greta leads the women toward the blood-red library adjoining the living room.

Huff follows. "I think I should be present, Jean."

"I think not." Jean closes the double doors in his face.

The doors click shut. Jean and Danya, the two Mrs. Sunderlands, stand staring at each other for a long moment. Danya is about to say something when Jean raises her index finger to her lips and presses her ear against the door. She waits a until she hears the lull of conversation start up in the next room. When she is absolutely sure no one is listening, she turns back to Danya who is staring at her intently.

Their grim expressions gradually melt into smiles. They rush toward one another and embrace. It is the heartfelt embrace of co-conspirators who are meeting for the first time after their plan has been set in motion. It is the encouraging embrace of accomplices who have come far, but who still have far to go.

They spend a good half hour in the library, whispering about the events which have led up to this meeting—some of which were expected, and one of which was not. They go over their stories like actresses, making sure they still know their parts.

Just before they go back into the living room, they raise an imaginary glass for a toast.

"To Maud, true blue!" Jean says.

"To Maud, true blue!" Danya echoes.

"Don't fold!" they say in unison.

Jean opens the library door.

The women enter the living room looking shell-shocked. Greta, Magma, Hobbs, and Huff bolt up, dying for news of the outcome. Danya and Jean don't say a word. Danya walks out of the living room, chased by Magma.

"What *happened?*" Magma says eagerly.

"Nothing. Let's go," Danya says.

Jean sits down to finish the rest of her scotch. Greta and Huff run to her.

"*How it did go?*" Greta says breathlessly.

Jean raises her glass. "It's a start."

Chapter Forty

It was an open secret at the Gypsy's that aside from dealing cards and taking care of the bank, Pratt supplied quality weed to players. On account of that, I first steered clear of him. I had a horror of drug dealers because of Alan. I swore I'd never befriend one.

Would that things in life remained so clear-cut!

It soon became apparent to me that Pratt was a decent guy, despite his avocation. He helped people out when they needed it, giving them money or a place to stay. Unlike some of my erstwhile "society" friends, when Pratt gave his word, he kept it. He didn't shy away from pals who got into trouble.

It was Pratt who took me aside and told me that I could actually use my "old bag" image to my advantage. He taught me how to play what I call Street Poker, which is about as far from classical, by-the-book poker as breakdancing is from the minuet. I learned that poker on the highest level isn't really about the cards, and that the greatest players in the game can actually *smell* fear in their opponents. Convincing bluffing is the real key to a successful poker career. And like pretty much everything in life, poker is about people. You have to know when and whom to bluff.

"Play the player," Pratt advised me. "Don't let the player play you."

Pratt's taking a big risk having me stay here in his cabin, and

I'm very grateful. He doesn't seem at all concerned I'm on the run. He's helped felons and fugitives before. He gave me his word he'd help me if the time came, no matter what I'd done. He has a strange honor code, like many of the poker players I've met. I always sensed a merry world of criminality bustling all around me at the Gypsy's. Because I loved poker, I chose to ignore it, never dreaming one day I'd be the most wanted criminal of all.

As I surf the web on Pratt's computer, I'm amused to see myself referred to as a "folk heroine," mainly because I shot a rich scumbag and evaded the police for so long. America loves outlaws. Pratt's in the kitchen sorting marijuana joints and pills into plastic baggies with a person he introduced to me this morning as "Cadillac Dan," despite the fact the guy drove up here in a beat-up old Ford pickup. Dan seems like an okay guy, although it took me a while to get used to the sight of his jowly face emerging from the primordial sea of prison tats covering his neck and arms. Unlike Pratt, Dan's a dealer who's done time. But that's because he grew up poor. By way of contrast, my brother's first dealer was his roommate in boarding school—a clean-cut preppy with the face of a choir boy and impeccable manners. Our mother loved him. He got a job in his father's company after college. But if he hadn't had money, he'd be in jail.

Surfing around the web, I'm interested to see that Danya Dickert Sunderland has given an exclusive interview to a blogger named Brent Hobbs. It's been picked up by all the news services. I read the piece very carefully. I especially like the part about the blue satin dress she wore for her wedding to Sun. In fact, she wore a white suit that day. When I finish, I know one thing for sure: This guy Hobbs may have thought Danya was talking only to him.

But, my true blue satin doll, I know you're really talking to me. Time to get myself captured.

The Turn

"Life is not always a matter of holding good cards,
but sometimes, playing a poor hand well."

—*Jack London*

Chapter Forty-one

Manhattan District Attorney Vance Packer has a headache. A big one. He's standing in the middle of his office with Detective Chen. The two men are watching a loop of breaking news on CNN.

"Here it comes," Packer says, wincing.

The CNN anchor speaks: *"And for those of you who are just joining us… Maud Warner arrived in New York this morning, two days after she was captured wandering in a daze through the streets of Washington, D.C. Appearing to be in shock, Warner hasn't spoken a single word since her arrest. She's currently under observation in a state psychiatric ward."*

The anchor does a recap of the crime, accompanied by stock footage. Scenes of Sunderland's star-studded funeral appear on screen, featuring a close-up of Packer descending the church steps amid the well-heeled mourners. Disgusted, he aims the remote at the TV like a gun, and switches it off.

"I hate funerals. Siddown, John," Packer says, taking a seat. "You think she's really in shock?"

"Could be an act," Chen says.

"You know who's going to defend her, right?"

"I heard. Lydia the Legend herself."

John Chen has been a detective in the NYPD for years. He's

known for his thoroughness and hunches that strike gold. This is his highest profile case to date, a challenge both he and Packer—as the new D.A.—are well aware of.

"So talk to me about our silent socialite. What'd you find out about her in D.C.?"

Chen gives a recap of his trip and the items he discovered in Maud's apartment, including the target practice sheets, the unused meds, and the article Sklar sent her.

"The most interesting thing about this woman…? She plays poker."

Packer shrugs. "What's so interesting about that? I play poker with a couple of women in a home game."

"Trust me, the dive where Warner plays ain't no home game. It's like a road company Rikers. I had to take a long shower afterwards. But forget all that. The point is not so much *where* she played. It's who she *met* playing poker."

"Like who?"

"Hear me out. I found this newspaper article in her apartment about an older lady poker player who also happens to be a lawyer. I think you know her: Joyce Kiner Braden?"

"Sure, I know Joyce. Terrific lawyer."

"She said to say hello to you, by the way."

"So you went to see her?"

"I did."

"Why?"

"A hunch. I read the article. It was mainly about a case she'd just won. A woman in Richmond killed her father who was once a prominent assemblyman. It made local headlines. Braden got her off using the E.E.D. defense."

"That makes sense. Braden specializes in that defense. Keep going."

"It happens that Sklar sent Warner this article. There's a note from him saying, '*Poker player like you… E.E.D. defense. Enjoy! Burt.*'"

"*Sklar* sent her the article? I wonder why?"

"Who knows? That's not my point. I talked to Braden and found out Warner met her at a poker tournament in Atlantic City. Coincidence? Maybe. Braden wouldn't say if Warner purposely sought her out. But I'm betting she did. I think she went up there with the express purpose of making Braden's acquaintance."

"Why?"

"So she could learn more about how people get away with murder."

"Because…?"

"Because she's *planning* to get away with murder. Walking into a restaurant and shooting someone point-blank is crazy, right? But not so crazy if you think you can use the *fact* it's so crazy to get away with it."

"E.E.D…" Packer says pensively.

"Exactly. Anyway, that's my theory," Chen says.

Packer considers. "It still takes balls to actually *do* it."

Chen chuckles. "You wanna talk about balls? This lady climbed three flights of a rust pile fire escape to play in poker hell with Satan and his crew almost every night of her life. *That* takes balls. She may be nuts. But she may be *smart* nuts too. You know all the stuff you have to avoid if you're planning to kill someone. You gotta think about DNA, cameras, cell phone records, eyewitnesses, getting rid of the body. It's a lot to plan. No…if you really want to get away with murder these days, do it in plain sight and play crazy. Gonna be hard to prove Grandma Moses wasn't nuts when she did this thing."

Chapter Forty-two

God bless Lydia Fairley! True to her word, she's defending me now. If I love her for nothing else, it's for getting me transferred out of the state's soul-crushing psych ward into the comforting chintzy atmosphere of the Payne Whitney Psychiatric Clinic.

Lydia hasn't seen me in years, not since I left New York. When I enter a room reminiscent of a granny's parlor she winces at the sight of me. I know I look like hell in my baggy gray hospital garb with my greasy, straggly hair, and sallow complexion. But that's the whole point. I'm *trying* to look like hell—not that I had very far to go, having been deprived of pricey cosmetic enhancements and peace of mind for years on end. Still, since my capture, I've totally perfected the slack-jawed, vacant-eyed, listless shuffle of the seriously deranged. I've studied Joan Crawford in *Possessed*. I feel my actress mother would be proud of my performance.

The attendant leads me to a chair and gently sits me down opposite Lydia.

"Hello, Maudie," Lydia says with great compassion, searching my lined, exhausted face for any sign of recognition.

I stare into space. A human husk. Lydia glances at the strapping female attendant, who shakes her head sadly.

"Call when you're ready," the attendant says and leaves.

Lydia clasps my limp right hand in both of hers, a gesture of love and reassurance. I don't react. I don't look at her. I'm a zombie.

"I'm not sure you can hear me, Maudie. I'm going to talk to you anyway. First of all, let me say how very sorry I am about Alan. I know how you two were close….I also know better than anyone the hell you've been through these past few years. I don't blame you for wanting to take a shot at Sklar. I'm just sorry things have turned out the way they have. But I'm your lawyer now. We're going to get you through this, Maudie. I promise."

I still don't react. She goes on.

"I don't how much you know about what's happened since the shooting…"

She proceeds to recap the whole Sunderland bigamy saga, and how Jean Sunderland has become Burt Sklar's latest financial victim in a scheme reminiscent of the one he used on my mother. I know all the things she's telling me, and a great deal more.

Much as I'd love to, I can't reveal my cards to Lydia. As my lawyer, she can't know the truth—not yet. I may be able to tell her the truth one day, if the two of us wind up together in some old age home, reminiscing in our rockers. But for now, she has to believe I'm off my rocker.

Only three of us are in on the series of events which have led to this moment.

Chapter Forty-three

After my mother died and I moved down to D.C., I tried my best to forget Sklar. I really did. But somehow, I couldn't help myself. I began to track him, which was easy. Sklar was a relentless self-promoter who constantly posted stuff about his glamorous life on Facebook and Twitter and Instagram. There were always squibs about him in the *New York Social Diary, Page Six, The Reliable Source*, and *Washington Life*. He loved posting selfies with tag lines like: '*Here I am at the Council on Foreign Relations with my best friend, Sun Sunderland*,' or '*Going to the Lincoln Memorial today to contemplate life,*' or '*Kennedy Center honors tonight! Box seat. Can't wait.*' Shit like that. I noticed he was down in D.C. a lot with his best buddy, Sun Sunderland.

My dear brother Alan died of an overdose on October 10, 2013. I blamed Sklar. My harmless guilty pleasure in tracking him amped up into an obsession. I was attracted to the thing I most despised, which made me very dangerous.

The week before Thanksgiving, I read that Sun Sunderland and his wife were coming down to D.C. for a gala dinner at the National Gallery. Sklar posted a picture of himself on Facebook outside the Hay Adams, where he was staying with his "best friend" Sun Sunderland. Sklar posted another picture of himself on Instagram with some ambassador outside Café Milano, where they were about to have lunch. I had nothing much to do until the Gypsy's game that night. So just for the hell of it, I drove to the restaurant and waited outside in my car, figuring I'd see Sklar in the flesh. I wasn't sure what I'd do if I saw him. I was so angry at him because of Alan. But, somehow, I liked the idea of spying on him, knowing I could ambush him at any moment. Stalking for stalking's sake. Then, just like at the poker table, luck changed everything.

Sklar left the restaurant alone at two o'clock and hailed a cab. I followed behind in my car. They drove to a house in a residential area off New Mexico Avenue in Wesley Heights. I parked just close enough to see and not be seen. Sklar kept the taxi waiting as he walked up and rang the doorbell. A woman in a bathrobe opened the door. She was holding a cloth to her face. A girlfriend, I wondered?

Moments later, who should appear at the door but Sun Sunderland! He tried to kiss the woman good-bye, but she quickly shied away and slammed the door. Sunderland gave Sklar a dismissive little shrug. Both men chuckled as they got into the waiting taxi. The taxi drove off. I stayed. Needless to say, I was intrigued.

I was even more intrigued when I found out from a neighbor that a Mr. and Mrs. *Sunderland* lived in that house. I decided to pay a call. I had no idea what I was going to say to this woman. I figured I'd just have to wing it. I rang the bell. When she opened the door, I saw the reason for the cloth. She was nursing a badly swollen eye and a split lip. She peered at me warily from her good eye.

"Mrs. Sunderland?" I said.

"Yeah?"

"May I come in for a moment?"

"Who're you? Whaddya want?" She sounded like she had a mouthful of cotton. She was obviously in pain.

"I…I'm a friend of Jean Sunderland," I blurted out, without even thinking.

That got me in the door *pronto*. I lied and told her my name was Sue and that Jean had sent me to talk to her. She told me to call her Danya. She wanted to talk. I sure as hell wanted to listen. I was fortunate to have caught her at a most vulnerable moment.

"How long's she known about me?" Danya asked, dabbing her face with the damp cloth.

"Oh, quite a long time," I lied.

"She knows about the marriage and everything?"

I was absolutely flabbergasted when she said this. It was all I could do to keep a straight face.

"She thinks you're just calling yourselves Mr. and Mrs. Sunderland," I said calmly.

"*Jeez*…No…We're married, all right. Illegally. He wanted it for the kid."

"You have a child?" I was stunned.

"I was gonna. But then I miscarried. Sun wanted a kid 'cause him and his son are kinda on the outs. He said he wanted to 'get it right' this time…He was just here. He doesn't have a fuckin' clue she knows. What a joke."

I was hoping to get as much information out of her as possible before I told her who I really was.

"What happened to your face?" I asked.

"Whatsit look like happened? A fuckin' door beat me up?"

"Sunderland did that to you?"

She nodded. "Jean's the fuckin' Madonna. I'm the whore he fucks."

I winced. "Why don't you leave?"

She guffawed. "They'd kill me if I left."

"They?"

"Yeah. Burt Sklar. You know him? Him and Sun, they're in this thing together."

"What thing?"

"You have no idea. It's so bad. Guess what? I'm glad Jean knows. I'm sick of all this shit! I wanna talk to her. I need to tell her something important. Have you got her number? I'm gonna call her. I need to see her."

Right then, I knew the jig was up. Jean didn't know a damn thing. I'd only stumbled upon Sun's secret life because I'd followed Sklar and seen Sunderland come out of the house. I had to tell her the truth.

"Look, um, Danya...I'm not... I mean, Jean doesn't know about this..." I stammered.

"*Oh Jeez! You're a fuckin' reporter!*" Danya cried, wincing in pain.

"*No! No! I swear I'm not!*"

She lept up. "*Get the fuck outta here now!*"

"Okay, but just please listen...My name is Maud Warner and—"

Before I could say another word, Danya drew back, staring at me in utter disbelief.

"*Maud Warner! Oh, my God...* I know who you are..."

And then she told me the rest of it.

Chapter Forty-four

That night, I cried more than I'd ever cried in my whole entire life. So many things made sense now. By morning, I'd managed to regain my equilibrium. I was cool and focused, with the strategic mindset of a poker player about to enter a big tournament.

I called Jean at her hotel around eleven, and asked if I could come by and see her. Though Jean had been a loyal friend to me in New York, we had lost touch. I was well aware I was an inconvenient friend, especially now that her husband was in partnership with my nemesis, Burt Sklar. But I knew Jean was a good egg, never one to shun an old pal who was down on her luck. She invited me up to her suite for coffee.

When I arrived, Jean was getting ready for a ladies' lunch. We greeted each other warmly and made some obligatory small talk. I told her I was still grateful to her for being one of the few people who didn't abandon me when I lived in New York.

"So how did you know I was in town?" she asked casually.

I was eager to get to the point. "Jeanie, I want to tell you a story."

"I'm listening, sweetie. Forgive me for primping. I need to look spiffy for these ladies I only see once a year."

As I watched Jean fiddle with her hair, I considered how best to begin my tale. I decided just to go for it.

"Jeanie, what would you say if I told you that your husband is a bigamist?"

She stopped mid-comb and let out a whoop of laughter. "Oh, Maudie! I see you haven't lost your old sense of mischief!"

I smiled. "I haven't. But in this case, I'm not kidding. Sun *is* a bigamist. Married to a gorgeous young woman who lives right here in Washington."

Jean turned away from the mirror to stare at me. "Maudie, dear, are you okay?"

"I'm fine, believe me. The woman's name is Danya Dickert Sunderland. She wants to meet you. We could go there now. I have a car."

Jean grew testy. "Is this your idea of a joke?"

"I wish it were."

At that moment, I could see she was a little frightened of me. She knew my reputation as "Mad Maud," on account of some of the crazy things I'd done to Sklar—like throwing an egg at him and parading outside his office with defamatory signs. I reached into my tote bag and pulled out a photograph in a Plexiglas frame. I handed it to Jean, who gave it a disdainful glance until she looked more closely. It was a candid wedding snap. The bride, a beautiful young woman in a white suit and veil carrying a small bouquet of white roses, was arm in arm with Sunderland in a suit and tie with a flower in his lapel. The happy couple were standing in front of a judge. Off to one side was Burt Sklar.

"*What…?* What *is* this?" Jean stammered as she examined the photo.

"Just what it looks like, I'm afraid: A little wedding in the Arlington County Courthouse four years ago. And if you have any doubts about its authenticity, turn the picture over."

As if in a trance, Jean did as she was told. On the back of the two-sided frame was the marriage license naming Danya Dickert and *Samuel* Sunderland as the bride and groom—Samuel being a substitute for Sean, Sunderland's real first name. Their witness was Burt Sklar.

Jean turned the frame over again and stared at the photograph.

"Where did you get this?" Jean said at last.

"First let me tell you how I found out."

I told her how I discovered the existence of Danya the day before by following Burt Sklar to her house. I told her the ruse I'd used to get Danya to open up and tell me the whole story. It was a lot to take in. But in the end, Jean cancelled her lunch and we drove to Wesley Heights.

Danya answered the door holding Mooncat in her arms. She was wearing jeans and a ripped sweatshirt, her eye swollen shut, her lip swollen too. She looked more like a terrified teenager than a sexy rival. Jean's first reaction was disbelief. Then she got angry.

That afternoon, I witnessed the physical incarnation of the old saw: *Hell hath no fury like a woman scorned.* The bruised, defeated Danya cowered in a corner clutching her cat, murmuring tearful apologies, as Jean ranted and raged around the room. She was not nearly as angry at Danya as she was at Sun for this galactic betrayal. Frankly, I never imagined that my prim, self-controlled friend had such passion in her, or that she would react the way she did. The discovery sent her careening over the edge. Her tearful wails were so heart-wrenching, I came to the astonishing conclusion that Jean hadn't married Sunderland for the bucks and the status like everyone in New York thought. She actually *loved* the bastard.

When she finally calmed down, Jean wanted to know every detail of Sunderland's relationship with Danya. Danya was eager to talk. As Sun's dark side was revealed to Jean, I thought of Humpty Dumpty and how nothing could put Sunderland back together again for either woman.

"I want to kill him," Jean said, like she really meant it.

"Me too," Danya echoed.

My opening.

"Danya, dear, I think you should tell Jean what you told me about the money. And the murder."

Jean listened to Danya's story in horror. We discussed it ad nauseam and eventually came to the conclusion that proving the facts of what we knew to be true would be impossible. Drastic measures were the only way. By the time I drove Jean back to her hotel to get ready for her gala dinner, one thing was certain: The two Mrs. Sunderlands and I were all in. We agreed we had to take these guys down ourselves. It was up to me, the wily poker player, to plan a way to do it.

Chapter Forty-five

Collusion at the poker table is very difficult to spot if the colluders are clever. Their covert signs and signals are invisible to the untrained eye. The main thing to watch out for is any sign the players know one another. It's vital that colluders never reveal they are friends so the fish will not suspect he or she is being targeted. It was with this insight in mind that I convinced Danya and Jean to put on their great charade. I knew the more they pretended to loathe each other, the more convincing their begrudging reconciliation would be—especially if it was due to their mutual desire to see justice done.

Over the course of five meetings in places no one would ever see us, I outlined my plan of revenge. I didn't give them specifics. But I did tell them it would involve violence. They both agreed and consented.

I made it clear that once my plan was in motion, I'd never be able to contact either one of them again. It was absolutely vital that no one suspect we were all in on this together. I was counting on both of them not to falter. But I said I might need reassurance if things got rough. Therefore, the mention or wearing of a blue dress at every opportunity was my signal each of them was still in the hand.

I warned them that things might not go just the way I planned.

And if, by chance, they went awry, I pleaded with them both to hold fast. It was our only chance to win. The three of us clasped hands. I said the magic words: "Don't fold."

Chapter Forty-six

Burt Sklar is curled up on the bed in the guest room of his apartment, cuddling a pillow that still smells of Danya. He never should have confessed his love to her as fast as he did, and the way that he did. He should have waited. But he was so sure she loved him. Otherwise, how could he have felt so strongly about her? He knows he's a great salesman. *So why couldn't he sell himself to the love of his life?*

The deep, searing pain Sklar is experiencing now is eerily reminiscent of the pain he felt as a child when his mother up and left their home with no warning. Young Burt regularly went to the car dealership where his father worked. His father wanted him to learn the business. He really liked to watch his father make a sale. Nathan Sklar could charm customers into more expensive models and options they swore they didn't want just by his smooth patter.

"Listen to your old man, son. The two cardinal rules of salesmanship are, first: Make people feel important. Second: Always tell them what they want to hear."

One day his mother stopped by to pick him and his father up to go to dinner. A burly man in a flashy suit was taking delivery of a black Lincoln Continental with custom leather seats and all the options. The man invited Burt and his mother out for a drive while his father filled out the remaining paperwork. Mrs.

Sklar sat up front with the man. His gray suit had a sheen to it. His tie was red with a little crown on it. He stank of aftershave. He had pockmarked skin and stubby fingers. He was not good looking, but there was an energy about him that drew people in. Whereas Burt's father had the cloying air of a man hoping to make a sale, this man had the slick confidence of wealth. Burt remembered how animated his mother was, giggling at the man's jokes, touching his arm, like they knew each other from before.

Two days later, Mrs. Sklar left without warning. Her mysterious departure didn't last long. She returned home in less than two weeks, looking drawn and defeated. It seemed to Burt that his father took her back, not out of love or pity, but just so he could resent her more in person. Eventually, Burt learned that his mother had run off with the burly guy in the flashy suit who bought the custom Lincoln. They'd had a fling. Then she found out he was married.

After that, Sklar's family life became a grim charade. The smell of those custom leather seats and his mother's coquettish laughter that day in the car were etched deep in young Burt's psyche, planting the seed in his young mind that money was the ultimate aphrodisiac. From that time on, Burt Sklar knew exactly what he wanted to be when he grew up. He wanted to be *rich*. Really, really rich. Way back then, he thought he might even kill to be rich. But when he grew up, he found out there were easier ways for a smart guy like him to make money. He didn't have to kill to get it. But he had to kill to keep it.

He flashes back to the day Lois Warner called him in a panic, screaming on the phone, "*Maud found the Durable Power of Attorney! She's been right all along! I'm going to the police!*"

Sklar had managed to calm her down, assuring her it was all a terrible misunderstanding. "*Candidly…?* When you hear the truth, Lois, I think you'll be thanking me, not going to the police. I've told you a thousand times, Maud is jealous of you because you are a great beauty and she's not. Besides, I've just made you a ton of money."

Sklar knew that Lois wanted to believe him. She always wanted to believe him. That was his power over her. He could make her believe anything he told her by dangling her two favorite carrots in front of her: Her beauty and her wealth. He also knew how star-struck Lois was by powerful people. Given that Sunderland was one of the most powerful people in America, he knew she would be impressed if Sunderland came to see her in person.

At first Sunderland was wary of going to see the old widow. But Sklar had insisted.

"Lois thinks I invested a great deal of her money into *our* company, Sun. You need to tell her how great the company is. *Truthfully*…? She'll be very impressed that you're there."

Sklar waited until Thursday, the day he always visited Lois, ostensibly to keep her company on her live-in maid's afternoon off. It was also the day he presented her with signature pages to sign without fear of interruption. Lois had no idea what she was signing and she didn't seem to care. She was more interested in talking about her problems. Sklar's assurance that he was making her one of the richest women in the country was enough to cheer her up, no matter what mood she was in.

Sklar and Sunderland had arrived at Lois' apartment at four o'clock on that Thursday afternoon. The old Irish doorman, who was used to Sklar's visits, bid the men good day and sent them up in the elevator to Lois' duplex apartment without hesitation. Sklar had his own key. He opened the door to the large foyer which flowed into the living room with its sweeping views of Central Park. Lois was ensconced in her bedroom, as usual. She was surprised and obviously flattered to see the great Sun Sunderland in tow. For a while, they all chatted amicably. Then Lois remembered the real reason for the visit. She confronted Sklar with the Durable Power of Attorney, handing it to him in a grand gesture.

"Burt, I never would have signed this! You know my family history," she said.

Sklar knew it well. He'd heard the story a million times. But Sunderland expressed polite interest, so it was a chance for Lois to tell the entire saga yet again, a role she relished. Sklar let her have the stage, knowing the longer she talked, the safer he was.

"So now you understand why I would never, ever, *ever* sign a Durable Power of Attorney after what happened to my father!" she concluded.

Outwardly, Sunderland was most sympathetic. Then Sklar stepped in.

"Lois, dear, you signed this because I needed it to make a *specific* investment—which, by the way, has made you millions."

Sklar knew that telling Lois he'd made her a fortune was always a powerful ploy. But this time she pushed back.

"No, Burt! I *never* would have signed this. Never in a thousand years! When Maud found it, I was *shocked*. And, frankly, very disappointed."

Sklar signaled Sunderland to intervene: "Lois, I know the investment Burt's talking about. And he's right. It's worth a fortune. It's lucky you signed this."

The two men double-teamed, trying to persuade Lois Warner she was sorely mistaken. But it was no use. The old lady kept insisting she never would have signed such a document, no matter what. Although she finally backed away from going to the police, she told them she was definitely going to let Maud have someone examine her portfolio of investments.

It was at point that Sklar took Sunderland aside on the pretext they needed to make an important phone call. The two men went downstairs to the library where Sklar told Sunderland that both their lives would be ruined if anyone credible took a look at Lois' finances.

"They'll find out everything, Sun. And when they find out about me, they'll find out about you. You know what *that* means."

It was a threat.

Sunderland understood all too well what would happen if

Sklar's larceny were ever detected, not to mention his own illegal marriage. They would both lose everything and go to jail.

Sklar recalled how shaken Sunderland was.

"*What can we do? What can we do?*" Sunderland kept repeating.

Sklar had made his decision. But it wasn't one he could talk about until the moment arrived. He led Sunderland back upstairs. The two men tried one more time to talk Lois Warner out of showing her portfolio to an outsider. By this time, Sklar knew she smelled a rat.

"I'm sorry, Burt. I'm going to trust my daughter. I'm sure I won't have to go to the police, but…"

It was at that point that Sklar moved closer to bed.

"Lois, you know how much I love you. You need to do whatever you like. Just let me know if I can help you in any way. Maud is welcome to have anyone she wants examine your portfolios. If she wants to go to the police, that's fine. Whatever makes you happy. Now be a good girl and give us a kiss good-bye."

As he leaned down to kiss her on the cheek, he grabbed a pillow and jammed it down on her face. But she was not as weak as he imagined. She fought back. He called out to Sunderland.

"*Grab her legs! Sit on her!*"

Sunderland hesitated.

"*For Christ's sakes, make her stop moving!*" Sklar cried.

Finally, Sunderland complied. The two men held the frail old woman down until she went quiet. Sunderland darted away as soon as her body was still.

"Just to make sure…" Sklar said, holding the pillow over her face for an interminable two minutes more.

When he finally lifted the pillow, Sunderland gasped.

"*Oh my God, Burt… What the hell have we done?*" He stared down at Lois' frozen face.

"She was old. It was necessary," Sklar replied.

Sklar remembered feeling curiously detached as he smoothed the bedcovers to hide any sign of a struggle. He picked up the book of Shakespeare sonnets Lois kept on the night table beside her bed, the one he had given her the day they met. He placed the book under her hand to make it look like she'd had a heart attack while reading. An old person's way to go.

The next day, Sklar was informed of Lois Warner's death by her physician. Sklar feigned shock and grief, saying, "I can't believe it! She wasn't just a client. She was family!"

The doctor told Sklar that old people with heart conditions often die without warning. "It's a relatively painless death," the doctor told him.

"Thank you for telling me that. I loved her," Sklar said with great sincerity.

When Sklar called Sunderland with the news they were in the clear, Sunderland broke down as if getting away with murder was almost as bad as the act itself. Sklar rushed over to see Sunderland, worried his Catholic friend might feel the urge to confess his guilt to the world. Sklar managed to calm Sunderland down, reminding him how much they both had at stake, as well as the dubious assurance they'd had "no choice." Though the two men never spoke of it again, Sklar knew Sunderland was haunted by the murder. The former altar boy's conscience was ticking away.

Sklar bolts upright in bed as he suddenly realizes that Sun might have told Danya *everything* about this crime. And by everything Sklar means his own involvement. Sunderland's cryptic outburst at the restaurant, "Lois, we killed you!" might not have been the only time Sun made reference to the murder. What if Danya knew the whole story?

Was that the real reason she fled? And where the hell was she?

Chapter Forty-seven

I hadn't uttered a single word since my capture. Not one freaking word! I wanted them to think I was crazy and in shock. But not everyone was fooled. The state's psychiatrist told the D.A. I was "malingering," the fancy term for faking. Meanwhile Lydia hired an expert who said I was in shock and a borderline schizophrenic. In other words, it was dueling shrinks at dawn. I liked Payne Whitney and wanted to stay there. Then I made a slight error. I bumped into a hospital attendant and inadvertently uttered the fateful words, "I beg your pardon."

Wouldn't you know the downfall of a deb would be manners? So it's good-bye psych ward, hello Rikers.

The jig is up. I can start talking now, although there aren't many to talk to. I'm in isolation in this hell hole because I'm a high-profile prisoner. Rikers makes the Gypsy's look like The Golden Door Spa. Nevertheless, I have plenty of time to go over crucial events to make sure I get my story straight. In order to go forward, I have to go backward.

Alan and I were estranged after our mother died. I felt betrayed he never supported me against Sklar. I just assumed he and Sklar were still in touch and that he was living on the trust fund

Mummy had set up for him. On Labor Day, 2013, four years after Mummy died, Alan called me up after a long period of complete silence.

"Hey, Maudie. Remember me?"

Hearing my brother's voice was a poignant reminder of the old days. He was the only family I had left. I didn't realize how much I'd missed him. I didn't care about Sklar anymore, or what he'd done. I was doing pretty well at poker plus working various temp jobs to supplement my tournaments. I'd quit doing the victim rag, although I did track Sklar occasionally on social media just to see what he was up to.

"Hey, stranger!" I said warmly. "How the hell are you?! *Where* the hell are you?"

"New York."

"Last I heard from you, you were in Santa Fe with another Ms. Right Now."

"Yeah. I was. Yeah…"

His voice was somber and hesitant, which was so unlike him.

"'Keeping your friends close and your enemies closer?'" I joked. Alan and I often spoke to each other in lines from *The Godfather*.

"My enemies are too close, Maudie. I'm in deep shit."

"I'm sorry, honey. What's up?"

"Sklar cut off my money….You were right about him, Maudie. I should have listened to you."

I was gratified to hear this. But I wasn't going to rub it in. "It's all just money under the bridge now, Bro. How can I help you?"

"I'm into some bad people for a lotta bucks."

"What's a lot?"

He paused. "Two hundred and fifty K."

I heard myself guffaw. "You're *kidding!*"

"I *wish*. These guys mean business, Maudie. I'm scared."

"Brother of mine, what makes you think I have that kind of money? I could scrape up fifteen K maybe. But that's about it."

"I gotta give 'em fifty thousand in a month. They give me time 'cause I've been a good customer."

"Who *are* these people, Alan? Please tell me you're not doing drugs again."

"No, no…Sports betting. I made a shitload of money at first. But you know how these things go…If I don't pay them, they're gonna cripple me, Maudie—or *worse*! These aren't *Godfather* people. They're *Scarface* people. I've tried to get in touch with Burt so many times. But he won't take my calls!"

"Why am I not surprised?"

"I know there's more money in that trust Mom set up. He's just keeping it."

Alan broke into childlike sobs. I felt so sorry for him. He was always a kid at heart, a beautiful dreamer, coddled by our mother who made him believe he was entitled to wealth without having to earn it. Sklar had abetted Alan's fantasy, steering him along on the old opioid road until he was so weak and dependent he didn't dare defy Sklar. But now that Mummy was long gone, Sklar had nothing to lose by stiffing Alan. I just wondered what had taken Sklar so long.

"Okay, okay…calm down, my little brother. What do you want me to do?"

"Come see Burt with me. He's scared of you, Maudie. I know that for a fact. Some people believed you. He doesn't want you badmouthing him again."

I agreed to go. Not because I thought it would do any good. But because I wanted to see my brother again and, I have to admit, I was curious to see Sklar again too. I'd always wondered whether Sklar had set out to pillage our family right from the git-go. Or if his larceny gradually evolved as a crime of opportunity, given my mother's neediness and dependence on him. I wanted to see what Sklar was like in person, now that he was such a success. Did his face reflect his corruption? Or was there a portrait in a closet taking the heat for him?

I took the train up to New York and met Alan in the lobby of Sklar's office building. I hardly recognized my brother. He was pale as the moon, and painfully thin, old beyond his years. He moved like he was in waist-high water, yet had jarring, nervous tics. He smiled when he saw me and we embraced. But I knew he was on something. I had to steady him as we took the elevator up to Sklar's offices on the fourteenth floor.

I hadn't been to those offices in years. Gone was the bland oatmeal décor which had comforted rich old lady clients like my mother. It was now a high-tech showroom of gray suede, glass and steel, far more suited to the glitzy crowd of celebrities and billionaires he represented.

I grabbed Alan's hand and we marched down the hall, ignoring the shouts of a perturbed receptionist demanding we needed an appointment. We barged past Sklar's secretary into his private office. Sklar was on the phone, his crossed legs stretched out on top of his desk. The second he saw us, he swung his legs down to the floor, murmured something into the phone, and hung up. I ignored his secretary sputtering her apologies behind us and got the ball rolling immediately.

"Burt, are you going to help my brother? Or do I have to start harassing you in public again?" I demanded.

Burt waved his secretary out of the room.

"Hello, kids! Long time, no see. An unexpected treat. Have a seat."

We plunked ourselves down on the leather chairs across from his desk. Alan physically shrank in Sklar's presence. He hung his head and grew teary. Seeing my brother reduced to an eight-year-old who'd been slapped for something he didn't do rekindled my burning hatred. I stared at Sklar with all the warmth of an enemy combatant.

"*Laudie, Laudie, Laudie Miss Maudie*...if looks could kill!" he laughed. "Tell me, what brings you guys to the Big Apple?"

"Gimme a break, Burt," I said angrily. "You know damn well

why we're here. Alan needs money and you won't take his calls. Where's the rest of his trust fund?"

Burt heaved a grand sigh and clasped his hands behind his head, leveling me with an amused gaze.

"So how's the poker coming along, Maudie?"

I was totally taken aback he knew I was playing poker.

I squinted at him. "You keeping tabs on me, Burt?"

He went on. "I met another lady poker player at a big gala at the Modern the other night. She's from your neck of the woods. A big-time lawyer. Very famous. Terrific gal. I'll send you an article they did on her in the *Washington Post*."

"You know my address too, eh?"

"I know more about you than you think, Ms. Maudie. I may know more about you than you know about yourself...." He leaned forward and folded his hands in front of him on the desk in a more businesslike pose. "Okay... What am I gonna do with you guys?"

"You're going to give my brother the money he needs," I said.

"*Honestleee*...? I know you kids blame me for everything that's happened."

"Enough with the *kids*, Burt. We're both middle-aged, like you."

"Maudie, I just wish to hell I could convince you that I'm not the devil here. Your dear mother, God rest her soul—fascinating, beautiful creature that she was—was also, to put it delicately, extremely *willful*. The bad decisions were all hers. Why don't you believe that?"

"Okay, fine," I said dismissively. "We're not here to talk about the past. We're here to talk about Alan. What happened to the rest of his trust fund?"

"He went through it. I warned him he would if he kept on spending," Sklar said curtly.

Alan finally piped up. "I'm right here, Burt! You always told me there was a lotta money...more than I'd ever need."

Burt shook his head. "Alan, do you have any conception of how much money you spent over the years? You never had a job. You just kept spending. You have no idea what it's like to earn a living, son. Now you understand. Money doesn't grow on trees."

"But you promised there'd always be enough," Alan whined.

"Enough didn't mean a bottomless pit. I *warned* you."

"You did not! You *encouraged* me!"

Alan was like a fly struggling to break free of a web. He finally just gave up.

"This is pointless, Maudie. Let's get out of here!"

Alan stormed out of the room, but I wasn't ready to go. I got up and shut the door so we wouldn't be interrupted.

"Okay, Burt. Here we are, alone at last. Nostalgic and touching as it is, if you want to stop meeting like this, you're going to have to help my brother. And I don't mean help him along the old opioid trail, like you did in the past. I mean financially. He owes a quarter of a million dollars to some *bad hombres who doan need no stinkin' badges.*"

Sklar whistles in disbelief. "Whoa, pilgrim! That's a helluva lotta money!"

"*Really*? You used to call it 'chump change' when our mother was alive. You told me I was going to be able to afford my own plane one day. I can hardly afford my five-year-old Toyota."

Sklar heaved another theatrical sigh. "You know, Maudie, we used to be friends until you went around town trying to ruin my reputation."

"Oh, *please*. You wouldn't have gotten anywhere if it hadn't been for me. You used me to get to Siddy. And you used Siddy's name to get all your other glittery clients. Don't deny it."

"It's not how you get in the door; it's once you're in that counts."

"How inspirational. Can I put that on a needlepoint pillow?"

Sklar rose from his desk, turned his back on me, shoved his hands in his pockets, and stared out the window.

"Views like this cost a lot…" he said almost to himself.
Then he turned to face me.

"*Truthfully*…? I've got a lot on my mind. I can't deal with your brother's crap right now."

"No problem! I'll just camp outside The Four Seasons where you and the great Sun Sunderland have lunch every Friday and tell people how you're gonna get my brother murdered." I got up to leave.

"*Siddown, Maud!*" Now he was angry. "The last fuckin' thing I need at the moment is for you to start making trouble for me again. *You hear me?*"

I stared hard at him and narrowed my eyes. We were in a poker hand now.

"Alan needs fifty thousand dollars. *Today*. And another two hundred K in six months. Are you going to give it to him or not?"

"How do you know he's not making it all up to get drugs? He's an *addict*, for chrissakes. Addicts lie!"

I wasn't folding. "Fifty K today, Burt. Two hundred K in six months. Or else I'm moving back up here to make your life P.R. hell."

He stared at me for a few seconds. Then a strange look came over his face, like he was trying to figure something out. He sat down. This change in position was the equivalent of a blink.

"Okay…" he said, more gently. "It just so happens there might be some money left over from an old investment."

"What investment?"

"An old investment."

"I want to see the paperwork."

"Forget the goddam paperwork! *Jesus, Maud!* Can't you see I'm trying to do your brother a favor here…?"

"*Oh, come off it…!*"

He raised his hand to calm me. "All right, all right… Let me be completely honest with you—"

"Gee, that'll make a nice change," I said.

"Ever the prep school smart-ass, aren't you, Maudie? It just so happens Mr. Sunderland and I have a very big deal pending. The last thing I need is for you to go rocking the boat right now."

"Burt, if I thought I *could* rock your boat, *believe* me, I *would*. But I know I'm the one who'd wind up sunk—*again*. So whether this money's from some so-called *investment*, or from another client you're going to rob, or just a plain old-fashioned gift out of the goodness of that thing in your chest which may once have been a heart—although I doubt it—if you want to bail my brother out, I accept *with pleasure*, as I used to say in my deb days."

"*Done!*" Sklar slapped the desk with his palm. "But I have one condition."

"Which is?"

He pointed his thumb and index finger at me like it was a gun, and said, "*Go. away. Go away for good!* I *mean* it. No more stunts, no more accusations, no more barging into this office, no more *bullshit!* Just accept the fact I did the best I could for your mother. *She's* the one who let you and Alan down, not me. Lois knew what was happening. She knew she was going broke. *Truthfully*...? Your mother was a raging narcissist who didn't want the party to go on without her!"

"Tell me what you criticize and I'll tell you who you are," I said.

"If you agree to go away, I'll help your brother. But for the *last time*."

I thought for a moment. "You know, in all those crime novels I used to give you for free, to *go away* is a nice euphemistic way of saying go to prison. So, in effect, you're ordering me to go to prison. And I guess being financially challenged *is* a kind of prison. And I'm already there. So if I do agree to *go away*, as you say, then what? Specifically."

"I'll give you fifty K in cash today, and the rest in six months," Burt said.

If I'd ever had any lingering doubts that Burt Sklar had stolen our mother's fortune, they evaporated in that moment. I knew that Sklar would never in a million years have agreed to give my brother this money unless he was truly guilty. I wanted to kill him right then and there.

Burt went on: "But I give you this money on one condition. This is it. No more money. *Ever*. Is that clear?"

"Crystal." I nodded.

Burt walked out of the room. He returned a couple of minutes later with a shopping bag holding ten bank bundles of crisp hundred-dollar bills, each bundle labeled $5,000.00. I was impressed he kept that kind of cash on hand. I wondered what other smarmy deals went down in that office.

He plunked the bag down on his desk in front of me. "Fifty thousand dollars. Do we have a deal?"

"That depends," I said.

"On what?"

"How do I know you're going to give us the rest of the money in six months?"

"How do I know you're not gonna badmouth me all over town again, picket my office, throw eggs at me, or post some of your bullshit about me on the Internet?" he shot back.

"Fair enough. Let's draw up a contract."

"*Fuck that*! I'm doing this for you as a *favor*!"

"Nothing formal! Just a piece of paper between friends."

"Don't you trust me, Maudie?"

I roared with laughter. "Is that a joke, Burt?"

Sklar threw his hands up in exasperation. "Whaddya want from me?"

"I want a piece of paper that says you owe me two hundred thousand dollars, payable in six months."

"Isn't your brother the one who needs the money?" Sklar said.

"That's right. But unlike you, I'm going to see my brother isn't tempted to spend it elsewhere before these goons get to him. If there's one thing we agree on, it's that my brother's an addict."

Sklar thought for a moment. "How do I know you're gonna keep your word and not trash me?"

"Because I'll sign a contract too. I'll agree to go away."

"*Done!*" Sklar slapped the desk.

He then drew out a thick black fountain pen from its holder and held it poised over a notepad headed: "*From the desk of Burt Sklar.*" He looked at me, and said: "How's this: '*I agree to give Maud Warner $200,000 in cash in 6 months. In exchange, she agrees to go away and keep her mouth shut forever.*'"

"Sounds good."

He pointed his finger at me. "Just understand this, Maud. I *will* call the police and have you arrested if you start harassing me again. You're sure you understand that, right?"

"Asshole," I muttered. "*Yes!* I understand that."

"Poker's done wonders for your vocabulary." He finished with a flourish, signed his name, and handed me the pen. "Your turn."

I wrote: "*Burt Sklar agrees to give me $200,000 in 6 months. In exchange, I agree to go away (to prison) and keep my mouth shut forever.*" I signed it.

We exchanged the notes. Burt chuckled when he saw the '*to prison*' addition I made.

"Ever the drama queen, Maudie. Just like your mother."

"Not quite. My mother loved you."

"I'll keep this in a safe place. On second thought, maybe I'll frame it," he said. "So…happy now, sweetie?"

Sweetie? I thought. Like we'd just had a nice dinner together. I knew that Sklar liked helping people with their problems almost as much as he liked helping himself to their money. He loved being thanked. Gratitude energized him. It was Sklar's unfailing optimism that made him so popular and indispensable. In the old days, long before I suspected him of being a crook, I was often comforted by his confidence. Now I was offended by it. To me, Sklar was no better than a killer who shows up at the funeral of his victim and gets a charge when the family thanks him for paying his respects to the deceased. But at least Alan was safe for the moment.

The *coup de grace* came when Sklar showed me to the door and actually made a move to give me one of his peppy How-To-Win-Friends-And-Influence-People handshakes good-bye. I swatted his outstretched hand aside like it was a crab claw.

Alan was waiting for me in the lobby. He couldn't believe I'd gotten the money. He hugged me tight.

"Thanks, Sis."

"Love you, Bro."

I told him we had to go directly to the post office. I mailed Sklar's "Go Away" I.O.U. note to myself in Washington, D.C. by registered letter.

I told Alan, "I'm not going to open this letter. It's proof that Sklar owes us the money. If anything happens to me, I'll put it inside a copy of your favorite book in my apartment."

We both knew what book that was.

Alan was so shaky I insisted on taking him back to his apartment. We took a cab to Ninth Avenue where he lived in a tenement wedged between a pizzeria and a dry cleaners. Alan led me up two flights of a smelly, dimly lit stairway.

The apartment faced the noisy street. The vague odor of pizza mixed with dry cleaning fluid was enough to put me off my favorite food forever. This was a far cry from the posh two-bedroom apartment on Beekman Place Alan was forced to sell years ago. Still, my brother always had a knack for making his homes cozy. I recognized some of his old furniture—the chintz couch and matching chairs from the library and several antique pieces, including the nineteenth-century painting of a spaniel which had hung over the fireplace.

I dropped the shopping bag down on the coffee table.

"We're going to talk about this," I said.

He thanked me effusively for helping him. But I wanted to know the logistics of how he was going to repay these goons he owed.

"So, let me get this straight. You're just going to meet them somewhere with a shopping bag full of cash and hand it over?" I said skeptically.

He didn't answer. He went into his tiny bedroom and came out proudly brandishing a gun. "Don't worry. I can handle it."

I was furious. "*Where the hell did you get that thing?!*"

"I stole it," he said sheepishly.

"*Jesus H. Christ, Alan!* Are you *nuts?* Do you have a permit?"

"No."

"You could go to jail if they catch you with this. Who the hell did you steal it from anyway?"

"Burt," he said with a sly smile.

I was dumbfounded. "You stole this gun from *Sklar? When?*"

"A couple of years after Mom died."

I crossed my arms. "Explain please."

"Okay, so Burt has this little house in Westhampton. He's had it since he was married to his first wife. He rents it out 'cause he has that big old mansion in Quogue now. He used to let me stay there off-season."

"Gosh, Alan. I had no idea you guys were *that* close."

"Yeah, well, I used to get drugs for some of his clients. But I thought he was really my friend too."

I shook my head in despair at how Sklar had used my brother. "So how'd you get the gun?"

"I was out there one winter. I got bored. I went poking around in the attic. There was a whole lotta junk up there. Ratty old furniture, boxes of old tax returns, receipts—shit like that. I found it hidden up under a rafter. I don't even think Burt knew it was there. So I just took it."

"Let me see it."

He handed me the gun.

"*Jesus!* It's *loaded!*" I cried.

"I know. Be careful."

"*Me* be careful? I'm Maudie Oakley, remember?"

I took the bullets out.

"You're an *idiot*, Alan. If you get caught with a gun in New York it's a mandatory prison sentence. What the hell are you *thinking?*"

Alan shrugged. "I like having it around. Just in case."

"In case of *what?*"

"I dunno. It's protection. This isn't the greatest neighborhood, as you may have noticed."

I looked hard at my brother. There was a defeated air about him that told me he needed protection more from himself than from any outside threats.

"Did you tell Burt you found this gun?"

"*Hell no!* Like I said, I don't even think he knew it was there."

"So, what's the plan? You're going to bring the gun along when you give these thugs their money?"

"I dunno… Maybe. I haven't really thought it through."

"Alan, look at me…" I said sternly.

It was hard getting him to focus. But when I finally looked deep into his eyes, all I saw was hurt and confusion. He was definitely on something.

"Alan, honey, are you *really* in trouble for gambling? Or do you just want this money for drugs? Please tell me. I won't be mad, I promise."

He leaped up from the couch. "*Quit badgering me, Maudie!* I'm grateful for your help. But you just gotta let me handle it. I'm a grown man. I know what I'm doing, okay?"

I stared at him, trying to "read" him. I knew he was lying.

"Maybe you do. Maybe you don't… But whatever you do, you're not doing it with this gun!"

I dropped the weapon into my purse.

• • ● • •

The next time I saw my brother was a month later on October 10th, 2013. He was on a slab in the Bellevue morgue—dead of an overdose.

I still get teary when I think of that pearly gray day when I sat on a bench by the East River with Alan's ashes in an urn beside me. I don't know how long I sat staring at the water with the breeze gently blowing my hair.

It was then that I began to think seriously about revenge.

I went back to D.C. and continued tracking Sklar, but with real hatred this time—not just idle curiosity. I was obsessed because, rightly or wrongly, I blamed him for Alan's death.

A month later, I followed Sklar from lunch at Café Milano to a house in Bethesda. I saw Sun Sunderland come out of that house and ride off in the taxi with Sklar. I asked a neighbor who lived there. When I found out, I rang the doorbell. A distraught young woman appeared, nursing some bad bruises. That woman was Danya Sunderland. She had quite a tale to tell.

That was the real beginning.

Chapter Forty-eight

Manhattan D.A. Vance Packer has just been told a story he finds too incredible *not* to believe. He's in a meeting with Jean Sunderland, Danya Sunderland, Squire Huff, and Detective Chen. Packer wonders if any of his predecessors ever had to deal with a more bizarre situation than the one confronting him now. His father always told him that politics makes strange bedfellows. But in this case, these bedfellows make even stranger politics.

The two Mrs. Sunderlands have apparently put aside their grievances and come to him for help. Danya Sunderland has tearfully revealed that Sun Sunderland made a deathbed confession to her. He admitted abetting Burt Sklar in the murder of Lois Warner years ago because both men were terrified the old lady was going to go to the police and expose them.

Packer thinks this revelation belongs squarely in The Land of Daytime Television. But the fact that Danya, the bigamous Mrs. Sunderland, is being wholeheartedly supported in her claim by Jean, the legitimate Mrs. Sunderland, is what catapults this astounding confession into the realm of the Planet Surreal. Packer clears his throat and directs his attention to Danya for a closer examination of the facts as she recalls them.

"Let me get this straight, please. You're telling us that when you were with Mr. Sunderland in the hospital in intensive care, he confessed to you that he and Burt Sklar murdered Lois Warner. Correct?"

"I mean, he kinda hinted about it before. But in the hospital he told me pretty much everything and said he wanted a priest," Danya says softly.

"And the reason he told you this was because...?"

"I guess he figured he was gonna croak. And he was, like, real scared of going to hell, like I said."

"Can you describe *exactly* what happened?"

"Well, he was out of it, y'know? Sayin' all this crazy stuff like, 'Burt made me do it...Burt made me do it...! I'm sorry, Lois! Go away, go away!' Like he'd seen a ghost or something.

Danya's childlike bearing—a gentle euphemism for stupidity—convinces Packer she must be telling the truth. After all, how could a person of her obviously limited intelligence make something this nuts up?

"When exactly in this delirium did Mr. Sunderland tell you he and Mr. Sklar killed Lois Warner?"

"Kinda at the end, sorta. I kept telling him the priest was coming and he was gonna be okay. But then he, like, pulled me real close and said, 'We killed Lois Warner. Burt and me. I saw her ghost... God forgive me.' He started choking. Then he just kinda, y'know, croaked."

"Those were his exact words? 'We killed Lois Warner...?'"

Danya nods firmly. "Yeah. Him and Burt."

At this point, Jean interjects. "We have a theory, Vance. Tell him, Squire."

Huff has been itching for an opportunity to show he's worth the thousand dollars an hour Jean is paying him.

He clears his throat theatrically. "Yes, well, we know that Maud Warner has always accused Burt Sklar of stealing from her mother, Lois Warner."

"I didn't know who Lois Warner was. Swear!" Danya interrupts.

Huff ignores her. "So we believe that Lois Warner found out Sklar was robbing her blind. Sklar and Sunderland went to see old Mrs. Warner, perhaps to talk her out of going to the authorities. When she refused to back down, they had no choice but to kill her."

Packer furrows his brow. "That's a little drastic, isn't it?"

Jean pipes up. "Is it, Vance? Really? If Lois Warner had gone to the police and they investigated Sklar, they would have found out about Sun who'd just been illegally married at that point. Maud Warner claims her mother signed a Durable Power of Attorney without knowing it so Sklar could loot her fortune. Is it just a coincidence that Sun signed his Durable Power of Attorney over to Sklar as well?"

"Finding out Mr. Sunderland was a bigamist would have ruined him socially and financially. Not to mention he would have gone to jail," Huff points out.

"They rape people in jail. Too bad he didn't go," Jean says.

Packer raises an eyebrow at Jean's bitterness. He turns back to Danya.

"You and Sunderland have been illegally married for five years, right?"

"About."

"And you knew he was married when you married him, correct?"

"Yeah! He said he loved me and wanted me to have a kid. He wanted the kid to have his name. I didn't think it was so wrong. I have a friend who's a Mormon. They do it, right?"

Packer and Chen exchange amused glances. "Where were you when Sunderland was shot?"

"In D.C. Burt called me from the hospital and told me to get up there. I was hysterical. I left Mooncat with my neighbor and got on a train and went to the hospital. Jean was there." Danya looks at Jean apologetically.

Packer turns to Jean. "And that's when you found out about your husband's other life."

Jean bows her head. "Yes."

"You both went into his room, as I understand it."

The two women say "Yes," in unison.

"Then what happened?" Packer asks.

"I left," Jean says curtly.

"He wanted to be with me," Danya says. "I'm real sorry, Jean."

"I know," Jean says.

"When did he ask for the priest?" Packer says.

"Um… Like, um, the next morning. He knew he was gonna go. I told the nurse and she went to find one," Danya says.

"And did he come?"

"*Finally*, yeah. Too late," Danya says.

Packer rocks back in his chair and makes a little cathedral of his hands. He reflects for a long moment.

"Did you think about going to the police after he confessed this to you?" Packer asks.

Danya reflects for a moment. "I know it sounds weird, but I kinda thought Sun was just, like, imagining it, y'know?"

"Imagining that he and Sklar killed Lois Warner?" Packer says.

"Yeah. See, when my mom died, she thought she saw this angel coming to get her. People think really crazy things when they're dying."

"So you didn't really believe him when he told you?"

"Well, I kinda did. But then I didn't."

"But now you believe him, right? What made you change your mind?"

She takes a shaky breath. "I'm real scared of Burt now."

Squire Huff picks up the ball. "We believe that Mr. Sunderland left it to Sklar to make sure Danya would be taken care of in the event of Mr. Sunderland's death. Sklar abused this opportunity and started transferring vast sums of money into offshore accounts which were in Mr. Sunderland's, Sklar's, and Danya Sunderland's joint names. In order to access those accounts, they all three had to sign. It was a tontine, survivors take all."

"Yeah! And I didn't know *a thing* about all that stuff! I *swear!*"

Danya cries. "All I know is that Sun told me to trust Burt and do whatever he said. Burt took care of my rent, my bills, credit cards, every damn thing! He gave me cash every month. He was, like, y'know, my guard dog or whatever."

Packer frowns. "But now you're scared of him...?"

"Yeah. *Really* scared."

"Because Mr. Sunderland confessed to you that he and Sklar killed Lois Warner?"

"Yeah! And because he killed my cat! And because he says we have to be together 'cause he's always loved me!"

Packer's eyes widen. "He told you he loves you?"

"Like he's been in love with me *forever*. If you ask me, I think he's happy Sun's dead."

"Show him the letter, dear," Jean says.

Danya takes Sklar's letter out of her purse and hands it to Packer. He puts on his glasses, reads it, and looks up. "When did you receive this?"

"Burt gave it to me in his apartment after Sun died. There's a whole bunch of 'em. He danced with me and told me he'd always been in love with me right from the beginning. It was icky. It really creeped me out."

Packer hands Chen the letter so Chen can read it.

"So you and Sklar were together in his apartment after Sunderland died?" Packer says with a furrowed brow.

"I went back to D.C. after the funeral. But when Jean went on TV and told about me and everything, Burt came down to pick me up."

"Why did you go with him knowing what you knew from Mr. Sunderland?" Chen asks.

She hangs her head. "He told me he was gonna put me up in a hotel. I didn't know he was gonna take me to his apartment and keep me a prisoner." A quick lie.

Danya musters up some tears. Jean thinks Danya deserves an Oscar for this performance.

"Burt wanted you to go to a meeting with his lawyer. But you didn't go," Packer says.

Jean sighs in exasperation. "For Christ's sakes, Vance! She's explained all that to you. Hobbs came to interview her. She saw him as a way to escape. She fled to him out of fear. And that's why we're here today. She wants to help me now. Isn't that right, dear?" Jean turns to Danya with a supportive smile.

"Right! I know y'all think I'm this lowlife gold digger. But you gotta believe me. *I didn't know what I was signing!* Sun said I should trust Burt! Burt said sign stuff, so I signed stuff. Burt said he was making me rich. But you can't be rich in fuckin' *jail*!"

Huff pipes up in a paternal voice. "Danya, dear, may I have your permission to tell the District Attorney the other fact you told us?"

Danya shrugs. "Yeah, sure, why not?"

"Ms. Dickert has a police record in Florida," Huff says.

"Mrs. *Sunderland*, if you don't mind!" Danya corrects him.

Packer winces. "For what crime?"

"I forged a couple of checks and used a credit card that wasn't mine, okay? I got probation. But I know it could look like I was in on whatever Burt's got me into. And I *wasn't*. I *swear*!"

"Why do you think it's something bad?" Packer asks.

"Because now I think Sun was telling the truth. I think him and Burt really did kill that woman on account of money," Danya says.

Jean looks pleadingly at Packer.

"Vance, you *know* she's telling the truth. She's just trying to do the right thing here."

"*I am. I swear I am!*" Danya cries.

"What Sun told her amounts to a deathbed confession. That's very powerful, isn't it?" Jean says.

Packer nods. "It can be. But with no corroboration, it's hearsay. That's why I wish the priest had arrived."

Jean sighs in frustration. The look on Danya's face is one of utter distress.

"At the very least, I'm sure you'll agree this merits further investigation," Huff says, rising.

"Oh, indeed," Packer says.

Packer escorts Huff and the two Mrs. Sunderlands out of his office. When he shuts the door, he turns to Chen and says, "You believe her?"

Chen shrugs. "What reason does she have to lie?"

"Right... She doesn't strike me as being, well, *capable* of making something like this up."

"You think she's dumb?"

"Obviously. But very pretty," Packer says wistfully.

Chapter Forty-nine

Over the next few days, Detective Chen investigates the death of Lois Warner. He reports back to Packer. Chen pulls out a pad with notes and begins.

"Okay, so I spoke to Lois Warner's maid, who said she and a chauffeur took care of Mrs. Warner. She said that Burt Sklar was a frequent visitor to the apartment and that he often came on her day off to keep Mrs. Warner company."

"And was the day she died one of the maid's days off?"

"Yup. Mrs. Warner told her that Sklar was coming to visit her that afternoon and that she seemed agitated. The maid asked Mrs. Warner if she wanted her to stay. Mrs. Warner said no. She doesn't remember Mrs. Warner mentioning anything about Sunderland."

"Did anyone in the building see Sunderland that day?" Packer asks.

"I spoke to the doorman who was on duty the night the maid came back and found her dead. He didn't see Sklar. He told me to get in touch with the day guy. But the day guy retired a few years ago. I spoke to his daughter. He has Alzheimer's. She says he can't remember his own name."

"So we can't put Sunderland at the scene," Packer says.

"No. The doctor who signed her death certificate was also her GP. I spoke to him. He said she had heart disease. The maid called him that night when she discovered the body. He went over to the apartment to examine her. He said it was clear she died of a heart attack. I asked him if there was any sign of a struggle. He said absolutely not. Signing the death certificate was just pro forma."

Packer leans back in his chair, massaging his hands together, deep in thought.

"Sunderland was dying. Why would he say this unless it was true?"

"It may be true. How do we prove it?" Chen says.

"Sklar's coming in shortly. Let's see what he has to say."

Sklar strides across Vance Packer's office, hand outstretched, brimming with confidence and affability. Mona Lickel was set to accompany him, but he refused, figuring the presence of his lawyer would make it look like he was guilty of something. However, he did take Lickel's advice when she suggested he ditch the hip black outfits he wears to show his celebrity clients he's on trend, and "dress like a nebbish accountant." He's got on a suit and tie. But it's a designer suit and an expensive tie. He looks sharp because today he's playing Michael Douglas in *Wall Street*—powerful, personable, and prosperous, with a you-can't-touch-me-no-matter-what-you-think-you-have-on-me attitude. *I'm Gordon Gekko!* a.k.a. *Burt fucking Sklar!*

"Vance, good to see'ya again. How'ya doin'? Sklar says, with a firm handshake.

"Thanks for coming in, Mr. Sklar."

Sklar takes a step back as if wounded. "*Burt!* Please! How long have we known each other?"

"Burt, this is Detective Chen and Kyle Michaels. I believe you and Mr. Michaels have met."

"Sure we did. Back in the day. Good to see you again, Kyle." Sklar grins to show he's let bygones be bygones.

Sklar recalls being questioned by Senior Assistant District Attorney Michaels when Maud first accused him of fraud. Lois Warner, along with her son, Alan, vigorously defended Sklar against her daughter's accusations, and refused to let Michaels look at her finances. Though Michaels had a hunch Maud was right about Sklar, he had no grounds to pursue the case.

The three men sit facing Packer at his desk. Sklar quickly assesses the gravity of the situation. He's here with Chen, the lead detective on the Sunderland case, Michaels, the head of the Fraud Squad, and the District Attorney himself. He understands how important it is to seize control of the meeting from the outset.

"So, Vance, what can I do for you?"

"Let's begin with a few things. First, what's your relationship with Danya Sunderland?" Packer asks.

"She's a good friend... Or at least, she *was*."

"What makes you say that?"

"I haven't heard from her in a couple of weeks. She missed an important meeting I specifically needed her to be at. And I understand she's joined forces with Jean Sunderland, who's suing me, as you probably know. So..." His voice trails off.

Uneasy glances fly among Packer, Chen, and Michaels.

"Who told you she and Mrs. Sunderland had joined forces, as you say?" Packer asks.

"My lawyer, Mona Lickel. In fact, she called me right before you did."

Packer leans forward, assuming a more prosecutorial air. "Tell us a little bit about how you met Danya Sunderland."

Sklar gives a thumbnail sketch of their meeting at the strip club and Sunderland's eventual involvement with Danya.

"And it was you who obtained the phony driver's license identifying Sunderland as Samuel Sunderland so they could marry?"

Sklar hesitates, worried Danya has told them everything. Better not to lie, he thinks.

"I did. Sun was my best friend. I basically did whatever he wanted me to do."

"You were present at the illegal marriage in Arlington?" Packer asks.

"I was. As best man."

"And Sunderland asked you to take care of Danya for him financially and otherwise so he could keep the marriage a secret?"

"Correct."

"Is that why Sunderland gave you his Durable Power of Attorney?"

Sklar has been expecting this zinger because it's the heart of Jean's case. It's why Kyle Michaels is there, to remind him that he's been accused of forging a Durable Power of Attorney before.

"*Truthfully*...? It's *exactly* why," Sklar says firmly, avoiding Michaels' probing stare.

Packer goes on. "Whose idea was it to set up a tontine between you and Danya and Sunderland?"

"*Candidly*...? That was all Sun's idea. Danya was the love of his life. He wanted her to be taken care. He was much older. He had a heart condition. The odds were he'd die first and he wanted her to have a good life."

"A very good life indeed," Packer says. "And he included you in on the agreement as well. Why?"

"It's obvious, isn't it? This poor kid knows nothing about finance. Sun knew she'd need someone to guide her and defend her against the very challenges she's facing now... I was the logical choice."

"Did Danya Sunderland know about this arrangement?"

"She signed all the documents," Sklar says.

"And she understood what she was signing?"

"Far as I know. Sun explained everything to her."

Packer narrows his eyes. "Is it fair to say you and Danya Sunderland spent a lot of time together?"

"Absolutely."

"Is it also fair to say that you developed feelings for her?"

Sklar feels his stomach lurch. He quickly makes the calculation that once again it's better to tell the truth here.

"I fell in love with her," he says softly.

"Was she aware of your feelings?" Packer asks.

"Not at that time, no."

"But she's aware of them now?"

"Yes. I told her. Which, in retrospect was clearly a mistake so soon after the tragedy. I suspect that's why she ran away," Sklar says.

There is silence as Packer, Michaels, and Chen contemplate Sklar's disarming admission.

Now it's Kyle Michaels' turn. "Mr. Sklar, as you know, we met years ago after Maud Warner came to me with her suspicions about you. At that time, Mrs. Warner maintained her daughter was meddling and she refused to give us permission to look at her finances. But she died broke. Now once again, we have someone telling us that you looted a fortune using a Durable Power of Attorney. Can you see why we have a problem here?"

"*Truthfully....?* The only person Maud should have been angry at was her mother. And the only person Jean should be angry at is Sun, rest his soul. I acted on his behalf with his full knowledge and consent, just as I did with Lois."

"So Sunderland was aware you were transferring the bulk of his assets into offshore companies and other entities in yours and his and Danya Sunderland's joint names?" Michaels says.

"He *directed* me to do it. The entities are in his name too. Look, he took a big risk marrying her, for Christ's sakes! But he did it because he wanted to prove to the world she wasn't just some bimbo! Danya was the love of his life. *Candidly...?* I have no idea why she's sabotaging herself like this."

"Is it also true that the last surviving member of a tontine gets everything?" Packer asks.

"Yeah, obviously. So what?"

"Do you know of any reason why she might be afraid of you?" Packer says.

"*Afraid?* Of *me? Hell no! Truthfully...?* I protected her from

Sun. I loved the guy. But lemme tell you, he made Dr. Jekyll and Mr. Hyde look like boy scouts." Sklar says with a grim chuckle.

"How so?" Packer says.

Sklar is now fed up.

"Look, gentlemen, the guy's dead. I don't wanna bad mouth my best friend. But I have photographs of Danya which prove he got too rough. If I committed a crime in aiding and abetting this marriage, I'm sorry. I'll have to take the consequences. Right now, though, as far as the law goes, I'm carrying out his wishes. *Truthfully…?* I'm mystified Danya is suddenly siding with Jean here when all I'm doing is protecting her rights. So if I've answered all your questions, I have work to do," Sklar says, rising from his chair.

"Just one more thing," Packer says, waving a hand at Sklar to stay seated.

Sklar makes a show of his annoyance, but sits back down. "What *now?*"

"Are you aware that your best friend Sunderland made a deathbed confession to Danya?"

Sklar scowls. "What confession?"

"She swears Sunderland confessed to her that you and he murdered Lois Warner."

Sklar is too stunned to react right away. He remains silent as he calculates how best to react to this accusation. Presence of mind is a vital tool in this situation. How would Gordon Gekko or The Wolf of Wall Street handle it?

"Poor guy must have been delirious," Sklar says, trying to sound nonchalant.

"He asked for a priest," Packer says.

"I don't know what to say, guys. It's hard to believe."

"What's hard to believe? His confession? Or her? Or both?" Packer asks.

Sklar shakes his head. "It's just sad. And, frankly, delusional. For starters, Lois died peacefully in her bed. You can check it out."

At this point, Chen pipes up. "How exactly did you find out Mrs. Warner died?"

He bridles slightly. "Guys, you're really gonna question me about this? Fine, I mean, sure... Her housekeeper discovered her and called Dr. Schneider. Schneider went over there and immediately called me."

"Why did he call you?" Chen says.

Sklar proceeds calmly. "Look, Lois and I were like family. She was estranged from her daughter. Her son was an addict. I basically took care of the woman. I was her emergency contact. Dr. Schneider and I had many, many conversations about her health. I loved Lois, okay? I was always concerned about her. Even though Lois was ninety years old, she looked on me like I was a father to her. We had an extremely close relationship, which is one of the reasons her daughter resented me so much. I'd have been furious if Schneider had *not* called me."

"Did you see Mrs. Warner that day?" Chen says.

"Yes, in fact, I did. It was Thursday. I always visited her on Thursdays because it was her housekeeper's day off. I'd sit with her and we'd talk about the news or investments she wanted to make. Sometimes she'd read Shakespeare to me. We really enjoyed each other's company. And that day, she was particularly lively—which is why I was so shocked when Schneider called that evening and told me she was dead."

"Was Mr. Sunderland with you that day?" Chen asks.

"Why would I bring Sun up to see Lois? He was an incredibly busy man."

"What if the doorman remembers you and another man going up to visit Mrs. Warner that day?"

"I'd say he was mistaken. How many years has it been now? Look, Lois was old. Old people die."

Chapter Fifty

After Sklar leaves, Packer, Chen, and Michaels sit in silence for a long moment.

"Sklar's a scumbag—pardon my French. Unfortunately, that's not a crime," Packer says.

"It should be. Except then half the world would be in jail," Chen says.

"Only half?" Michaels says. "I just can't get over the fact that Sklar's done the exact same thing with Sun Sunderland as he did with Warner's mother—getting their powers of attorney."

"You've seen the document. It's Sunderland's signature with two witnesses. One of them being Mona Lickel, his lawyer," Packer says.

"She signed the one before too. No chance it could be a forgery?" Michaels asks.

Chen shakes his head. "I talked to Lickel. She said she and a paralegal witnessed it. When I asked her if I could speak to the paralegal, she told me I'd need a medium. The woman died of lung cancer shortly after Sunderland signed it. They had to know this woman was going to die."

"Let's face it, Mona was Lucretia Borgia in another life," Packer says.

"She's Lucretia Borgia in *this* life," Chen says.

"You think she knew about the bigamy?" Michaels says.

"She says not. Again, who knows? She's Sklar's lawyer, right? She can't say too much. Look guys, the way I see it Sklar thought he was going to get the money and the girl," Chen says.

"So what's he going to do now that she's refusing to cooperate with him?" Michaels says.

"Not our problem. *Yet*," Packer says. "I'd love to charge him with fraud, believe me. But right now it's just their own legal nightmare, right Kyle?"

"Unfortunately, yes. No proof….Should she be scared of Sklar?"

Packer shakes his head. "I don't see him bumping her off, do you? Plus he loves her. He's still got a lucrative business and many, many powerful friends. People are afraid to offend the guy on account of his impressive client list."

"I disagree," Chen says. "Sklar's gone to a lot of trouble to set all this up. He's obsessed with her. Read the letters. Unrequited love plus a billion dollars is an explosive combination. I think he's potentially very dangerous."

"Maybe, maybe not," Packer says, heaving a sigh. "Maybe he was just pretending to be in love. Maybe he's using her to get to the billion. In any case, there's nothing we can do for now."

"One thing's for sure. The lawyers are loving it," Michaels says.

Packer raps his desk with his pen. "All right, gentlemen, we can't prove any of this, so let's move on. Lydia's going to defend Warner with E.E.D., like you predicted, Detective. They're going to say Warner was so unhinged by the death of her brother last year and all this other financial chicanery with Sklar that she didn't know what she was doing. But we all think she knew *exactly* what she was doing, right? She planned to get away with murder using E.E.D. She doesn't know we're onto her. How wrong she is."

"She's still a sympathetic figure," Michaels says.

"Plus she has The Legend defending her. And if they put the victim on trial, she might get off," Chen says.

"She's not walking. *Not On My Watch*," Packer says, stabbing the air with his pen. "She wasn't confused. She knew exactly what she was doing. She *planned* to shoot Sklar, and missed. The fact she accidentally killed a scumbag is irrelevant. It's still premeditated murder. This AARP pinup is going to prison for life."

The River

"Whoever coined the phrase 'a man's got to
play the hand that was dealt him'
was most certainly one piss-poor bluffer."

—Jeannette Walls, *The Glass Castle*

Chapter Fifty-one

Lydia came to see me in Rikers. She was wearing black as opposed to her usual bright pastels. A bad sign. I could see it pained her to tell me the news.

"Maudie, they're charging you with Murder One," she said solemnly.

Lydia explained their theory to me. They believed I *intended* to shoot Sklar, then use the E.E.D. defense to get a lesser sentence. She said the prosecution had evidence that I knew about that strategy beforehand. She explained that Detective Chen had found the Joyce Kiner Braden *Washington Post* article Sklar had sent me with his note about E.E.D. Not only that, Chen had gone to interview Braden in her office. The detective surmised I got the idea for that defense from the article, then purposely sought Braden out at a poker tournament to find out more about how it worked.

They also believed that my nerves caused me to miss Sklar and hit Sunderland instead. I sensed that Lydia believed their theory as well.

I have to say they weren't exactly wrong. But they weren't exactly right either. Here's the truth: Walking into the restaurant that day I admit I was in an *eye for an eye, tooth for a tooth* frame of mind. But I'm a good shot, and I didn't mean to shoot anybody. I aimed at the banquette *between* Sklar and Sunderland, knowing that the mere notoriety of such a brazen crime would serve my purpose just as well as wounding or killing one of them. If Sklar hadn't pulled Sunderland in front of him, the man might be alive today. Everything would be playing out just as I'd planned—only I wouldn't be a murderer.

What surprises me most is how little effect Sunderland's death has had on me, purely from the moral point of view. I know I should feel tons of guilt and buckets of remorse that I killed a man. But, *truthfully*—to use one of Sklar's favorite words—I don't really give a damn. Certainly not for *that* man who helped kill my mother. I find this odd, given the way I was brought up—going to church, obeying rules, curtsying to everyone in sight, and all that sort of thing. I keep waiting to feel a debilitating gash in my psyche, but so far, I'm cool with it.

My only real concern was what Sunderland's death might do to my confederates, Danya and Jean. Would they crack under the pressure? Were they equipped to handle the guilty conscience that usually comes with complicity in a murder? I wasn't sure. However, I was sure that if just one of them folded, the game was over. Luckily, they both seem to be holding up very nicely. Then again, they aren't the ones who actually committed the crime.

I have to wonder if long exposure to Sklar had somehow acted as a catalyst for the dormant sociopath in me—much like exposure to a carcinogen suddenly causes cancer in people who are genetically predisposed.

Or did the game of poker embolden me? Poker is mental war. You must be willing to die in order to win. I've been on the front lines for years playing against my "enemies" in tournaments, living and dying on a regular basis at the tables. Did poker somehow inspire me to war against my enemies in real life? I wonder...

I confess I don't recognize my face in the mirror anymore—and it's not just because I'm older. It's because I'm not the person I once thought I was, or would ever be.

If the cards have taught me anything, they've taught me this: No matter what kind of hand we're dealt in the beginning of our lives, who we become depends on heart, guile, and a little luck.

Chapter Fifty-two

I'm now playing the biggest poker hand of my life with no cards. Lydia and I are in court for the first day of jury selection. She's explained to me that getting a panel of sympathetic jurors is key. She tells me picking the right jury is both an art and a science. She's hired an expert consultant. However, finding a jury of my "peers" is going to be a challenge. I'd say I'm relatively peerless when it comes to the highs and lows of life. What other woman has bowed to "*le tout* New York" at her own debutante party, then gone on to commit one of the most brazen murders in the city's history? I've lived it all from the top down, and now from the bottom up.

I notice the perspective jurors glancing at me. Will older women be more kindly toward me than younger ones? Will men dislike the fact that, as a woman, I took matters into my own hands? Will I be resented for being a privileged person? It all depends on Lydia's ability to get a "read" on the juror, as we say in poker.

I'm hoping they will see me as something more than a child of wealth who spun out of control when life didn't go my way. I wish I could explain to them that too much money can be as damaging as too little; that neurosis, dysfunction, and addiction can flourish just as easily in wealthy homes as in poor ones; that money is a matter of luck, and class is a matter of character. How can I convince them it was money that first attracted a shark like Burt Sklar to my family; money which amplified my mother's narcissism; and money which cemented Alan's addiction? And finally, how can I tell them that the loss of money was *not* my motivation? I never would have risked this for money alone. No…I am an avenging angel. Or devil. Whatever.

After two intense days of *voir dire*, a jury is selected. Because it's such a high-profile case and may take long, the judge sets the trial date a week away to give jurors time to get their affairs in order. Lydia says she's hopeful that the men and women who have been chosen will at least be understanding when they hear my entire story. Poor Lydia. I know she's just trying to bolster my spirits. But I saw them all looking at me like farmers with pitchforks. I suspect to most of them I'm just another spoiled brat who thinks she can get away with murder.

Lydia and I go back to Rikers where she tells me for the ump-teenth time that using E.E.D. is a long shot, particularly now that the prosecution has proof I investigated it before I committed the crime. She feels bound to tell me that Vance Packer is out to make an example of me to prove the system is as tough on privilege as it is on poverty. No plea deal has been offered. But she's not giving up. I so admire her for that. Let's face it, loyal friends are few and far between.

As we're so close to trial now and the jury looks to me like a lynch mob, I feel the time has come to "confess," which in my case means the time has come to bluff.

When you bluff in poker, you're essentially telling a story that you hope your opponent will believe so that he or she will fold their hand. You have to make your story convincing, or else your opponent will call you and you'll be out. I've been in many a tournament where I knew I had the losing hand. Yet I mustered the courage to bluff my way out of it. Part of that has to do my "table image"—which is the way people think I will play because I'm an older woman. My opponents never imagine I have the guts to play risky cards. People don't like their preconceptions challenged and that's what I'm banking on here. I'm hoping my image as an older lady will confound the D.A., as it has confounded my fellow poker players on occasion.

The prosecution is now patting itself on the back because they have discovered my plan to pretend I was crazy when I committed this crime. But they know now I wasn't crazy. I went there intending to murder Sklar, even though I missed. That's what they think. What's more, they have the evidence to prove it. But once again, this older lady has been underestimated, just like at the poker table.

"Lydia, I've been lying to you," I announce.

I have her full attention.

"I wasn't out of my mind when I walked into the restaurant that day. I knew what I was doing. Things didn't go as planned. But I need to come clean with you now. I want to tell you the truth."

At first, Lydia seems slightly annoyed that I didn't trust her from the very beginning. She's attentive, however, obviously interested to hear my new story. I need to spell it out for her so she understands there's concrete proof of what I'm telling her.

When I finish my tale and tell her there's hard evidence to back it up, Lydia's face is frozen in a comic book stare.

Eyes out on stalks, all she can say is, "*You've got to be kidding!*"

Not kidding, I say to myself.

Bluffing.

Chapter Fifty-three

When I was in the ninth grade at Miss Wheaton's, an all-girls boarding school in Providence, Rhode Island, I played Sidney Carton in an adaptation of *A Tale of Two Cities*. Everyone said I ought to be an actress, like my mother. But the stage really wasn't for me. However, that talent has come in mucho handy at the poker table. I've often played the part of a ditzy older woman, pretending not to know where to sit or when it was my turn to bet. While players are looking at me with smirks in their hearts, dismissing me as "dead money," I'm taking careful stock of each of them. If I've learned one thing in poker and in life, it is: *Never underestimate your opponent.*

One Hogan Place in Manhattan is where I'm going to tell my story to the District Attorney. It's time for penitence on parade. I've lost a lot of weight and I'm further dwarfed by the baggy prison jumpsuit. They really need to get Michael Kors in here to redesign these ghastly uniforms. Inmates need a lift. My hair's gone completely gray. I take mincing steps, as if unsure of my balance. Though I'm acting the part of a frail and frightened little old lady, I'm thinking to myself: *Time to shuffle up and deal, baby!*

Alan, Mummy, Siddy, I hope to heaven—or hell—you're watching…

I'm led into Vance Packer's office. Packer, Detective Chen, and Kyle Michaels are all waiting for me like a trio of grand inquisitors. Lydia is there too, having assured Packer that I have a fascinating story to tell, one he'll definitely want to hear.

Packer greets me with a solemn nod, then motions to Detective Chen and Kyle Michaels.

"I believe you know these two gentlemen," he says.

I give each man a wan smile. I want my deep remorse to show. I perch on a chair, kneading a handkerchief in my hands as my eyes dart from one person to another. I'm a frightened bird, trapped by fate and folly.

"So, Ms. Warner," Packer begins, "your lawyer says you have an interesting story to tell us. I believe she's explained to you that we are offering you what's called 'Queen for a Day,' which means anything you say will not incriminate you, as long as you tell us the truth. Do you understand?"

I whisper, "Yes."

"You understand this is your last chance to tell us the truth before trial?"

"Yes."

"Any time you're ready," Packer says, glancing at Lydia as if to say, this better be good.

All eyes are on me, just like at the poker table when I'm about to act. Just like at the poker table where players always underestimate my ability to carry off a "triple barrel bluff," I'm banking on the fact the District Attorney will underestimate my ability to carry off a triple barrel lie.

I swallow hard and take time to gather my thoughts before going "all in," as we say when we move all our chips into the middle of the table for our tournament life…or death. I know that everyone in the room is looking at me for "tells," any little gesture or offhand remark which will give me away, and make them suspect I'm lying. When I'm good and ready, I take a deep breath and say to myself: *It is a far, far bigger bluff I do than I have ever done before…*

I begin my story.

"The truth is…Burt Sklar promised to pay me a quarter of a million dollars to kill Sun Sunderland."

I pretend not to hear the low guffaws or notice the incredulous glances flying between the three men. Packer folds his arms and rolls his eyes impatiently at Lydia, as if to say, *Are you effing kidding me?!*

"Just listen to what she has to say," Lydia snaps. She nods at me to continue.

I clear my throat. "As you all know, my mother, Lois Warner, died broke. I blamed Burt Sklar. I hardly spoke to my brother, Alan, after she died because I believed he was in league with Sklar against me. About a year ago, Alan called me up out of the blue. He sounded desperate. He told me he owed a quarter of a million dollars to some very dangerous people. He said they were going to kill him if he didn't come up with at least some of the money. He was convinced there was still a lot of money in the trust fund our mother had set up for him years ago with Sklar as the sole trustee. But Sklar had stopped taking his calls. He asked me if there was anything I could do to help him with Sklar. I told him I'd have to think about it. Meanwhile, he was hiding out and there was no way to get in touch with him until he called me.

"I read in one of the columns that Sklar was down in D.C. at a dinner in honor of Sun Sunderland. I found out he was staying at the Jefferson. I called him up and said I wanted to see him. He didn't want me to come to the hotel so we went for a walk. He was curiously friendly. I was surprised to learn that he'd been keeping track of me. He knew my address in Washington and he knew of my obsession with poker.

"Then we got down to business. I told him that Alan owed a quarter of a million dollars to some very bad people and his life was in danger. I asked him about the trust fund and why he wouldn't take Alan's calls. Sklar said he'd explained to Alan ad nauseam that the trust money was long gone. But he said he'd think seriously about a way to help Alan. He was kind. I really believed him.

"Sklar got back in touch with me a few days later. He said he was coming down to D.C. again and told me to meet him at the Lincoln Memorial. I met him and right away asked him if he was going to give Alan the money. He said he was working on it. What I didn't know then was that he was also working on *me*...."

I pause. Lydia nods at me for encouragement. I continue.

"My mother *refused* to see through Sklar. I could never understand how she kept falling for his lies. I knew he had this Svengali-like ability to persuade her of *anything*! I deeply resented her for being so blind... But you know how they say all women eventually *become* their mothers...? Gentlemen, you're looking at Lois Warner right here in front of you!" I thump my chest for effect.

The men seem a little taken aback by my histrionics, but they don't say a word. I go on.

"Sklar worked on me to get my sympathy. I see that now. My former nemesis was being kind to me. Had I misjudged him? He planted that seed very convincingly. He said I could help him. That drew me in. He said he was in love with a woman who was in love with a very bad man, and he'd just found out how bad that man really was. He wouldn't tell me who the man was at first. But he said it was ironic that I was the only person he could confide in, and that if I knew the whole story, I'd know why. He said he was afraid of what this man would do—not only to the woman, but to himself as well. He said this man had committed a murder.

"Then he asked me if I played poker with any hit men. I said I probably did, but they didn't exactly advertise. I asked him jokingly if he was thinking of killing this man. He said he was. And I knew he wasn't kidding. He asked me if I'd ever thought of killing anyone. I said, 'As a matter of fact, I've thought of killing *you*!' He laughed, then nodded as if he understood. He knew I was slightly unhinged given my past behavior. He knew I was taking meds because I told him. He said I was lucky I didn't kill him because he wasn't the real culprit in my life."

Packer interrupts. "Ms. Warner, we need to get to the point here."

"Sorry... He finally told me who this bad man was. He said he was Sun Sunderland, his best friend. I was shocked. But I believed him. He told me that it was actually *Sunderland* who'd stolen all my mother's money. And that Sunderland was terrified my mother was going to go to the police because that would expose everything. He told me that Sunderland *killed* my mother! And the thing is, I knew Sunderland had gone to visit my mother the day she died because she told me he was coming and she wouldn't say why. I remember she sounded upset when I spoke to her. So when Sklar told me that Sunderland *killed* her to prevent her from going to the police about him, I knew it was possible."

This little tidbit raises eyebrows. I burst into tears. Lydia immediately rushes over to comfort me. The men in the room are shifting wildly in their seats and looking at each other. They are all wondering what I want them to wonder, which is: How could I possibly know all this unless Sklar *himself* had told me?

I go on and on about how insane this revelation made me, and how Sklar knew just how to whip me up into a frenzy.

"Sklar knew how crazed I was. He worked on me. I told him I was going to kill Sunderland if I got the chance. I don't know if I really meant it then. But I wanted to kill him and I said it to Sklar like I might actually go through with it. It was then that he said—and I remember this very well—'How far are you willing to go to help your brother?' That was the beginning of everything."

"How so?" Packer says.

"He sent me a clipping of an article on a famous defense attorney named Joyce Kiner Braden. Maybe you've heard of her?"

"She's well known," Packer says tersely.

"She's also a poker player. He suggested I go to this poker tournament and make her acquaintance, then talk to her *specifically* about the 'E.E.D. defense.' You know what that is, right?"

"Of course," Packer says irritably.

"Well, I didn't know. I'd never heard of it. But I was going up to play in that tournament anyway so it wasn't a big deal to meet this woman and ask her about this weird defense."

"How'd you know she'd talk to you?" Packer says.

"Poker's a small world. Joyce and I are older women. Trust me, when you're surrounded by three hundred men who think you're easy prey, you're happy to find a kindred soul. We bonded like old bat Rosicrucians. When we met on the break, I told her I'd read the article about her in the *Post*. And like Burt instructed, I got her talking about the Extreme Emotional Distress defense. I learned a lot about it."

"Like what?" Packer asks.

"Like it's difficult to prove. But if you're clever, you can get away with murder."

I glance around. The men seem more interested now, like kids waiting to hear the end of a gruesome fairy tale.

"Go on," Packer says.

"Sklar said he'd give Alan the money if I killed Sunderland. It's hard to explain, but there was a kind of gangrene spreading through my system at that point. I couldn't stop thinking about Sunderland and my mother… I won't lie to you. I *wanted* to kill him—and not for the money. I just wanted him dead."

"So the plan was…?" Packer says.

"Sklar said that if you want to hide something, hide it in plain sight. The plan was for me to walk into The Four Seasons when he and Sunderland were having lunch. I was to shoot Sunderland at point-blank range. I'd be arrested, obviously. Then I'd pretend to be in shock and not utter a single word, no matter what. Sklar said he was sure I could get off using the E.E.D. defense. Sklar swore to me he'd back me up and help me get out of it. He'd tell people I was crazy and I should definitely get off."

"And you believed him?"

I pretend to consider this question. "I didn't really care what happened to me then, if that makes any sense."

"You didn't care if you killed a man?" Packer says.

"I wanted to kill *that* man. And I really thought I could do it for my mother. So I agreed."

"Then what?" Packer says.

"So then Alan and I went up to New York to see Sklar. Alan had no idea about the murder. He just believed I'd gotten Sklar to help him pay off his debt. Sklar gave us fifty thousand dollars that day as a down payment. I told Alan to leave the room while I talked to Sklar in private. We agreed I was going to kill Sunderland. And when I did it, Sklar would give Alan the rest of the money. But I was worried that if something happened to me, Sklar might not keep his word. So we exchanged notes."

"Notes?" Packer says.

"I wrote that I was willing to go away to prison and keep my mouth shut if Burt gave me two hundred thousand dollars in six months. Sklar basically wrote the same thing to me."

Packer sniffs. "I see. And where exactly are these notes?"

"I don't know where his is. But as a precaution, I mailed mine to myself in D.C. by registered letter the day we signed them. I never opened it. I wedged it into my brother's favorite book and told Alan that if anything happened to me, it was there. Sklar owed him the money."

"What book?" Packer says.

"*The Godfather*. It's still in my apartment if you guys didn't take all my stuff."

Chen makes a note.

"Then Sklar gave me the gun."

Packer, Chen, and Michaels immediately perk up like prairie dogs.

"Sklar gave you the *gun*?" Packer says, unable to disguise his amazement.

"Yeah. He put it in the bag along with the fifty thousand. He said it was untraceable. I was supposed to say I got it in D.C. from one of my poker buddies."

"Go on," Packer urges.

"So then not long after that, my brother died of an overdose. He didn't need the money anymore. I suspected he wanted the money for drugs the whole time. I could have dropped the whole idea. But at that point, my hatred for Sunderland was burning brighter than ever. Sklar called me up to say I'd be in an even better position to get off using the E.E.D. Defense because of Alan's death. And he promised me the two hundred thousand. But I really didn't care about the money. I wouldn't have had any use for it in jail anyway. I *wanted* to do it. As the poet says, 'You ain't got nothin', you got nothin' to lose.' But I decided to wait until October 10th, because it was the one-year anniversary of my brother's death. The real truth is…? I was actually planning to shoot them *both* that day."

Lydia sees that Packer, Chen, and Michaels are now riveted.

"Walk me though the crime," Packer says.

I explain in detail the events leading up to my final confrontation with Sunderland and Sklar at the restaurant.

"So Sklar and Sunderland are sitting on the banquette. My purse is open. I grab the gun. And it's right then with the weapon in my hand and those two men in front of me that I realize *I can't go through with this*! I'm standing there completely frozen. Sunderland looks at me and blurts out, '*Lois! No! We killed you!*' And I was so startled and horrified, that the gun just kind of *went off*! I wasn't even aiming. There was this deafening thunderclap. And, *candidly, honestly, truthfully*," I say, echoing Sklar just for fun, "I don't remember a damn thing after that."

"You don't remember dropping the gun, walking out of the restaurant, getting on a train to D.C.?" Packer says.

I shake my head. "Nope. The final irony is I really *was* in shock at that point."

"And you don't remember what you did or whom you saw when you were down there?" Packer says.

Lydia interjects. "I don't think she needs to answer that, Vance. She's told you what you need to know."

"So what's the next thing you *do* remember?" Packer asks.

I look to Lydia for help.

"Vance, she's just told you the truth about the shooting. What happened in Washington isn't important," Lydia says.

"It *is* important. She pretended to be in shock when she was arrested. She lied then. How do I know she's not lying now?"

"Because there's physical proof to back up her story," Lydia says. "First, there's the article Sklar sent her on Joyce Kiner Braden. You have that. Along with Sklar's notation about the E.E.D. defense. You can find her note from Sklar in a registered letter in her apartment. I bet if you search his office, you'll find her note to him. And you have the gun. Proof enough?"

Packer clears his throat. "Maybe. If her story checks out."

I see that these men are still skeptical. But the thing is, there's no way I could have known about a lot of this stuff unless it happened the way I said it did. I've thought this bluff through. I took all the facts and twisted them around to suit my story. I've watched enough crime shows on TV to know that my story— farfetched as it may sound—isn't a patch on some of the wild schemes people dream up in order to get away with murder. Most important, I don't look like someone who could have made all this up. I'm a frail old woman. Just like at the poker table, I will be underestimated. My invisibility makes me invincible.

Chapter Fifty-four

A week later, Chen reports back to Packer and Michaels. The three men sit in Packer's office, discussing the evidence. Chen has the floor.

"We already had the *Post* article Sklar sent her on Joyce Kiner Braden, plus the notation he made on his personal *From the Desk Of Burt Sklar* pad which says '*E.E.D. defense*'. I went back down to D.C. The unopened registered letter *was* in the copy of *The Godfather*, like Warner said. This is a photocopy of both the envelope and the note Sklar wrote." Chen hands the documents to Packer and Michaels.

Michaels reads aloud: "'*I agree to give Maud Warner $200,000 in cash in 6 months. In exchange, she agrees to go away and keep her mouth shut forever.*' Signed '*Burt Sklar.*' That's his signature."

Chen goes on. "We're getting a search warrant for Sklar's office. There's a chance we'll find her note to him there. We also know from his travel schedule that he was down in D.C. during the times she says they met."

"How do we know that?" Packer says.

"The travel schedule from his office, plus pictures he posted on Facebook, Instagram, and Twitter."

"How did you get the travel schedule?" Michaels says.

"He's being very cooperative. He maintains he wants to help Ms. Warner in any way he can. He says she's nuts. Which fits with what she says about him backing her up," Packer says.

Michaels crosses his arms. "I still don't see how we get from there to him hiring her as a hitwoman."

"Bear with me," Chen says. "Warner says Sklar gave her the gun, right? One of the first things we did, of course, was to check out the gun when she dropped it at the scene. It was registered to a deceased person. But when Warner told us Sklar gave it to her, I had a hunch. I followed it up and got lucky."

"Do tell," Packer says.

"The gun Warner used was a Smith and Wesson .38. Very loud. These guns used to be standard issue for police departments in the seventies and eighties. This gun was issued to a person now deceased: Police Sergeant James J. McCaffey of the NYPD. McCaffey died in the nineties. His widow's still around. I went to see her. McCaffey was her second husband. She had a daughter by her first husband, a guy named Gugliantini. McCaffey was fond of his stepdaughter. He was very upset when she got cancer and her husband left her. She now lives in an assisted living facility in Long Island City. I went to see her. She's in a wheelchair. She suffers a lot. She told me that her husband left her when he discovered she was sick."

"Very nice," Michaels says in disgust.

"Yeah. She remembered the gun very well. Her stepfather gave it to her for protection when she stayed alone in the country. She and her husband bought a little house in Westhampton when they were first married. The husband got the house in the divorce. But when they were married, she used to stay out there in the summer while her husband commuted back and forth to the city where he worked as an accountant. Three guesses who her husband was?"

"*Sklar?*" Packer says wide-eyed.

"You got it. Sylvia Gugliantini Sklar is the first and only *Mrs. Burt Sklar*. And, man, does she hate his guts," Chen says.

Michaels whistles in appreciation. "Nice work, Detective. Very nice work."

Packer leans back in his chair, folds his hands behind his head, and begins an uncharacteristic of stream-of-consciousness patter.

"The improbability of this case on all fronts is mindboggling, starting, of course, with the crime itself…I always found it hard to believe that a woman of Warner's age and background could have dreamed up something this crazy all on her own. I mean, if she only wanted to get rid of Sklar like everyone first assumed, there were other ways she could have done it and maybe even gotten away with it. Shoot him in a dark alley, not in a crowded restaurant."

Chen and Michaels both give contemplative nods of assent.

Packer goes on: "So let's examine the possibility she's telling us the truth… That Sklar is the mastermind behind this… Given their history, how is it Sklar felt he could even approach her with an idea like this? Gentlemen, any ideas?"

"I think it's *because* of their history, and because he was chomping at the bit to get Sunderland out of the way," Michaels says. "He knew Warner was vulnerable and he knew she was volatile. I knew her as 'Mad Maud' when she came to see me all those years ago accusing Sklar. I thought she was a little nuts then. It's actually one of the reasons we didn't pursue the case. She was passionate about saving her mother back then. She loathed Sklar. But I sensed an element of Stockholm Syndrome here when she was talking about him. She was scared enough of him to obey him. Sklar knew she desperately wanted to save her brother. He figured he can control her like he controlled her mother. That was his way in," Michaels says.

"So Sklar knows how volatile she is. Knows she's on meds. Knows she's a good shot. He senses there's some of her mother in her. And we all know he was great at manipulating Mom… Like she said, she *became* her mother…" Packer says.

Chen shakes his head. "I don't know… I still can't get over the fact she plays poker—not to mention that hellhole she used to play in. This isn't your typical older lady here. She could be trying to frame Sklar."

"If that's the case, how the heck does she know all the things she knows?" Packer says. "How the heck does she know Sklar's in love with Danya? She didn't even know Danya existed before this. How does she know Sunderland's a sadist who killed her mother? How could she possibly know all this shit—pardon my French—if Sklar didn't tell her? And there's actual physical proof. The love letters Sklar wrote to Danya, the article he sent Warner, the note, the gun… And if we find her note in his office…? That's a lot of evidence. Sklar gives Warner money to save her brother and the chance to avenge her mother by killing Sunderland. He knows she's unstable, so he convinces her she can get away with it… Meanwhile *he's* really the one with the powerful motive. With Sunderland gone, *he* gets the money from the tontine *and* the girl of his dreams."

"Sex and money, the dynamic duo," Michaels agrees.

Chen is still skeptical. "I don't think we're giving her enough credit. She may be tougher and cleverer than we think."

"You saw her when she was here," Packer says. "Did she look like a tough, clever woman? To me, she looked like a defeated debutante. I think she's telling the truth."

Chapter Fifty-five

I'm escorted into the courtroom for the opening day of my murder trial. I have to say that I look and feel better than I have in years. I'm wearing a chic little black dress with a fetching bow at the neck that Lydia kindly bought for me. Let's face it, it gives a girl a lift to wear nice clothes, no matter what the circumstances.

Before taking my seat, I look around the courtroom, which is jam-packed with reporters, society folk, gawkers, and the like. I'm thinking, this is just like a New York gala, and I'm the entertainment.

I see Sklar sitting in the front row of the peanut gallery next to his lawyer, Mona Lickel. They are Robespierre and Madame Defarge come to see Marie Antoinette on her way to the guillotine. Lickel is knitting me into oblivion. Sklar has come to see "the spoiled little prep school girl," as he used to refer to me, get creamed at last.

However, his triumph over me is dimmed by the sight of Danya, cozied up to a buff African American man who looks like an ad for a fitness gym. I catch Sklar turning his head to sneak a peek at his beloved, then quickly turn back to face front with a facial expression that is a trifecta of jealousy, sorrow, and rage.

On the other side of the aisle in the middle of the bleachers are Brent Hobbs, Magma Hartz, Greta Lauber, and Jean Sunderland, a tight sheaf of insiders, whispering amongst themselves. Brent,

Magma, and Greta are looking at me with sympathetic eyes. But I know Danya and Jean are on tenterhooks wondering how I can possibly avoid going to prison.

I see Kyle Michaels and a smattering of famous faces, as well as many people I once knew socially. I'm surprised to see the maître d' of The Four Seasons, who led me to the table on that infamous day. A murder trial makes a nice change from the hurly burly of feeding the overstuffed.

In the way back of the room, I spot some of my poker buddies: Billy Jakes and his wife, Gloria, home from Spain; Adam Kenmore and his wife, Anita; Lyles and Sarah; Julius and Rachel; Eric, Barry, Dave, Loni, Lara, Marsha, Roxanne, and even The Gypsy himself in his red bandanna. And there's Night Fox, and the Great North American A.J., and Big Ober and his wife, Veronica, Asian Corey, Tipps, and Cowboy, and, of course, good old Pratt. It's like a whole contingent has travelled up to see me and root for me, even though they know it's probably hopeless. I love them because they were my friends when no one else was.

Vance Packer and his associates are sitting at the table directly across the aisle from me and Lydia. They don't look at one another.

The courtroom has the grimly festive air of the ancient Colosseum with spectators anticipating an exciting spectacle leading to blood—mine, to be precise. I sit upright with my hands crossed in my lap and my ankles crossed primly, just like I used to sit in dancing school, waiting for the music to begin. I wear my stoicism with quiet confidence, like I once wore a Chanel suit. Lydia gives me a supportive pat on the hand.

As we wait for the judge to arrive, I think back to one of the very first poker tournaments I ever played. I was heads up against a very tough and very nasty opponent who had been picking on me the whole time. He announced to the table that he hated playing poker with women in general, but particularly older women.

We were both "all in" before the flop. We both had fairly

equal chip stacks, so whoever won this hand was going to win the tournament. Because we were both all in, we had to turn our cards face up before the dealer dealt the hand out on the board. I remember being dismayed to see that this odious man had Aces, the best starting hand in Hold'em—the ace of spades and the ace of diamonds, to be precise. I had Queens—the queen of clubs, and the queen of hearts. Being an overwhelming favorite to win the hand, and the trophy, he was practically licking his chops.

The Flop came: Ace of hearts, Four of clubs, Nine of clubs, giving the man three Aces, and me nothing but a pair of queens for high. My odds of winning got even worse. The Turn card was the Jack of clubs. The man was still way ahead with his trip Aces. I had a long shot flush draw. And, lo and behold, the River card was the five of clubs! He still had three aces. But I had the Queen of clubs, which gave me the club flush and the winning hand.

The man was furious. He slammed his fist down on the table so hard chips flew up in the air. He stormed away, cursing, "*I had that game won!*"

I was thinking of this when the words, "All rise for the Honorable Burkett J. Jamison!" snap me out of my reverie. Along with the rest of the court, I stand up with Lydia by my side. The jury box is still empty. My heart is pounding. I can feel Burt Sklar's eyes boring into the back of my skull. I know I shouldn't turn around, but I can't help myself. I glance backward. My eyes meet Sklar's. There's a guttering smile on his face. I know exactly what he's thinking: *I have this game won, Maud Warner!*

I remain expressionless and face front again.

Judge Jamison settles into his chair, tells the court to be seated, makes some comment I'm too nervous to hear, and gets right down to business. He looks directly at Vance Packer.

"Mr. Packer, I have before me a plea deal and written allocution from the defendant."

"That's correct, your honor," Packer says.

"Ms. Warner, please stand," the judge says in a stentorian voice.

I obey like a biddable child. Lydia stands up beside me and grips my hand.

"Is everything in your written allocution truthful?" the judge asks me.

"Yes, Your Honor."

"Do you agree to testify truthfully in future proceedings?"

"Yes, Your Honor."

"Do you understand that you are pleading to a second-degree manslaughter charge with jail time of three to five years?"

"Yes, Your Honor."

"Did anyone force you to make this plea?"

"No, Your Honor."

"Are you doing this of your own free will?"

"Yes, Your Honor."

"Are you happy with your lawyer's services?"

"Very happy, Your Honor."

Lydia squeezes my hand tight.

The judge clears his throat.

"Then it is the judgment of this court that you be sentenced to a total of three years in prison counting time served."

When he utters these words, the courtroom explodes in a collective gasp of amazement. I hear Burt Sklar's angry voice above the din. I turn around to see his face distorted with fury as he points his finger at me and screams at the judge:

"*Three years! That's outrageous, Your Honor! The woman is a murderer! My best friend is dead because of her!*"

The judge bangs his gavel and orders silence in the court. Sklar calms down. Vance Packer rises from his chair as Detective Chen marches down the aisle accompanied by two beefy bailiffs. They stop at Sklar's row. Chen says: "Burt Sklar, I'm arresting you for Murder in the First Degree. Stand up."

Sklar doesn't appear to understand what's happening. Turning to Mona Lickel, he says, "Is this a *joke*?"

Lickel, on the other hand, seemed to grasp the seriousness of this charge, given the way she leapt up like a jumping bean and rushed over to Vance Packer. They have a brief consultation. How I relish seeing Lickel's angry face turn to stone as Packer tells her what's going on. She shakes her head in utter disbelief. Packer is nodding smugly, like he's saying, "Sorry, lady, we have proof."

Sklar cries out to Lickel as a bailiff is slapping handcuffs on him.

"*Mona! What the fuck…?!*"

Lickel walks back to him like she's in a trance.

"Maud Warner is accusing you of hiring her to kill Sun Sunderland. They have proof."

"*What?! Are you fuckin' nuts? WHAT?!*"

The bailiffs have to restrain him as Lickel whispers in his ear. I can't hear what she's saying. But as she's speaking, Sklar's face turns, as they say, a whiter shade of pale.

"*No! No! NO! What gun? What contract? What defense? What the FUCK!?*"

His head snaps around. He glares at me with an expression I once saw in a horror movie where this guy's prom date morphed into a life-size insect just as he was about to kiss her.

I look back at Sklar with my innocent doe eyes, and say, sadly, "I'm sorry, Burt. It was time for me to fold and tell the truth."

Chapter Fifty-six

I served three years in the Bedford Hills Correctional Facility for Women in New York. Bedford is the alma mater of Jean Harris, another infamous socialite who murdered a famous man. It wasn't exactly cushy, but it could have been worse. I liked a lot of the women I met there. I taught some of them to play poker. I told them the importance of bluffing, adding that I, myself, have never been very good at it.

"It's the part of my game I'll definitely have to work on when I get out," I said.

I lied, of course. The bluff was my specialty, in poker and in life. But then, all poker players lie—just to keep in practice.

When I finally did get out in 2018, much had changed in the three plus years I'd been incarcerated. The original Four Seasons had closed, sailing off into New York history like a great ghost galleon, until someone got the bright idea to re-open it in another location. I wish it well, though I doubt I'd ever get a good table there.

F.A.O. Schwartz is gone. No more live Santas for kids to tell what they want for Christmas. The Internet is Santa now. Click and get. Who knows? Maybe there will be reindeer drones one day.

The Gypsy's game was held up at gunpoint and closed down. Its demise marks the end of the longest running illegal poker game in D.C. The Gypsy started another game in a sterile and far less dangerous locale. Players say it's not the same. It seems that dicey back alley venue added a certain piquancy to the poker that was played there. They all miss it.

Magma and Brent Hobbs are married, living in sexy bliss in Magma's apartment. Magma looks younger than ever. Brent's book on the whole Sunderland-Sklar-Warner affair, titled *Hell Hath Fury: Bigamy, Larceny, and Murder for Hire*, is on the best-seller list and climbing.

Lydia Fairley got her own TV show. Her first guest was Joyce Kiner Braden. They discussed the trial and the E.E.D. defense.

Vance Packer and Detective Chen received good reviews on how they handled the case, particularly because I didn't totally escape doing time.

Jean prevailed in her lawsuit against Sklar and Sunderland's estate. Sunderland's Durable Power of Attorney was ruled a forgery by four out of five forensic handwriting experts. The probate judge threw it out of court and awarded her Sunderland's entire estate. The assets in the tontine were gradually recovered. Jean reached a deal with Danya, to whom she was publicly grateful. The lawyers made out like bandits, but my gals are both happy.

Danya married the handsome guy she was with at the trial. They opened a luxury fitness center in Boca Raton.

Jean is back in the advertising business. She won a Cleo Award for an ad she created for AARP. She tells people she's no longer bitter about the bigamy, or Sun's betrayal. She's embracing life as a stronger and wiser woman. She watches her fortune closely.

Burt Sklar is now serving twenty to life. They found the note I exchanged with him in his office, adding to the evidence against him. They didn't believe him when he said he'd never seen that gun. His dramatic arrest made headlines all over the country, which prompted Mrs. Lurlene Meers of Oklahoma City, Oklahoma, to come forward. October 10th, 2014, was the day Lurlene was having an illicit lunch at The Four Seasons with a man who was not her husband. It was her very first trip to New

York and she was thrilled her paramour had taken her to the famous restaurant. While they were waiting for a table in the Pool Room, Lurlene took a cell phone video of the Grill Room and happened to catch the crime on camera. Her husband eventually found the video on her phone. After he called his divorce lawyer, he made her call the D.A. But that's another story.

The video clearly showed Sklar pulling Sunderland in front of him to avoid what he knew was coming. Detective Chen testified to all of this in court. He said that video erased any doubts he had about my accusation that Sklar had hired me to do the job. He totally believed me now. I was let out of jail to testify. I can still see Sklar's eyes boring into me as I tearfully recounted how manipulative he was in recruiting me to carry out his heinous plan to get the money and the girl. The jury found him guilty.

Sklar's in Attica now, appealing his conviction, continuing to protest his innocence, along with almost every prisoner there. Only, in his case, it's true—at least the murder for hire part.

Jean and Danya and I may all meet again one day. But probably not. The Vagina Vigilantes vs. the Viagra Villains tournament is over.

We won.

I'm back in D.C., playing poker with my old pals. Billy Jakes gave me a welcome home poker game. I never did recoup any of the money Sklar stole from my mother. But Jean's secretly backing me in all the poker tournaments my little heart desires.

One thing that hasn't changed since I've been in prison: A woman has yet to win the Main Event of the World Series of Poker. You need luck and a lion's courage to win that tournament. You also need to be great at bluffing. If you bluff, you can't falter. You must tell a story your opponent can believe, and *make* him believe it. In an odd way, you must believe the story yourself. And you can only do that if you believe *in* yourself.

I'm going to Las Vegas this July. I plan to enter the Main Event. And who knows? With a lot of bluff and a little luck, I might win.

Showdown

Fiction is the greatest bluff there is. Writers are abetted by imagination, our own, and that of the reader. Imagination is the most powerful deck of cards in the universe. It has no limits.

If you are reading this, it means you have played the entire hand with me. If you have enjoyed the book, I thank you as a writer and a poker player. If not, I can only say: Next book, next hand.

Acknowledgments

My deepest thanks to my dear friend, Linda Fairstein, and my "poker sista," Linda Kenney Baden, for their invaluable guidance and support. Thanks to Marion Elizabeth Rodgers, a wonderful friend and editor. Thanks to my great poker buddies Ken Adams, Billy Jacobini, and Ken Oberle, who taught me No Limit Hold'em and introduced me to the poker world. Thanks to my beloved husband, Jim, who read endless drafts of this book and spurred me on through the many occasions I wanted to fold. And, finally, a special thanks to Chloe, my little "alien from the Planet Adorable," a furry little ace of hearts at my feet.